Eden to Orizaba

Jerry Wilson

Floricanto Press

Floricanto Press

7177 Walnut Canyon Rd.

Moorpark, California 93021

(415) 793-2662

www.FloricantoPress.com

ISBN-13: 978-1726019590

"Por nuestra cultura hablarán nuestros libros. Our books shall speak for our culture."

Roberto Cabello-Argandoña and Leyla Namazie, Editors

This novel is dedicated to my parents, Wesley and Mary Wilson, who welcomed the first immigrants from Mexico to their small Oklahoma farm town, never asking if they had papers, and to those new neighbors who in turn enriched my parents' lives.

Chapter One

Lantry Barton lurched ahead when the driver hit the brakes. He'd been dozing again, the troubled slumber after a sleepless night. He rubbed his eyes and pulled the curtain back. Beyond the window a sunbaked plain of mesquite and cactus rolled by. Pale greens and browns stretched to infinity, fading to the neither earth nor sky mirage that danced above the burning sand. The driver braked hard and the bus stopped with a jolt. Now Lantry's spattered window defined a single frame, what looked like a large recreational vehicle beside the road with a sign that read U.S. Border Patrol. A semi loaded with fruit, a line of cars and a couple more trucks waited to move north. The bus door opened and a man in uniform stepped up. "Just the routine check," the officer said to the driver. He inched his way down the aisle.

So, they must be near the border. How long had he slept? The last town that registered was a place maybe an hour south of Abilene. That would have been hours ago. He must have dozed through two hundred miles! He likely would have remembered nothing about the town had it not been for the billboard and the name, Eden. The very idea of an Eden in this god-forsaken arid plain had amused him. It was of course inevitable that the town would make the most of its association with the garden of Adam and Eve; inside the "D" in EDEN was a bright red apple with a hunk bit out. The slogan was "Experience the Blessings." The sign said the population was 2,700, which raised the question, what kind of jobs would keep that many people in such a bleak spot on the map?

The bus had caught the one red light on US 87. What 2,700 people did was clarified by another sign pointing to the Eden Detention Center. Squinting east, Lantry saw a sprawling complex of concrete, surrounded by a tall steel fence. He wondered vaguely whether the population figure included the inmates, whoever they might be. He chuckled again at the irony. The "blessings" that kept this Eden alive was not the freedom of the biblical garden but locking people behind walls.

Lantry glanced around the bus at fellow travelers. Most looked like Mexicans, but half of south Texas was Mexicans anyway, so how would you know? The officer made his way down the aisle, his steely eye sweeping across the passengers, pausing when it fell upon younger men with brown faces. In the fifth row he stopped and demanded papers. The man dug in his pocket and pulled out something green, likely a Mexican passport. The officer moved on, toward the rear where Lantry sat.

A siren broke through the silence of the bus, and Lantry glanced back out the window. Two vehicles with flashing lights sped around the trucks and cars and came to a stop behind the load of fruit. Both the SUV and the van were Border Patrol. Four agents jumped from the SUV. One headed for the truck driver, two converged on the open semi-trailer and the fourth released a German shepherd from the back. A pair of agents boosted the dog onto the load. The shepherd worked his way forward, pawing and sniffing. Now three agents were on top too, throwing aside bags of what looked like oranges.

The officer on the bus reached Lantry.

"Going to Mexico?" he asked.

"I guess so," Lantry replied.

"And what is your business there?"

"No business. Just going to hang out for a while. At least that's the plan."

"OK. Be careful at the border," the officer said, and moved on.

Now Lantry saw that the truck driver had climbed down and was escorted to the RV. The officers on the load were dragging a man from beneath bags of fruit, then another and another. They quickly cuffed the three, led them to the back and pulled them down to the highway. The detained men stood on the blistering asphalt while the last officer tossed down an assortment of backpacks and small plastic bags. Agents grabbed the three by the arms and guided them to the waiting van, shoved them in the back, slammed and locked the door.

Now Lantry's bus was moving again. He gazed back at the receding checkpoint until it left his field of vision and only the sea of mesquite remained, the tableau broken now and then by another truck or car heading north. He was well awake now and becoming acutely aware of the throbbing in his head. Nothing unusual for this time of afternoon, but still he wished he'd brought something to drink. Undoubtedly, it wasn't too much farther to the border.

Lantry had sunk back to a stupor when the driver again braked, and he saw that they were entering Laredo. It had to be Laredo, since that was the only town of any size north of Mexico. The bus crawled through now-dense traffic until finally the long low valley of the Rio Grande came into view. A few minutes more and the bus stopped a block north of the bridge. Lantry joined the slow procession off the bus, retrieved his backpack from the baggage compartment and walked toward the border.

Crossing was no problem. Lantry's passport was in order, purchased little more than a year earlier when he and Linda were talking about Paris. Mexico was the first stamp. The agent handed it back with a ninety-day visitor card, and Lantry walked south. "Taxi, taxi," men were barking. He waved them off. A dirty-faced boy who didn't reach Lantry's waist was hanging on his shirtsleeve, trying to sell Chiclets.

"No thanks," he said, before remembering the phrase from college Spanish, "No Gracias." "Beat it kid!" he added in English.

Lantry's thirst could no longer be ignored, for alcohol yes, but also his body was dehydrated, his throat parched. He'd left Abilene just after sunrise and had forgotten to grab his water bottle from the pickup. He walked a block west to escape the roar of trucks on the main drag, the Pan American Highway, and found himself on Avenida Benito Juarez. He ducked into the first bar he came to, a dark, smoke-filled cantina with border ballads, *corridos* blasting from the jukebox. In the corner three men hunched around a table playing cards.

The bartender was washing glasses. "*¿Qué quieres?*" he called over his shoulder.

"Give me a beer," Lantry said. "A Carta Blanca," he added, reading a sign on the wall.

The bartender set a cold, perspiring bottle on the bar and Lantry tipped it back.

"Might as well bring another," he said, setting the empty bottle aside.

"Ah, *mucha sed*," the bartender said with a chuckle. "Very thirsty," he added in English.

Lantry reminded himself to sip the second beer. Anyway, his head already felt better, and a whole evening lay ahead.

Lantry paid and went back out, now into twilight. Even at this latitude days are still short in February, and light was dying fast. What day was it? "February 14," he mumbled. "Valentine's Day." He strolled south on Juarez a few blocks, glancing over his shoulder when the street started looking dicey. With darkness falling he remembered stories he'd read in the *Morning News* about border towns, this town in particular. He recalled with some chagrin that he'd even written one referencing Nuevo Laredo, although he'd never been there. A violation of the first rule every journalism student learns. But for at least a year, rules hadn't meant that much.

The streets were crawling with people, including people he guessed had no good business here. He'd easily crossed the border south, but how many were lurking in the shadows, waiting to slip into the dark river, or maybe angling for a coyote to guide them north? He remembered the three guys dragged off the truck at the border checkpoint. Who were they, and what had happened to them, he wondered vaguely. Whoever they were, it was probably good they'd been caught. On the next corner a gang of ruffians huddled against a wall, passing a bottle of wine. Their voices hushed until he passed, but he felt their eyes on his back.

He turned back toward the main thoroughfare, where streetlights were coming on. Walking felt good, his legs uncramping from eight hours in the bus. Two beers had cleared his head a bit, and now he began to feel hunger. Ahead he saw trees, and in a couple more blocks he arrived at a sizable leafy plaza. He ducked into a place called Tacos Caballo and ordered three. He wolfed down the first, and in the middle of the second another word from his Spanish surfaced. Caballo. Wasn't that horse? Was this horse he was eating? Whatever it was, it was spicy good. He polished off the third and went back out into the night.

By now the plaza was hopping. Old women sat on the curb roasting meat and onions on little charcoal grills. Grackles squawked in the trees, just as in Dallas. An ice cream vendor pushed his cart by, calling *"helados, helados fríos."* He found a bench and sat down. Within moments a shoeshine boy arrived, scoffing at Lantry's boots in need of polish. He couldn't deny that they were scuffed and dirty. He'd paid little attention to such things for a long time. Anyway, it was a pleasant evening, and he certainly had nothing better to do, so he set a boot on the boy's stand. Teenagers strolled by, knots of boys, knots of girls, and now and then one of each peeled off from their friends and a pair went arm in arm into the shadows.

Lantry remembered again that it was Valentine's Day. An entire year had passed. If only he'd gone home after work as he'd promised, and they'd gone out to dinner like they'd planned. But the guys in the office had persuaded him that one quick drink on the way home would do no harm. When he'd finally dragged in at ten, drunk, she was gone.

He contemplated the absurdity of his last couple of days. What in hell was he doing in Mexico, anyway? True, he had no good reason to be anyplace else, but why here? Lovers strolled by and kissed in the shadows, and he was alone. Surely a year should be long enough to get a woman out of a man's head, but the irrelevant fact that it was Valentine's Day—and more importantly an un-anniversary—that brought it all back.

He certainly couldn't blame her. She'd given him too many second chances to count. But at least on this night last year he still had a job. The possibilities were still there, and he'd promised himself—and Linda in the letters he'd sent to her parents' home in Iowa—that he would get himself together and come for her, if she would have him back. That didn't happen. There'd been too much water—or booze—under the bridge, and now he had no wife, no job, no apartment, and as of this morning, not even a car. Worst of all, he had no plan. At least he had the roll of bills in his boot.

He paid the *lustrador*, stood unsteadily in his shiny cowboy boots and wandered aimlessly until he found a liquor store. He bought a bottle of cheap tequila, downed a slug, then tottered on until he came to a dumpy hotel and rented a room.

Chapter Two

The van jolted to a halt and uniformed officers swung the back doors open. "Alright, get your asses out!" one officer barked. Pablo and the others struggled to rise, their hands cuffed behind their backs, their legs shackled and stiff from the two-hour ride. They were jerked to the pavement and hustled clanking toward a building that read South Texas Detention Center, Pearsall, Texas. The guards pushed them through an automatic door, across a lobby, down a hallway and toward a cell already crowded with men who looked much like them. Steel-barred gates rolled open, the officers shoved the trio through and the gate clamored shut behind them.

"*Hola, amigos,*" one voice said.

"*¡Silencio!*" growled another.

"*¡Yo digo quién habla aquí!*"

Men stepped aside as a short, muscled Mexican with a dagger tattooed on his neck stepped forward.

"My name is Oscar," he said in English. "I say who talks here."

He grabbed Pablo by his shirt and shoved him against the wall. "*¿Comprende?*"

"*Sí,*" Pablo replied.

"*¿Y los otros dos?*" the man demanded of the other two.

"*¡Sí, Sí!*"

Pablo stared at the concrete floor but glanced furtively around the cell. There were eight others besides himself and Geraldo and Hector, with whom he'd arrived. Most were ragged and dirty like him. They had not arrived at the border in style. Had they ridden La Bestia, he wondered. The freight train was the cheapest way to get to the border—that is if thugs didn't rob you of whatever you possessed along the way—but also the most dangerous. Would any of them be stuck in this cell if they'd had money? How many had been double-crossed by a coyote who'd promised to bring them over?

Maybe he wouldn't be standing in the stench of this crowded dungeon if Angélica hadn't caught the flu. He had arrived back in Guadalupe Victoria before Christmas with over four hundred American dollars in his pocket, enough to pay off his mother's debts and to buy beautiful dresses for her, his three sisters, and of course for María. And for María, there was also the ring from a pawnshop in Sioux Falls, a thin gold band with a tiny stone that looked like a diamond.

Like most fellow workers, he'd sent *envíos* from Sioux Falls after every paycheck, everything he could spare after buying food and paying rent on the little apartment he shared with three other guys. With the money he sent, his mother had purchased the books and uniforms to send his sisters to school. She had even paid the lawyer, though in the end he failed to regain the title to their land. Pablo's plan when he returned had been to get a job in Victoria and never need to cross the river again. He and María would marry, maybe not in the church, because that also took money, but at least get a little house for themselves and move in together. But that was before he heard about *la lista negra*, the blacklist that meant he would not be hired for the only job to be had. And before the flu that started in La Gloria found its way to Victoria.

So, after Christmas he'd headed back north, the only choice he saw. The bus from Victoria to Mexico City and from there to Nuevo Laredo was just over 1500 pesos, almost a hundred American dollars. He'd saved back more than enough, but with Angélica sick, who knew how much the doctor's bill might be, and the medicine, and whether the mysterious flu would spread to the others. So, at the last minute he pressed the hundred into María's hand. *"Para emergencias,"* he said. María cried and begged him not to go, but they both knew there was no other way.

"No llores, por favor," he begged. Please don't cry.

He promised that the separation would be brief, not more than a year. He would send money as usual, and when he returned he would have enough to buy a little piece of land. Or if that couldn't be done, they would move to a city where he could find a job.

So that meant riding the Beast. Pablo caught the van and the local bus to Orizaba, where he filled his backpack with provisions for the journey—tortillas, fruits, two cans of beans and a liter of water. He figured he could refill the bottle along the way. He waited behind a rail yard warehouse. When the train rounded the bend, crouching figures disappeared, flattening themselves on boxcar roofs. The train slowed, and he raced across the tracks, grabbed a ladder and swung himself up. He climbed to the top, only to find the car covered by prone bodies. The next vehicle back held just two. Without any calculation he leaped across the divide to that car, the momentum of the train carrying him across the ten-foot chasm under which steel wheels screeched and ground against creaking rails.

Pablo hit the flat steel roof on hands and knees, skidded and rolled and came to rest dangerously close to the edge. He pulled himself to the center and lay panting for breath.

A sharp pain seared his back. A can of beans had broken his headlong tumble. He dragged his pack off and opened it. One can was deeply dented and seeped juice onto his spare jeans, underwear and shirt. The bananas were smashed flat. The oranges and avocados had fared a little better. He pulled a kerchief from his pocket and cleaned up the mess as best he could. He stood the ruptured can upright, hoping it would leak no more.

Pablo now had leisure to survey his circumstances. The knot of people on the car in front of him were all facing his way, their faces contorted by what looked like fear. Glancing back, he saw why. Besides his two fellow riders, a third had appeared—and was now approaching him with a gun in his hand.

"¡Dame el dinero!" the man snarled.

The gun was now at Pablo's head.

"¡Ahora!" the man shouted. "Give me your money now!"

Pablo reached into the pocket his mother had sowed inside his belt. Why had he kept the small roll of pesos all in one place? If only he'd stashed some in his shoe. Too late now. The man smacked Pablo's forehead with the pistol, and Pablo handed over the money. The man spat in his face, stuck the roll in his pocket, and prepared to leap to the car Pablo had vacated, the roof where two dozen people recoiled in terror. A pair of boys jumped from the boxcar and skidded down the embankment. The thief turned his back to spring, and without a single thought Pablo stood and swung his backpack with all his might, striking the thug in the lower back. The robber sailed spread-eagled into the abyss, the pistol flying from his hand. His body glanced off the wall of the now-speeding boxcar and careened screaming to where steel wheels met tracks. Pablo felt a tiny bump in the split second the body was severed, the upper half expelled in a burst of blood, body parts, the gun and a flurry of bills scattering down the embankment.

A great cheer rose from the crowded car ahead, shouts of "*Gracias amigo!*" "*Gracias a Dios!*" Pablo sank to the steel roof. What had he done? He had just killed a man. The thought of taking another human life had never entered his head, and yet a man was surely dead, and at his hand. He began to weep. A very long journey had just begun, and now he was a murderer, his money pouch was empty, even his food mostly ruined.

He raised his head and the smoky diesel wind blew the tears from his eyes. The loud commotion continued from the other car. A woman threw flowers toward him with a shout of joy. Marigolds sailed across the abyss and scattered on the wind. Now the two who shared his boxcar were at his side, boys really, younger than him, probably not more than sixteen. They embraced him and joined in his tears. But then one opened a plastic bag and produced a loaf of bread. He tore it in three pieces and handed one to Pablo. The trio clung to the roof in gathering darkness and munched the drying bread.

Chapter Three

Lantry opened his eyes to a dingy ceiling. Where was he? The events of the previous day slowly coalesced—if in fact it was only yesterday—meeting the guy from Craigslist in the Wal-Mart parking lot in Abilene, turning over the title and keys to the pickup and pocketing the five grand in cash, riding with the buyer to the bus station, sleeping across a broad span of Texas. The parts after he crossed the border were closer to clear, at least up until the tequila. The bottle stood on the nightstand half full, no lid.

Pain stabbed at a place behind his eyes as it did most mornings. He stared at the peeling paint, wondering what to do. His bladder was full, so he threw off the sheet and tried to pull himself up. Blood rushed to his head and he fell back on the pillow. On the second try he rolled to the edge and swung his legs off, then stood shakily. Holding to the wall he edged toward the toilet. When he finished with the commode he splashed water on his face and looked in the mirror. His eyes were bloodshot, and his cheeks had a three-day beard. Somebody had smashed a cockroach beside the mirror.

Lantry bent and sipped at the faucet before he remembered that in Mexico you aren't supposed to drink the water. He shuffled back and collapsed on the sagging bed. He eyed the bottle for a long while, then took a swig—just one—and found the cap. He gathered crumpled clothes from the floor and pulled them on. Now what? He gazed out the dusty second story window at the Mexicans passing by. They looked uniformly poor. Dirty, ragged children, old women with fruits and vegetables, in fact anything and everything in baskets and tubs balanced on their heads—plucked chickens, pottery, something wrapped in corn husks, maybe *tamales.* He glanced at his watch. It was after eight o'clock.

Lantry stood, shouldered his pack and went out. He clomped down the stained wooden staircase into the street and stopped at the first open-air hole in the wall, and took a chair nearest the sidewalk. He ordered café *americano* and huevos rancheros. Even though he'd never been particularly interested in Mexico, he did like Mexican food. Eggs and toast didn't measure up to greasy fried eggs with incendiary salsa and fresh tortillas.

A scrawny dog lay at his feet with begging eyes, scratching lazily at his fleas. Lantry paid his bill, tossed the last scrap of tortilla to the mutt and went out. His head spun worse when he walked. He came to a *farmacia* and thought of going in for aspirin, but instead crossed the street and ducked into a bar that was already open and downed a quick Dos Equis beer. The combination of food, coffee and beer revived him a bit, and he strolled aimlessly until he came by chance to the little plaza of the night before. He found a bench, and was immediately surrounded by children, boys with shoeshine kits, girls hawking Chiclets. He wondered why they weren't in school. He shooed them away.

As his head cleared, Lantry began to consider his options. Except for the pleasant weather, he saw nothing to hold him in Nuevo Laredo. He knew little about the country, wondering now at how indifferent he had been. After all, he'd grown up in San Marcos, two-hundred miles from the border, and had lived all his thirty years in Texas. But now that he was in Mexico, the question was what next?

It wasn't too late to reverse course. With his American passport he could come and go as he pleased. But going back to Dallas seemed out of the question. He'd burned every bridge. He thought of a last desperate run to Iowa, where Linda was staying with her folks, at least last time he'd heard, which was months ago. But it wasn't just the February weather that was cold there. She'd made it pretty clear that their relationship was done.

In the year since she'd left he hadn't cared much about his work, or about anything else. The drinking that drove her out, that was what he had instead. Yet in a year of crazy decisions and mostly the absence of judgments of any kind, the folly of yesterday almost amused him, that he would do what he'd done with so little thought or plan. His pickup was gone—sold too cheap he knew. He couldn't get that back, and he had no job or even prospects for a job. No question his flight had been crazy, but on the other hand he'd chosen a direction and he couldn't think of any good reason to turn back now. With nothing to lose that he hadn't already lost, Mexico seemed as good a place as any to be.

Lantry reminded himself that in Texas the roll of bills in his boot wouldn't last long, so that was one obvious reason to be here. He wasn't sure, but he thought he'd paid just twenty bucks for the hotel room, and he'd heard lots of tales about how cheaply a person could survive in Mexico. Even booze was cheap here. Plus, the weather was warm.

As if to contradict him, a gust of north wind kicked up scraps of paper and swept them across the park, also bringing a chill despite the warming sun. It certainly wasn't like Dallas, and especially not like Iowa, but he felt sudden goosebumps on his arms. He sat facing south, toward the sun, and suddenly, without more weighing of options he stood and walked back toward the bus terminal. "If I need a reason," he said aloud to himself, "I'll just say that it's warmer if I go south instead of the other directions I might have gone." But that didn't answer the question of where to with any specificity.

It wasn't just yesterday. Everything he'd done for the past week was impulsive, rash. He should have seen it all coming when he showed up two hours late on Monday and the editor called him into his office. Had he thought he could ride his reputation for incisive work forever? Not realistic, he knew. To be honest, he hadn't really been worth his pay for some time. Missed deadlines, sources not double checked, sloppy writing. He remembered a story he'd written on his last day. The perspective was not necessarily a problem for the paper, an unsympathetic story about undocumented Mexicans taking jobs that might have gone to Texans, so it raised no questions in the newsroom. But even at the time he'd wondered how accurate it was. He hadn't checked out the senator's statistics, partly because it would have been too much trouble and partly because he hadn't really cared.

It was nearing nine o'clock and he hadn't found the bus station. He realized that he was lost and asked for directions. When he saw the terminal, he studied the *horario*, the names of possible destinations and the departure times. Monterrey was the closest city, and he considered that for a moment. The final destination of many buses was Mexico City, with one leaving every hour or so. Some were direct, through Monterrey, west to Saltillo, then south through San Luis Potosi to the capital. But that bus had just left, and the next one on the schedule

16

took the old Pan American Highway, Mexico 85. Since Lantry knew little about the geography, the route mattered little to him. Also, this bus was second-class, so it cost even less. He stepped to the window, bought a ticket and got on the bus.

After Monterrey, the arid Sierra Madre came into view and the first ascent began. The bus groaned and climbed and wound slowly into the mountains. Lantry began to wonder whether he should have taken the faster bus. Then they descended to a fertile plain, and the pace picked up. But the stops to release and add passengers in Monterrey, Ciudad Victoria, Ciudad Mante, Ciudad Valles and a dozen smaller towns seemed interminable.

South of Victoria they passed a sign marking the Tropic of Cancer. As if by command, vegetation grew dense and tall. Tropical flowers, pink, lavender and orange, were reflected in the colors of houses. Brilliant birds flitted amongst banana groves. Twenty-five-foot bamboo became common, and as tropical foliage grew thicker, so did men carrying machetes along the road. Women bearing pots or baskets or bags on their heads trudged from home to market or back. Exotic gardens surrounded tiny huts, some shaded by poinsettias higher than the roofs.

By Ciudad Valles, light was fading fast. Lantry had been riding for eight hours, but unlike on the previous day's long ride across the Texas plains, he had not been tempted to sleep. In fact he had found that in spite of the slow pace, pretty much everything about this trip was exciting his senses. He admired the quaint town plazas, the sprawling vegetable and flower markets, the small farms and tiny houses beside the road, the flocks of colorful chickens that scattered off the highway as the bus approached, the vendors holding everything from oranges to carved wooden figures up to passing motorists, the flower-decorated crosses that marked the sites of traffic deaths.

Now the bus ascended again, climbing back into the increasingly lush Sierra Madre. It crept slowly around tight curves and giant ceiba trees, and finally, finally, descended to the Moctezuma River and the *pueblo* of Tamazunchale. For reasons he couldn't define, Lantry was powerfully drawn to the little mountain town, rich in fruits and flowers, butterflies and birds. But his ticket was through to Mexico City, still hours away. When the bus stopped he got off and bought street tacos and a beer. Back on the bus he weighed whether to stay on for the ride, or to get back off. After all, every decision he'd made for days now had been impromptu, so why not this one? He had just decided to get off when a new driver mounted the steps and closed the door and they roared off into falling dusk. But Lantry felt somehow that the mountains had called him, that he would need to return. He finished his food and beer, and as darkness fell he sipped the last of his tequila and fell asleep.

Chapter Four

When Pablo had crossed the border in 2007, it had been easy. Yes, there was the night in the pasture south of Fort Worth, but that turned out OK. It was June that time, and the Rio Grande was high. But 2007 was before the crash. The US economy was still booming then, and demand for cheap labor took some of the heat off men who crossed the border to do jobs that North Americans didn't want to do. The drug gangs pretty much controlled the Mexican side even then, determining who crossed, when and where and how much it would cost. Women and girls without money sometimes had no choice but to pay with sex.

Pablo was almost as broke then as now, so he'd had no way to pay. His family had lost their land, his father was dead, his mother and sisters bought tortillas and beans by washing the laundry of others in a small lake near their home. But that was before a torrential rain flooded a manure lagoon at Granjas Carroll and washed across the valley to their laundry spot, also the place where the poorest residents got their household water. Now even washing clothes there was beyond question, let alone drinking the water. With only a few pesos in his pocket, Pablo had to find another way to cross.

He'd bought a patched inner tube from a tire shop, then stumbled through brush all night, making his way upriver until he passed both the fence built by the US Marine Corps and the lucrative region controlled by the Zeta cartel. It was a moonless night, even the stars obscured by clouds. He picked his way to the edge and blew until the inner tube was hard. He waded in, positioned himself atop the craft with his backpack on his lap, and let the current take him. Eventually the river found a bend where the current carried him to the other side. He left the tube behind and began the long walk back downriver.

At the first hint of dawn Pablo had crawled under a cluster of mesquite, washed down tortillas with the last sips from his water bottle, and gone to sleep. He awoke with the sun at its zenith. Brushy leaves sheltered him from the sun, but his thirst was almost unbearable, and his eyes refused to focus. Flies and mosquitoes buzzed around his head. The foliage that hid him from the river shimmered in the sun, first as a mirage, but then it began to move. Then it was not the cactus and mesquite that moved, but men in uniforms the gray-green color of cactus and mesquite, crouching and creeping toward him, guns at the ready. And then it all disappeared, the men, even the low brush that he knew surrounded him. When he woke again his mouth was open, his tongue swollen. He thought of creeping to the Rio Grande to drink, but that carried too much risk, sickness as well as being seen from the helicopter that passed every few minutes. Instead he worked at conjuring bitter spit on his tongue and licking parching lips. He sliced open prickly pear leaves and sucked scant juice. At last the sun sank lower, and eventually evening fell. At dusk he crawled out of his refuge and hobbled eastward toward Laredo's glow.

Pablo had a few pesos in his pocket that time, but he was reluctant to spend them. He crept furtively into a McDonalds beside the highway, dodged to the room marked Men and Caballeros, turned on the faucet and drank his fill. He filled his bottle, drank that down and filled it again. Back outside he found French fries and half a hamburger in a dumpster. He sat in the shadows on the curb devouring the meal. So intent he was that he didn't see the figure approach until the other spoke.

"*¿Necesitas trabajo?*" Do you need work? the quiet voice asked, a young man about his age.

"*Sí,*" Pablo replied.

"*Vamos a South Dakota mañana,*" the man said. "*¿Quieres venir conmigo?*"

"*Sí,*" Pablo answered.

He didn't know where South Dakota was, though the word "south" probably meant it was someplace near. But it was the word "work" that he had indeed heard. It was for work that he had crossed. And for the money that work would bring. Pablo walked with the man to a room where half a dozen others waited.

Before sunrise they packed themselves and the few things they had brought into a windowless van.

"*¿Cuantos años tienes?*" the driver asked. How old are you?

"*Dieciocho,*" Pablo replied. "Eighteen."

The driver, a Mexican who spoke some English, handed Pablo a card with a number and a name.

"In Sioux Falls you are José," he said. "Your first paycheck comes to me for the trip and the card. Until your second check I will give you food and a place to stay."

The van bounced over rutted dirt roads and across endless roadless stretches of cactus and mesquite desert, tacking east and west but always north, until at last they returned to a four-lane highway. The driver turned the music

21

up, Mexican music, and the human cargo hurtled north at seventy-five miles an hour.

Pablo's second crossing had been very different. He had climbed down from the nightmarish boxcar ride as the train rolled into the outskirts of Nuevo Laredo, his pockets as empty as his stomach. He checked every dumpster he found, but there was nothing to scrounge; he wasn't the only person without money or food. He walked the streets, wondering what to do, until an elderly woman called out to him. A dead tree had fallen against her house. She handed him an ax and told him that she would pay him to chop the trunk and limbs into pieces he could carry to the alley. Before he went to work she gave him tacos and pan dulce, which gave him the strength to wield the ax. When he had finished the job she gave him fifty pesos and more tacos and pointed him toward the river.

But how to get across? Everybody knew what had happened north of the border. The economy had crashed in the fall, and even though there was a new president named Obama, the country was far from recovery. A man told Pablo that even if he got across he might not find a job. Worse yet, the border crackdown meant he probably couldn't make it this time by himself. Even if he hadn't been robbed, from what he'd heard the money he'd lost would have been far short to pay a coyote to take him across. Now that he was here, he had no idea what to do next. His only certainty was that the only option was to cross. He walked toward the Rio Grande.

Pablo stopped to rest on a park bench in front of a large statue. His gaze was returned by the tall bronze figure of Benito Juárez, the Indian president from the south who had liberated Mexico from the foreigners, a hero every Mexican knew. He was wondering what independence had brought Mexico when his reverie was interrupted by a voice.

"Going across?" the man asked.

"*Sí,*" Pablo replied.

"I can take you for $200," the coyote said. "And that is cheap. Most people charge more."

"*Lo siento,*" Pablo replied. "*No los tengo.*" He explained that he had been robbed and that all he had in his pocket was enough for another meal.

"There is another way," the coyote told him. "All you have to do is carry a small package. On the other side a man will meet you and will take you where you want to go."

"What kind of package?" Pablo asked, but of course he knew. It was only a question of what kind of drugs.

"Just marijuana," the man said. "Just a kilo. It's no problem. We do this all the time, and nobody gets caught."

Like every teenager back in Victoria, Pablo had smoked marijuana. He knew how it made you feel, and he knew there was no great harm. But he'd also heard plenty of stories about what happened to people caught at the border with drugs. There had to be another way and he would have to figure it out.

"*No gracias,*" he said.

"*¡Cobarde!*" the man barked. "Cowards can rot in Mexico for all I care. I tried to help you, but I can find others who want to go."

He got up and strode away. Pablo sat staring after him. *¿Cobarde?* The man had called him a coward. Nobody had ever said that to him before. Was he a coward? He'd killed the man who robbed him, and those he'd saved thought he was a hero. But that had nothing to do with what happened. It was his legs that stood, his arms that swung the backpack. His head was not involved. So far as he could tell, neither cowardice nor heroism was behind what happened. But he had ridden the beast so his sister could see the doctor and get medicine, and though he'd told them all that he'd be safe, he'd known very well how dangerous the journey might be. The more he thought about it, the angrier he became. No, he might not be a hero, but he certainly was not a coward.

Pablo walked on north until he reached the river. There he saw others, mostly young men, but also women and kids, waiting for a way to cross. As night fell he saw that the crowd drifted east, downriver, and he followed until he came to a low scrubby floodplain where scores of dark figures sat or lay or cooked by glowing fires. He stood in the shadow of a willow tree and watched a middle-aged woman rise from the earth to check the blackened pot that hung above her fire. She glanced up and saw him and returned his stare. After a time, she motioned for him to come. Instead of three bowls, one for herself and one for each of her children, she dipped the thin stew into four. Pablo squatted with them and ate.

When they had finished, Pablo thanked the woman for her kindness and crawled under the willow tree. He gazed through drooping branches at the stars, wondering what courage or cowardice had to do with doing what a person had to do, including crossing the Rio Grande. Finally, he drifted off to sleep.

When Pablo woke it was from a dream in which Angélica had gone to the doctor and spent all the money he had left her, but still was on the edge of death. Then it was María who was sick too, or maybe both, and there was nobody to help. When he opened his eyes, the sun had not

24

risen, but the first hint of day had come. Dense fog blanketed the sleeping camp. He stood, dusted sand and debris from his clothes, urinated against the trunk and shouldered his pack. He turned back up the river trail he had come.

When he reached the railroad tracks he followed them to a warehouse where men were loading trucks with bags of avocados, bananas, oranges and other vegetables and fruits. Lurking outside the gate was the man he'd met in the plaza. Anger rose again in Pablo's throat. He walked straight to the man and looked him squarely in the eye. "I am not a coward," he said, "but that has nothing to do with it. I have to get across."

In the same moment he agreed, Pablo had known it was a bad idea. Despite what he'd said, he had fallen for the coyote's taunt. If he'd taken more time, maybe he could have found some other way, though he had no idea what that might have been. But he and two other guys, Geraldo and Hector, were each handed a bag of marijuana. They were loaded into a truck almost full of big bags of oranges, then covered over with more bags. Breathing wasn't easy with fifty pounds of fruit on his belly.

Chapter Five

Lantry woke with the sun in his eyes. The bus had descended from the mountains and was rolling fast across a broad flat plain. Ahead lay a vast valley surrounded by mountain peaks. Even from a distance he saw that the valley's lid was a blanket of solid gray sky. For another hour they crawled through smoking industrial works and shantytowns toward the heart of the great metropolis. The bus jolted to a stop in a terminal bigger than any he'd ever seen. He stood on legs stiffened by the round-the-clock ride, stepped down and claimed his pack. He had no idea where in this sprawling hive of twenty million souls he stood, but a sign told him he had reached Terminal Norte.

In Nuevo Laredo he had spent America dollars, and in Tamazunchale he had bought his tacos and beer with change from Nuevo Laredo transactions, but now he realized he'd need pesos. It wasn't hard to find a moneychanger; they seemed to be on the lookout for dazed *gringos*. He had no idea what the official exchange rate was, so he'd have to take what they offered. But to minimize the likelihood of being ripped off, he changed just fifty dollars. He judged that would get him by until he could find a bank.

Lantry had taken the required year of Spanish in college, but it hadn't interested him much. Too bad he hadn't paid more attention. But somehow, he conjured the words to ask the man at the ticket booth which metro line would take him to El Centro.

"*Línea cinco a línea tres a línea dos,*" the man said. "Five to three to two."

Lantry bought a token and rode the escalator deep into the bowels of the city to the metro station. Once on the subway car, he realized that a system map was clearly presented on the wall. He studied it and followed the color-coded lines toward the *Zócalo* — another word he recalled — the city center. But two stops before the *Zócalo* was Bellas Artes, next to Alameda Park. A vague memory arose of a magnificent classical structure the professor had raved about. Why not get off there and walk to the center? His cramped legs could use the exercise.

Lantry emerged into hazy sunshine at the edge of Alameda, a broad swath of trees that stretched west as far as he could see. Before him was the Palace of Fine Arts. It was magnificent for sure, but it could wait for another day. Just now he needed food — and drink. He realized that in spite of the haze and the exhaust-laced air he was breathing, his head felt almost clear. After all, he'd spent twenty-four hours on the bus with little alcohol to drink. But he also hadn't eaten for twenty-four hours except the street tacos in Tamazunchale, so food was the more immediate need, a need spurred by a strong spicy aroma wafting from a white cart a man was wheeling by. On the side was painted a giant hotdog, bursting with onions, relish and *chile*, and below it the word "*Exquisitos.*"

Lantry sank onto a park bench and devoured the sandwich. Not far from his bench was a large mounted sign that bore a map of the historic downtown zone. He finished his lunch, shouldered his pack and went to study the map. Just beyond the Palace of Fine Arts was a major north-south thoroughfare called Lázaro Cárdenas, named for some president if he remembered right, and to the east lay the

Zócalo. Two blocks south was La Torre Latin Americana, which the sign claimed was the highest building in the hemisphere. His eye measured the structure. Tall yes, but surely not as tall as the Empire State Building, which he'd never seen, and certainly not as tall as the Sears Tower in Chicago, on top of which he had once stood. He puzzled over the claim until he realized that the phrase "*más alta*" had to mean highest, not tallest. After all—again if his vague memory served him—the sidewalk on which he stood was some 7,000 feet above sea level.

The light turned green and he crossed Cardenas and walked east on Cinco de Mayo. In Texas the Fifth of May was a party day promoted by Corona and even American beers, but what was the significance of the date? Memory provided no clue. Lantry was not an ignorant man, nor was he uneducated. Besides a college degree he'd attended law school, and many scraps of information were stored away somewhere in his head. But he was also aware of how little he knew about the country he had entered, the country just across a river from his home state. He marveled uncomfortably at how incurious he had been.

Just across the thoroughfare he came to a restaurant named Sanborns, housed in a grand building called the Casa de los Azulejos. "*Azulejos,*" he muttered, searching for the meaning. "Yes, that means tiles," he said, surprised that the word had returned, but after all, his memory had been prompted by the fact that the entire exterior was an elaborate design constructed with ceramic tile. A plaque beside the door said it was the palace of the Counts of Orizaba, built in 1596. "Whoever they were, they must have been rich," he said for nobody else to hear. He knew he'd heard the name Orizaba, but no connection came to mind. But what amazed him as much as the beautiful building was the realization that it was built before the first European settlers arrived in what would much later become the United States.

At the first corner Lantry saw a sign announcing La Opera Bar. "Opera" held little appeal for him, but "bar" got his attention. So, which was this? He swung open a massive wooden door and stepped inside. Immediately before him lay a long, heavily ornate dark wood bar. He stood just inside the doorway, waiting for his pupils to widen. Every detail was obscured by darkness, but as his eyes adjusted he saw that everything about the place was dark, heavy and old, the soaring metal ceiling, the almost blackened heavy wood furniture and booths, the massive carved mirror frames. He stepped toward the bar. A grainy photograph on the wall pictured a man who looked familiar, a man on horseback. Yes, it was Pancho Villa, the general of the north in the 1910 Revolution.

Another fuzzy photograph pictured a group of men. A typed caption said that when Villa and the handsome mustachioed peasant leader Emiliano Zapata and their allies took control of the capital after a decade of fighting, they made themselves at home in the Opera Bar. According to the story it had already been open for nearly half a century, and before the revolutionaries, had been a hangout of president-for-life Porfirio Diaz. That would stand to reason, since the bar stood in the historic city center, surrounded by the palaces of the Spaniards who ruled the country for centuries before independence. Lantry scrutinized the fuzzy, dim background of the second photograph. Something else looked familiar. Finally, he realized what it was; the revolutionary heroes in the photograph were leaning against this very bar!

Lantry stepped to that bar. Two other men drank at the far end; otherwise the cavernous place was empty as far as he could see. But after all, it wasn't even noon. It was the time of day when bars were inhabited only by woeful men, men who—like him—required drink. Of the many beers on tap, he recognized a few. "Dos Equis," he said, and the bar tender set a pint in front of him. The beer was cold, and so good, the first alcohol since Tamazunchale. Yes, that was just the previous evening, but it seemed much longer ago and in another world. He downed the first beer, sipped a second more slowly, paid his bill and went back out into the hazy sun.

Lantry sauntered east on Cinco de Mayo toward the *Zócalo*. Sitting on the sidewalk, her back against a wall, a teenaged girl played at a battered accordion, a tune he didn't know, but a phrase of which the squawky instrument repeated again and again. Huddled against her was a tiny girl sucking on a lollipop, her daughter? He walked past, but something in the young mother's eyes gripped him. He stopped, listened to the painful music for several moments, handed her a bill and walked on.

After four or five blocks the street opened into the *Zócalo*, a vast open plaza four blocks square. To his left stood a huge cathedral, which a bi-lingual sign told him was the largest in the Americas. He crossed the street and stepped inside. The roof of the gigantic Gothic structure rested on massive stone pillars, and from the ceiling dangled a series of long chains and corroding candelabras. Lantry stared at the chains and the pillars, puzzled that the chains did not hang parallel to the columns. Gravity would guarantee that the chains hung plum, so how to account for this phenomenon? Certainly not just two beers.

30

Lantry ventured forward. Immediately he felt the sensation of descending to a lower plain. Then he recalled something he had once read about Mexico City. The city was built on a former lakebed, and given the many major earthquakes the place had known, an explanation for this strange phenomenon emerged. The stone floor on which he walked had sunk under its own weight, and earthquakes had caused the columns to tilt. And now he recalled that a great earthquake sometime in the 1980s had killed thousands here, an eight on the Richter scale if he remembered right.

Lantry shivered. He needed to be back outside in the sun. Was it the coolness of the huge dark vault, the aroma of votive candles, the realization that at any moment the earth might tremble and sink beneath his feet? Or perhaps just his presence in the sacred but foreboding place? He strolled quickly toward the altar, glancing in passing into sixteen richly-ornate side chapels, and retreated to the sunny *Zócalo*. He crossed to look at the two-block-long building that spanned the east side, the National Palace.

To his surprise he was permitted to enter, though a soldier at the door asked to hold his passport while he was inside. Here he found a broad courtyard, itself probably a square city block, with a two-story edifice surrounding all. On the steps to the second floor Lantry encountered vast murals painted by Diego Rivera in the 1930s and 1940s, murals that reached around two walls of the palace. They depicted the story of Mexico from the pre-colonial days of the Aztecs and even their predecessors to the Spanish Conquest, to the struggle for Independence, Revolution against the dictatorship of church and state, the class struggle of the 1930s and the fight against fascism in World War II.

His head spinning from the abrupt submergence into the long and dramatic history of a neighbor he had largely ignored, Lantry reclaimed his passport. For some time, he realized, a beating drum had penetrated his consciousness, and now he saw that a crowd had gathered near the center. He made his way through the crowd and found a band of dark-skinned men dressed in snakeskin loincloths and elaborate feathered headdresses, dancing in a ceremonial circle around the drums. A cloud of fragrant smoke rose from a sensor beside the drummers. Lantry watched in a trance until he became aware of his rumbling stomach, of the fact that he had eaten only a hotdog since the night before. He walked north in search of food.

What he found instead beside the cathedral was Templo Mayor, the major temple of the ancient sacred center of Tenochtitlan. He momentarily ignored his hunger, venturing inside to view the foundations of the sacred site, dismantled by the Spaniards both to destroy the conquered culture and to obtain the stones to build their own edifices, including the cathedral. Interpretive signs in English as well as Spanish told Lantry that before Conquistadors arrived, above him stood twin pyramids thirteen stories tall, temples to ancient gods of water and war. It was here that the symbol of modern Mexico first appeared, the eagle with the snake gripped in its talons and beak.

Reeling from his unanticipated immersion, not only into "modern" Mexican history—that is the past few centuries—but into an unknown ancient world, Lantry emerged from the recesses, back to the plaza once more, this time determined to find food. A block west of the cathedral he encountered Café Popular. Peering through the yellowing glass he saw that the name fit the place; it was packed wall to wall. He entered and was ushered to a tiny table for two. He was familiar with *tamales* from a couple of Tex-Mex places in Dallas, so he ordered a *tamal Oaxaqeño*, and of course a beer.

The meal came quickly, but he was not prepared for what he found. Wrapped in a fresh banana leaf, the *tamal* covered the plate. Inside he found highly seasoned pork wrapped in a generous blanket of *masa*, all covered with a delicious peanut and chocolate-flavored sauce the waitress told him was *mole negro*, a specialty of the southern state of Oaxaca. This meal, Lantry had to remind himself, was not to be devoured as had become his habit, but savored. It was one of the tastiest things he had ever encountered. He chuckled at the realization that after a single day he'd found a very good reason to be in Mexico. When the *cuenta* came, he owed the equivalent of five US dollars for the meal and the beer. Mexico wasn't a half-bad place to be, he thought as he strolled back to the street.

The pale sun had set as he ate, and it was time to find someplace to sleep. Several nearby hotels looked cheap enough, especially if accommodations in the capital were as inexpensive as the food. He chose the Juarez, partly because it shared its name with a city that every Texan knew.

"*¿Cuánto es?*" he asked the clerk.

"*Ciento ochenta,*" came the reply.

"*En dólares?*" he asked, struggling unsuccessfully to convert the currency in his head.

"*Trece,*" the clerk replied. "Thirteen."

Lantry pulled the newly-acquired roll of bills from his pocket and handed over 180 pesos. The key dangled from a well-worn and oily scrap of wood, the number 321 carved in the side. He mounted the stairs, found his room and collapsed on his back on another sagging bed. The ceiling was higher than the one in Laredo—so long ago it might have been another life, but the room was just as dingy. A scrap of painted wallpaper dangled above the door, waiting to fall, but those things couldn't matter. In some way he had not experienced for many months, Lantry felt something like satisfaction. Maybe it was the *tamal* and the beer, or perhaps the stimulation of all that he had seen, heard and felt since he'd crossed the Rio Grande.

Yet, alone in the little room, the loneliness that had followed him for many months, the despair that had taken up residence in his head, could not be long suppressed. His life was in shambles, no question about that. He'd lost his job, abandoned his apartment, closed his meager bank account and sold his pickup. Probably the truck had been worth six or seven thousand, but he'd jumped at the first Craigslist offer of five from a guy he'd never met. Yet, all those things he'd lost he could live without, he told himself—but could he ever be happy again without Linda? "Linda, Oh Linda, I miss you so much," he whimpered, and tears clouded his eyes.

Lantry sat up on the bed and pulled off his boot. He unfurled the thick roll and counted out fifty-seven hundred-dollar bills. How long could that last, he wondered. He took out a ballpoint pen, and on a scrap of newspaper somebody had left behind he did the math. Thirteen a day for a bed, maybe a little more than that for food and drink. If he drank cheap stuff in places cheaper than the Opera Bar and tried to drink less than he had in recent months, maybe he could get by on $30 a day. At that rate his cash might last half a year. "And then what?" he said aloud.

34

Lantry wanted to stay in the room, wanted to pull the covers over his head and fall asleep, to sleep well and perhaps never wake up, or if he did wake, rise somehow refreshed, leave the past behind and instead discover the other wonders this great city might hold. But he doubted he could sleep. He pulled his boots back on, stuffed the roll beside his ankle and went back out into growing darkness.

When he returned, he was his old self again. He staggered through the front door and past the desk clerk without raising his eyes, gripped the handrail and guided himself up three flights of stairs, eventually found the door that matched the number on his key, and collapsed fully clothed on the bed.

Chapter Six

"Wake up punks!" the jailor barked.

The steel bars slid open and two uniformed guards stepped in.

"You," one said, jabbing his finger into Pablo's chest. "Time to go see the judge. That's when the fun begins," he added with a heartless chuckle. "No more living in the country club. Course you don't know what that means, since you don't even know English."

He cuffed one of Pablo's wrists, jerked it behind his back and bound it to the other. The second guard was ready with leg irons. Pablo hobbled out of the cell and down the hall, a guard gripping each arm. They threw him into the back seat of a waiting car and belted him in. The driver, separated by a heavy mesh wall, drove through the gate and headed north on Interstate 35.

More miles of flat brushland rolled by. Something like two weeks had passed, so it must be about the first of March. The driver glanced over his shoulder.

"Your papers says they got you as a drug runner illegal. They gonna lock your ass up good," the man said gleefully.

"Maybe twenty years. If it was me, I'd say life, but you know these liberal judges we got down here, you might get off light. Hell you might be dumped back across the border in ten or fifteen. But I'm bettin twenty."

He chuckled again. Pablo understood most of what the man said, but gave no reply.

In Pearsall, Pablo had had no contact with the outside world. He'd asked for an *abogado*, but the guards, even the Latinos who spoke English, pretended they didn't understand the word. Even after he learned to say "lawyer," they only laughed.

"Who do you think is going to pay for a lawyer for you?" one demanded.

"What makes you think a wetback drug smuggler has rights in this country anyhow?" More than a lawyer, he wanted to talk to María, to let her know what had happened, where he was, but that was out of the question. Men who had the cash were allowed to make one call, or if they wanted to call somebody in the US they could call collect. Pablo had zero money, and even if he'd had a hundred dollars there would have been no way to call home. The only public phone in Victoria was at the *farmacia*. He'd used it once to call the lawyer who was supposed to help get back their land. But he had no idea what the *farmacia*'s number was or how to find out, and even if he'd been able to call, it wasn't likely that anybody would go across town to find María.

What must she be thinking? He told her he'd try to send a message once he'd safely crossed, and now more than two weeks had passed since he'd left Victoria. Did she think he'd deserted her, or that he hadn't made it across? Or maybe that he was dead?

The driver had said he'd be locked up for ten or twenty years. Could that be true? Surely when he saw the judge he could explain and the judge would understand. What he did wasn't so bad, and he wasn't a bad person. He just wanted to take care of María and his family. There was the other thing he'd done, the thing nobody besides the people on the train knew, and he didn't plan to tell that. He hadn't intended to kill a man, and maybe the guy deserved to die. No doubt he'd saved other people from being robbed, or maybe killed. Anyway it was something he couldn't undo, and it had nothing to do with why he was here.

The San Antonio skyline came into view and the driver slowed for heavy traffic. Pablo recalled his first trip through the city in 2007. They'd slept that afternoon in the van somewhere in a neighborhood that looked like Mexico, but when night fell they were back on the road north. This time San Antonio was as far north as he was going to get.

The driver pulled off the freeway and headed toward a cluster of tall buildings. They arrived at an underground parking garage and the attendant waved them in. The driver parked and called on a cell phone. Two uniformed guards showed up, pulled Pablo from the car and hustled him into an elevator. When they emerged, high above city streets, he was led through double doors and past a string of offices. He was seated in a small guarded room with other shackled detainees and told to wait.

An hour passed, and finally his name was called. He was ushered into a small cubicle, where a lawyer sat behind a desk. The lawyer did not look up from the papers he was reading. His head was bald and round with a thin layer of gray above his lip. Eventually he raised his eyes to stare at Pablo over his glasses, but he said nothing. Having sized up his client, the lawyer returned to a paper before him.

"So," he said at last, "undocumented alien charged with drug smuggling, is that right?"

Pablo didn't comprehend the first part, but he knew this was mostly about the marijuana. In a way he was relieved.

The man he'd killed had haunted his dreams every night for two weeks, and even with daytime distractions the crime had never been far from his thoughts. But this was simply about crossing a river with a bag of smoke.

"*Soy Pablo Real,*" Pablo said. "*Por favor, puedo explicarlo.*"

"Speak English," the lawyer demanded. "I don't speak Spanish. I don't know why they gave you to me anyway. I told the clerk I don't do drug runners."

"*¿Hay otra persona que hable Español?* Pablo asked. "I understand only little English."

"Sorry pal, you're stuck with me, and English is the language in this country. And don't think you're gonna get off, cause you're not. Best I can do is maybe get you two years, which is better than you deserve. I don't know why you couldn't just stay where you came from and get a job instead of trying to get rich bringing drugs into my country."

A clerk was at the door.

"Pablo Real," she said. "The judge is ready for you."

The lawyer hefted his belly from the chair and motioned for Pablo to precede him out the door. Pablo stood and followed the clerk down the hall toward the courtroom, his chains clanking with every step.

A man in a black robe was perched behind a long, dark desk. Pablo sat on the front row as instructed, a few seats from two other men, one in a suit and the other in a uniform, one of the border agents that had apprehended him. Behind them were other Mexican men in handcuffs and leg irons. The judge looked up from a paper he was reading.

"So, Pablo Real, arrested by the Border Patrol on February 14, 2009, charged with illegal entry and drug possession with intent to distribute approximately two and one-half pounds of marijuana. How do you plead?"

Pablo's expression was blank. Besides his name and the word marijuana, he had comprehended little of what the judge had said. He'd heard English spoken in Victoria by the Americans who'd brought the hogs, and he'd learned more words from TV in Sioux Falls, but not the words that came from the judge's mouth. He glanced at the lawyer for help, having little idea how to respond. The lawyer only shrugged. The only thing Pablo could think to do was to explain how he came to be here.

"*Mi hermana está inferma,*" he began, but the judge cut him off.

"Agent Schmidt, you speak some Spanish don't you? You can tell me what the defendant says."

"Yes, your honor," the man in uniform said. "He said his sister is sick."

He turned to Pablo and addressed him in Spanish.

"So what is it you have to say?" he asked, "and make it quick. We all have jobs to do."

Pablo knew this was his only chance to explain, and he didn't know where to begin. He couldn't begin at the beginning, with his family losing their land, not with what happened to his father, because that was all over now. So he would begin again with Angélica, about the flu and the doctor bills, about his new wife María, about no work for him in Mexico and how badly he needed money for his family. He started to tell about La Bestia, but thought better of that because of what had happened on the train. He mentioned Sioux Falls before he realized that would reveal that he'd crossed once before.

"Alright, that's enough of that," the judge growled. "I'm not interested in who your sister is or what you did or didn't do in Mexico. What I want to know is, do you admit that you snuck across the border, an illegal alien, and that you carried drugs?"

The border agent interpreted what the judge had asked.

"*Sí, señor*," he said, "*pero puedo explicarle.*"

"I don't want an explanation," the judge thundered. "What I want to know is do you plead guilty, or not."

Pablo cast another bewildered glance toward the lawyer, who seemed barely awake in a drama in which he neither wished nor played a part. Finally the lawyer spoke.

"Your honor, on behalf of my client I will enter a plea of guilty as charged, but would ask for leniency, that the sentence you impose not exceed two years."

The gavel's smack still rang in Pablo's ears.

"Two years it is," the judge said. "Mr. Real, I find you guilty as charged, and I sentence you to two years incarceration at a facility of the United States Bureau of Prisons. Case closed."

Pablo's lawyer rose and motioned for Pablo to do the same. He was escorted from the chamber and down the elevator to join three other shackled men in a waiting van.

Chapter Seven

The chaos on Cinco de Mayo never stopped, though once the bars closed the rumble settled to a drone accented by roaring motorbikes and blasting horns. But Lantry slept — until a siren screamed through his dreams and opened his eyes. Morning had come once more.

It was August now, two months into the rainy season, and the traffic din was softened by the swish of tires on sodden streets. Lantry had purchased a flimsy plastic raincoat in the *mercado* that kept him mostly dry, all but his legs and feet. The soles of his boots had worn thin and the leather was cracked, so his feet were often wet. But the rain was warm, and he had adjusted to minor discomforts and paid them little heed. Usually the sun was up long before he was, and by the time he needed them, both boots and streets were sometimes dry.

Weeks ago he'd moved to the cheapest room, a tiny cubicle with one small window that opened onto an airshaft. The view was a brick wall six feet away. The shaft led down to an alley, so it brought not fresh air but a moldy stench to his room. He'd grown so accustomed to exhaust and other foul odors that congested lungs and watering eyes seemed normal, though this morning seemed worse than usual. He sat up in bed, finger-nailed the crust from his eyes and rose groaning on shaky legs. Holding to the wall, he edged toward the bathroom. He turned on the faucet and splashed cold water on his face. He was powerfully thirsty, but remembered his bouts with what Texans called Moctezuma's revenge. He'd forgotten the rule more than once, and had paid the price. Now, even drunk he didn't drink the water. Half an inch remained in the bottle of water he had purchased. He tipped it up and cleared the phlegm from his throat.

He tried to focus on the visage in the mirror. "Hm, not a pretty sight," he mumbled. His hair was long and ragged, his face covered with stubble, his bleary eyes sunken and red. He traced a sour odor to his armpits. He turned the hot tap full blast in the shower and tested it periodically with a finger until eventually it began to warm. He stepped in, shampooed his hair, soaped and scrubbed every inch of his body, and toweled dry.

His head was splitting worse than usual. He found three aspirins, but there was no water left to wash them down. He threw them into his mouth and drained the last sip of Tierra, a cheap wine that was ubiquitous in neighborhood convenience stores. He'd found the name amusing when he was half sober. *Tierra* meant earth — or maybe dirt?

He looked through the jumble of clothes on his open pack, sniffed several shirts until he found the one closest to fresh, and put it on. His jeans lay crumpled by the door, a nasty-smelling stain on one leg. The filthy pants took his mind to vague images from the previous night, he and two other men passing a bottle of wine that had even more bite than Tierra. Where exactly he'd been he wasn't sure, but he vaguely remembered entering an alley somewhere near Mercado La Lagunilla. The next thing he remembered was waking up on the pavement, dragging himself to his feet, brushing off the worst of the filth and staggering south toward the hotel, his stomach heaving and his head throbbing.

Lantry dropped to his knees beside the soiled pants and thrust his hand into the back pocket. His wallet was still there. He pawed it open. There was Linda's picture, his Texas drivers license, a few other cards and scraps of paper. The money was gone. Frantically he grabbed the mattress and jerked it up. The small lump remained in the corner, stuffed in a hole probably gnawed by a long-gone mouse. He pulled out the wad, then released his breath. He removed the rubber band and counted out the money, six hundreds, three twenties and a few peso bills. All told about seven hundred dollars. Most of the money he'd brought across the border — it seemed like a lifetime ago — was spent. When he'd moved to the tiny interior room of the Juarez months ago he'd negotiated to pay by the week; otherwise the money would have been gone by now. Just the same, this couldn't go on much longer. In another month he'd be flat broke. Something had to change.

Why was he still here, anyway? No answer to that. He'd long since grown bored by the exotic culture that surrounded him, indifferent to the rich history. He still enjoyed the food, when he was sober enough, and he'd found that even the cheapest street food was delicious if you got it in the right places. He'd long since stopped eating at Café Popular and now and then splurging at Café Tecuba or Sanborn. At hole-in-the-wall taquerias he could fill up for a dollar or two. But spring and half of summer had passed, and all he had to show for it was that he'd become more proficient with the language, though on a narrow range of topics. He'd made no friends, not even acquaintances beyond hotel clerks and maids, a few waitresses and other men who hung out in cheap bars or drank in alleys. Even them he knew almost nothing about, and they knew nothing about him. He realized with some shock

44

that he'd pretty much stopped thinking about women, maybe because Linda's face and her lovely body always appeared, but also because women he met on the streets steered clear when they saw him coming.

Lantry dragged out his other jeans and guided in a leg. His boots were still wet, so he pulled on the tire-soled sandals he'd bought in the market and slapped his way downstairs to the street. On sunny mornings he sometimes paused, even in his stupor, to gaze through glazed eyes at the amazing array of color the daily rains had brought, the most brilliant and varied flowers he'd ever seen. On such mornings the sights and the aromas sometimes brought brief moments of joy, but this was not such a morning. A light rain was already falling. Hot coffee might help, and Café Popular was close. He staggered across the street, sloshing through potholes and puddles, but dodging the drenching spray of passing cars.

By the second cup he felt slightly more alive. The aspirin was kicking in and his head was clearing. But the unsightly image he'd seen in the mirror came back to mind. "You're killing yourself," he mumbled over a second cup. "This can't go on." He didn't know what to do, but one thing was clear; he had to get out of the city. He remembered how the mountains had called him, the clear sky and fresh air. He pictured the Sierra Madre and the little valley town of Tamazunchale. Maybe he should catch a bus back there. But what would he do for money in a tiny village like that? Maybe it would help get his head straight, get his life together before he starved, but then what? He ate an omelet and shuffled back to the Juarez.

He stared again with bewildered eyes at the drawn and haggard face in the mirror. His hair was at least clean now, but long and stringy, his beard tangled with some debris he'd missed. The man in the mirror looked much older than Lantry's thirty years, older in fact than the last time he'd faced himself. When was that exactly? He couldn't say. Honesty had gone out the window with the job, with Linda, with everything worth saving.

He lathered his face and shaved as carefully as his shaking hand would allow. He threw the covers across his bed and spread out his possessions to be packed. To his surprise he found a clean shirt in the bottom of the pack, even a fresh pair of underwear. He put them on, descended again to the street and found a barbershop. While the barber worked Lantry thought about options. Whatever else, he had to get a job of some kind. Maybe he could have found something in the city, but he'd had too much of noise and bad air. Getting a job in a place where he might afford to live probably meant a smaller city, but not a tiny *pueblo* like Tamazunchale. He might as well head on south, he concluded, but it had to be someplace where he could breathe mountain air.

A couple of times wind had blown enough smog away from the city that he'd glimpsed the big mountains to the southeast, capped with snow. That would be too high and too cold, but he knew that beyond them lay the Sierra Madre Oriental, the long, wild range the bus had twice climbed and which he knew extended much farther south. He paid for the haircut, went back for his pack and caught the metro to Terminal de Oriente, the station for buses east and south. To his surprise, when the train emerged from the earth the rain had stopped and the sky had grown bright.

Inside the terminal he found a tattered Mexico map somebody had left behind. For several minutes he perused the names on the departure board, matching them to places on the map. He traced the routes with his finger, muttering the names as he read. A hundred miles or so to the southeast, on the border between the states of Puebla and Veracruz, rose a soaring peak called Orizaba. The map listed the altitude as 5,611 meters. He calculated roughly that that would be well over 18,000 feet high! In the valley below the peak lay a string of towns with enchanting names like La Gloria, La Libertad and Guadalupe Victoria, wonderfully appealing names, but for him full of irony. "Glory, Liberty, Victory," he muttered. "Everything I don't have." The towns were off the main road, and beyond them the map showed a huge expanse of green. "At least I can have green," he mumbled to himself. He bought a ticket to Guadalupe Victoria.

Chapter Eight

They had no idea where the van was headed. It rolled northwest out of San Antonio on a broad four-lane highway, climbed through the hills to a higher plateau and finally turned north for another hour across dry, scrubby plains. The vehicle had no side windows, but Pablo and his companions caught glimpses of the landscape through the meshed front glass.

In late afternoon the van slowed and entered a small town. The name of the place was announced on a billboard, Eden. "Eden?" one man said. The four shared puzzled stares. Could Eden mean the same thing in English as in Spanish? The place the priest talked about where God created man, the place of beauty and plenty, the place where life began?

At the center of the dusty little town the van turned east, then pulled off at a sprawling array of grim concrete buildings surrounded by a tall steel fence topped by a roll of razor wire. The sign at the entrance read in big letters "Eden Detention Center." As the driver waited for the gate to roll open, Pablo made out the smaller letters below, "operated for the Federal Bureau of Prisons by the Corrections Corporation of America."

The van was met by a phalanx of guards, mostly steely-eyed white men. Two looked more like Pablo and his fellow passengers, but they didn't seem like friends. The guards hustled the prisoners into a room, and the one who appeared in charge ordered them to strip. Another searched their clothing, then flung everything into a bin.

"Grab the floor and spread your cheeks," the first guard ordered.

Another handed each man a bundle, baggy orange shirts and pants, socks, canvas shoes and underwear. Stains in the crotch told Pablo that the briefs were far from new. Now clad in orange, they were escorted to another room to be photographed and fingerprinted. A guard jabbed a needle into each man's arm and drew blood. Then it was down a hall and through a heavy barred gate. There the four were separated and moved out, two guards per man.

Pablo's escorts guided him around a corner and toward the dark end of the hall. One selected a key from the ring that dangled from his belt and unlocked a steel door. The other produced a key that fit Pablo's handcuffs and leg irons.

"I hope you enjoy life in the hole," one guard said with a venomous snicker. "You'll have plenty of time to think about why you're here."

He gave Pablo a shove and slammed the door shut with a clank that still echoed in Pablo's head.

When his eyes had adjusted to the dim light Pablo examined his new dwelling. He was not a tall man, and his arms were not long, but standing in the center of the cell he could almost touch both gray concrete walls. A narrow steel shelf on the wall held a lumpy mattress, and beside that stood a toilet. A narrow barred window near the ceiling admitted the only light. The smell was that of a dank tomb. It had not occurred to Pablo that he would be deprived even of the company of other men. If this was to be his confinement for the next two years, he would surely rot.

With nothing else to do, he stretched out on the mildewed mattress. An hour passed, maybe two, before the slot in the door clanked open and the evening meal was shoved through, a small piece of tough meat he couldn't identify, a potato and a slice of white bread. Gradually true dark fell, dark except for the bluish glare of the guard tower floodlights on the concrete wall. But sleep would not come, could not overpower the clamor and roar, the cacophony of voices—murmurs, conversations shouted from cell to cell, curses screamed. He caught phrases in Spanish, but in such a jumble he comprehended little. He was alone in a solitary cell, but it seemed he would be tortured by the agony of others who shared his fate.

Far into the night he fell asleep at last, only to be jerked back to consciousness by a coyote's howl. For the first moment it was the wily predator of Orizaba, come down from the mountain to test the chicken coop. But he opened his eyes and reality descended. When the howl came again, he realized it was a crazed human voice echoing down the corridor from another solitary cell.

Pablo stood on the mattress and stretched to see out the window. If he'd been as tall as the guards he might have peered out, but it was beyond his reach. He measured the window with his outstretched hand, two spread palms wide, the glass smeared inside with fingerprints of other men, the other side splashed with dirt by some long past rain. He could see nothing but the close concrete walls, lighted by the guard tower glare. He'd been in this hole for only a few hours, but it was already clear that if he were to remain sane, it had to be through some escape of his mind. He decided to begin by recalling details of his dismal day.

Already he missed not only the sunshine and the air, but companionship, even of those who shared his misery.

His fellow prisoners had revealed scraps of their stories in the back of the van. One, like Pablo, had been sentenced for bringing drugs across the border, another for illegally entering the country a third time. The third was beginning a second term, busted for driving drunk.

After the convicts had changed to orange, a woman at the desk had given the guards a sheet of paper with the numbers of four solitary cells.

"Why, what did we do to be thrown in the hole?" the man convicted of drunken driving demanded in English.

"Because that's what you deserve," a guard shot back.

The clerk added that the prison was overflowing with criminals, so it was prison policy to house new inmates in solitary.

"Maybe you'd rather be stuck with six others in a cell with four cots?" she said. "You could sleep on the floor, or maybe there's a faggot who'd share his bed."

The guards had guided them down the hall to the processing room, then to the isolation wing, then to this dark hole, and now Pablo's mind had already rejoined his body in the solitary cell. There was clearly a flaw in the idea of escape by reliving the past. Regardless of where his mind might take him in the outside world, the story would inevitably wind back to a dungeon behind walls and bars.

After what seemed an eternity, the bluish gray of the concrete gained a hue of grey, and then the yellowish pink of dawn. More time passed, and the slotted door slid open again, a hand shoved a tray through and the door slammed shut. Pablo rose from the mattress and urinated, then shuffled three steps to see what the tray might hold. A bowl of cereal with thin gray milk and a glass of water.

He choked down the cereal and drained the glass. The cell had no sink, no running water except what rushed into the stool when it was flushed. The mere lack of running water was itself not so bad. After all, the only time in his nineteen years that Pablo had experienced the luxury of piped-in water was during his months in Sioux Falls. On the tiny farms of his childhood, a water faucet in the house had been beyond the imagination of his family and their neighbors. Pablo's house had consisted of three small rooms, the kitchen where his mother cooked over a wood stove and where they crowded around the little table to eat, a room with a battered couch where he slept and a mattress where his sisters slept, and a third room big enough for his parents' bed. All water, both for humans and for livestock, was drawn a bucket at a time from the well. He could easily live without piped-in water, but here there was no well dug by a grandfather, no sunshine or air, no snow-capped mountain to gaze upon. Not even a window he could see out, even if there was something to see.

Yet Pablo had survived worse, he reminded himself, and he determined that one way or another, he would survive this. Sitting on the bunk he put his mind to work at coming to terms with two years behind walls. Two years was a very long time, but unless he could convince himself that he would survive, perhaps he would not. Some day, he told himself, he would emerge and go home. The hard part now was wondering what was becoming of María, of his mother, of Angélica and the younger girls. He sprawled on the cot and imagined María's face, remembered her warm body next to his. If only he had a photograph. More important, if only there was some way to let her know where he was.

Had the flu reached María too, his mother and the other girls? It had started in La Gloria, people thought, right after Granjas Carroll hauled truckloads of dead pigs from the barns and piled them to be burned. Then came the big rain in January, the sort of rain that only the oldest villagers had seen at that time of year, and putrid water spread across the plain. The money Pablo had left was probably enough to pay Angélica's doctor bill and to buy medicine for her, but if the others had fallen ill, by now the money was surely gone.

Chapter Nine

Lantry's bus rumbled through endless city streets and idled amidst knots of honking cars at congested intersections. People walked beside the streets, darted through traffic, clogged overpasses under which the bus passed, people everywhere. Finally the bus entered a freeway and headed east. After an hour of urban sprawl and smoking industrial plants, they began to climb at last from the sprawling valley. The bus leaned into the first hairpin curve, providing a panoramic view of the vast metropolis Lantry was leaving behind. The city spanned the wide valley and crawled up every hill. An east wind had brought fresher air to the streets that morning, but the blanket of gray hovered as always above the seething cauldron.

They continued to climb, and soon two snow-capped peaks came into view, what people called Popo and Itzi, rising against a sky that was almost blue. How long had it been since he'd experienced untainted atmosphere, breathed fresh air? February to August, half a year, time for most every facet of his former life to fade, even the memory of clear blue sky. The rainy season had begun in June, settling the dust, producing magical new flowers and sometimes thinning the smog. Lantry knew few of the flowers, but in more sober mornings he'd marveled at the array of color and the aromas that sometimes overpowered stale fumed air as he passed. But even when wind followed cleansing rain, the great gray dome had never truly yielded to blue.

Last night's booze was wearing off, and his head had resumed its usual throb. Typically that called for the relief of alcohol, a beer or two by noon, but today there'd been only the splash of wine to wash the aspirins down. He cracked the window and inhaled the first sweet breeze in months, and with it a moment of delight. He hadn't decided whether leaving Texas had been a good idea or a mistake, but for sure this escape to the mountains was right. He found himself wishing that the bus would never stop, that it would wind on and on through the mountains, past the modest but flowery roadside homes, higher and higher, past every temptation and bitter memory until at last he would emerge purified on some unknown side.

But the bus could not climb forever. It reached a high plateau and rolled on toward a city that his map showed to be Puebla. In Dallas, Cinco de Mayo had been little more than an excuse to drink a few extra Coronas on the fifth of May, but he recalled from somewhere that it was in Puebla that Mexicans defeated the French 1862.

The bus pulled off the freeway and into the edge of the city to exchange passengers. Lantry was tempted to get off and look for a drink, but he gritted his teeth and kept his seat, diverting the need by studying the passengers departing and climbing up. They seemed different than in the capital, darker, more shabbily dressed for the most part, some in country garb and sandals. Instead of suitcases or backpacks many carried what they'd brought in plastic tote bags. But regardless of their circumstances, they carried themselves with quiet dignity.

With new passengers aboard they were on the road again, more miles of freeway before finally exiting at a town called Atatzingo. Lantry bought a bottle of water and a mango and changed to a second-class bus, no more air conditioning or bad American movies blasting from TV monitors overhead. That bus rumbled northeast, up a less traveled two-lane road across a broad agricultural plain that spread toward the towering Sierra Madre and the cities of Perote and Xalapa. Clouds rolled in from the Gulf to meet him, blanking out the mountaintops, but flashes of color replaced the long view that had held his eyes.

Even after months in Mexico, Lantry was unprepared for the realities framed in his window. Unlike Texas, where ranches might run for miles and giant tractors worked agricultural fields, here fields were small, sometimes an acre or two, sometimes stretching for what he judged might be a few city blocks. Men followed teams of horses or sometimes a single horse or mule, working a row or two at a time. Fields of vegetables were dotted with human figures, bent low over hoes and harvest bags. He pulled out the water and the mango and watched the scene unfold.

At last they left that highway and headed east on a narrow blacktop toward the *pueblo* of Derrumbadas. On the edge of town the driver braked for a herdsman and his flock of goats to cross, then proceeded toward Guadalupe Victoria. They stopped at every tiny *pueblo*, most unnamed by a roadside sign or on his map, collections of small houses that seemed to have erupted from the soil from which they were made, some well advanced in returning to the earth. Besides people, the *pueblos* harbored cattle, horses, chickens, sheep, goats, cats and dogs.

The afternoon sun was intense on the lowlands, and the plain shimmered in the August heat, but rainclouds were building in the foothills to the east. It was the rainy season here too; the corn was tall and garden crops were green. Lantry searched the clouds for a glimpse of the Sierra Madre he'd seen from afar, and a few kilometers before the bus rolled into Victoria, a hole opened briefly in the veil. Before them rose the unbelievably tall and spectacular peak his map called *Citlaltépetl*.

"*El nombre Nahuatl,*" his seatmate offered, seeing Lantry's finger underlining the mountain on his map. "*El Pico de Orizaba, también.*"

The mountain's tremendous thrust into the sky took Lantry's breath away. The magnificent snow-capped peak loomed far above surrounding mountains. From the west it seemed an almost perfect cone. The height of the glacier verified what Lantry's map told him, that Orizaba was far taller than the two extinct volcanoes they'd passes outside the capital. But most thrilling, Orizaba towered not over a blanket of gray that obscured the struggles of twenty million souls, but above a broad valley that rose toward the vast swath of green on his map. Through the gap in the clouds he saw that brownish foothills led to green slopes, then to treeless rock and earth, and finally to ice and snow. Lantry could not take his eyes off Orizaba. So entranced he was that for a time he forgot his throbbing head. He gazed out his window at its magnificence until his neck was cramped. But then as quickly as it had opened, the window beyond his spattered window closed. Thunderclouds boiled up from the foothills, the mountain disappeared and it began to rain.

As Guadalupe Victoria came into view, Lantry became aware of an unpleasant odor. He couldn't place the smell, but it seemed familiar and it was growing stronger, something sour, a hint of ammonia. He sniffed and searched his memory for where he had smelled the stench before. Then he saw in the valley to his north a sprawling complex of long, low corrugated metal buildings, and beside them a giant green lagoon. Now he knew what he smelled. It was hog manure. Beyond the first complex of buildings lay another, and then another, row after row of long steel roofs glinting in the sun. They passed a large field of what looked like carrots irrigated with brown, foul-smelling water, although it was the rainy season.

They crossed a stream, foamy and green. Beyond the turn-off to the first complex, the two-lane highway was clogged with semi-trucks, some bringing loads of corn, others loaded with hogs bound for slaughter. The bus dodged and bounced through potholes, then rolled into Guadalupe Victoria. They crawled down a bumpy side street and past a sprawling outdoor vegetable market where people were rushing for cover from the rain. The bus squalled to a stop across the street from a large church with dual yellow and red towers.

Lantry recovered his backpack from the overhead rack and stepped down into the rain. His head was beyond throbbing to splitting now, and his stomach rumbled for food. He ducked under a tarpaulin shelter and wandered through the vegetable stands, past the vendors of plucked chickens and slabs of meat, finally to the zone of market restaurants. He ate a chicken taco, then stopped at a tiny shop that sold tequila and mescal. He bought a fifth of the cheapest tequila they had, cheaper even than what he'd been drinking in the city. He didn't recognize the label, but the moment he pointed to the bottle and uttered the word "tequila" to the clerk, the self-loathing he'd hoped to leave in Mexico City was back. But the bottle was in his hands and fifty pesos lay on the counter.

Lantry stuffed the bottle into his pack and waited for the rain to stop. When it eased to a drip he emerged from shelter and walked back toward the church towers, what he assumed would be the center of town. Unlike other villages they'd passed through, he found that the church fronted on the main street, not on the plaza.

He spread a plastic bag on the protruding root of a sprawling cypress tree for a dry seat, pulled out his bottle and took a long swig. As if prompted by the booze, he heard music — a trumpet, a guitar, a base, maybe something else, then men singing. It sounded like a Mariachi band, possibly from a nearby bar, he thought, but it was early in the day for that. He stood and wandered idly in the direction of the music. It grew louder, until finally the band rounded a corner and proceeded toward him. Four men in metal-studded black jackets and pants led the procession, playing and singing as they came. Behind them four others bore a simple wooden coffin on their shoulders. As they drew near Lantry saw that the coffin was small, big enough for a child. He stepped behind a tree to watch unobtrusively as the procession passed, perhaps fifty people or more, some with tear-streaked faces, others stoic, most carrying long-stemmed white flowers. The mourners passed, turned another corner and proceeded toward the church.

And then the rain resumed. After three months he had grown accustomed to afternoon showers in the capital, but he had no idea how much rain might fall on the western slope of the Sierra Madre. He splashed through puddles for a couple of blocks until he encountered a plain two-story building with a small sign announcing a hotel.

"*Buenas tardes,*" the clerk cheerfully greeted him as he stood dripping before the desk. "*Bienvenido a Guadalupe Victoria.*"

The room was a hundred sixty pesos, eleven dollars. Lantry pulled out his wallet and paid, and the clerk handed him a pile of coins and a key. He started for the stairs, then turned back.

"*¿El funeral?*" he asked.

"*Sí, un muchacho, solo ocho años*" the clerk replied. "*Gripe, la primera muerte que ocurre aquí, pero mucha gente está enferma.*"

Gripe. Lantry was pretty sure that was flu of some kind. Maybe this town wasn't such a good place to be, not just the stench, but apparently lots of sickness and an eight-year-old dead? He climbed the stairs to the room at the end of the hall, number fourteen. The key turned with difficulty and he opened the door to a musty room with a bare light bulb hanging from its cord, yet another sagging bed, a battered nightstand, a lavatory and a stool. He used the toilet, which flushed sluggishly, and dropped onto the bed. His head was still throbbing, but more tequila would ease that, at least for a while. He pulled the bottle from his pack and drank.

Chapter Ten

The barred gate rolled open with the usual reverberating thud. The keepers took obvious pleasure in banging it open, even more in slamming it shut. How many times in a day or night did that terrible clang echo down the corridor of Cell Block B? Besides the incessant jumble of voices, the shrieks, curses and threats, the din was punctuated now and then by blows. But it was the clatter of crashing bars that echoed relentlessly in Pablo's head, even in his sleep when all was quiet besides his cellmates' snores. Even when the bars flew open instead of shut there was no comfort or hope. Except for the hour in the sun, when they took a man out of his cell it was usually to someplace he didn't want to go.

Two guards were at the door, a shackled inmate gripped between them. One unlocked the legs and then the hands, and the other flung the new man into the crowded cubicle. Four bunks, a lower and an upper on each side and four men, and now, again, number five. Pablo's first thought was more nighttime hours standing by the window, staring out at the floodlights that blinded every view besides glimpses of fence, or sitting on the toilet, or lying on the concrete floor. Those were the options when five or six men shared four beds, or at least the best options. But he tried to think of himself as lucky. At least in a regular cell he could see out the window, even if there was nothing of interest to see. In some cells the same man got the floor every night, and in some, he'd heard, lying unmolested on the floor was preferable to the abuse he might endure.

Before the last number five left Pablo's cell a few days earlier they had agreed on an arrangement that was fair to everybody. Each man had a bed four nights out of five. Now Pablo sized the new man up. Could he take the guy down if it came to that? Number five raised his head. His cheekbone was a swollen purple bruise. But didn't Pablo know the man? Where had he seen him before? Their eyes met, and Pablo saw the same light of recognition in the new inmate's eyes.

"Pablo?" the other called. "I'm Vicente, from La Gloria."

"Vicente, of course!"

They had met in the market long ago, and one fall they had worked together shocking corn.

"What are you doing here Vicente?" Pablo asked.

"What do you think? Same as you I guess. Working construction in San Antonio without papers. I made a fight when the boss didn't pay my wages, and he called *la migra*."

"So when did you leave La Gloria?" Pablo asked. "Do you know my sister Angélica?"

"I left two months ago. No, I don't know Angélica."

"She was sick when I left in February," Pablo said. "I wish I knew how she is."

"*Sí, la gripe,*" Vicente said. "The flu. Half the town was sick when I left. They made the men go to work anyway, and they came home sicker than before. Some men quit, and some families where sickness had not yet come left the valley. There was nothing there for me except the hogs, so I went north."

"And María," Pablo inquired. "Do you know María?"

"I know lots of Marías," Vicente said with a laugh. "Which María?"

"My girlfriend," Pablo said. "My wife. We were together before I went to South Dakota, but we got our own place at Christmas time."

"No, I don't think I know her," Vicente said. "I'm sorry, but in La Gloria we don't know a lot of people in the big city of Victoria." He laughed again.

"So, Vicente, where do you think you're going to sleep?" growled Roberto. "There are four beds here and you don't have one."

Vicente studied Roberto and the other two men. "I don't know," he said. "I didn't ask to be here."

"You can have my bunk tonight," Pablo offered. He faced Roberto with cold eyes. "I guess we'll do like last time," he said. "Take turns."

He stared unflinching at the other two.

"*Sí*," Carlos assented. "That's fair." Juan nodded his head.

"You'll get my place last," Roberto snarled, knowing he was outnumbered but asserting his rank as the tough guy who couldn't be trodden under foot. "And don't ever forget why I'm here," he added. "Not because I swam some damned river or helped build some *gringo*'s house. I'm here because I buried my switchblade in a man's belly, and I'd do it again."

Nobody in the cell doubted Roberto's story, but nobody replied. There were four of them now, and one of him, and so far as they knew he didn't have a knife. Pablo turned his attention back to his friend.

"Tell me all you know about things in the valley," he said. "We know some of the same people. What's happening at Granjas Carroll? So the sickness has continued to spread?"

"I know little," Vicente said. "Half of La Gloria was sick and two kids died. The company said it wasn't from the pigs, and of course the governor agreed. Everybody was scared when I left, but I haven't talked to anybody since. In San Antonio I met a guy in a park where I was sleeping, and he offered me a job. I worked one week, and on Saturday he said I didn't work hard enough and I wouldn't get my pay. In truth I worked very hard, pouring concrete for a big house. When I said I'd beat the hell out of him if he didn't give me my pay he pulled out a gun. He got on a cell phone and called *la migra*, and that was that. He told them I was a lousy worker. He lied that I'd said I had papers when I didn't. They took me away and locked me up, and now I'm here for two months before they dump me back across the river. That's all I know."

The trap door slid open and in came a tray with five plastic plates of food. Each plate held a mound of beans with scraps of gristly meat and a pile of spaghetti. The five took their plates and fell to eating.

"What the hell is this damned so-called meat?" Roberto growled.

"At least it's not rotten like the fish they brought yesterday," Carlos said meekly.

At three o'clock the guards returned and herded the five out to the exercise pen. It was a concrete slab maybe a dozen meters across with a basketball goal at one end. There was no basketball, and even if there had been, basketball was not their game. If they'd had a soccer ball they might have kicked it around, even though the outdoor cell was far too small to actually play the game. Anyway, there were maybe fifty other men in the yard, so thick that the only thing an inmate could do was pace around the perimeter and hope not to bump into

64

one of the thugs that was looking for a fight.

It hadn't taken Pablo long to learn who they were. Some were gang members doing hard time, others were like caged tigers who thought the way to survive was to stare everybody down, or knock them down if they got in the way. Most of the prisoners were Mexican like him, some from Guatemala, Honduras or El Salvador, but some weren't like the people he'd grown up with in Victoria. The word was that two had raped other men in their cells. But most, at least the few he'd talked to, had stories similar to his. Illegal crossings, no papers, some carrying drugs, whether by choice or not. One thing most had in common was no lawyer, or a lawyer that didn't care what happened to them, or maybe who thought they should be here and helped lock them up.

Roberto was not the only man here for violent crimes, and some claimed to have weapons hidden in their cells or under their clothes. Those were the men who spoke with others only to threaten or to fight, to let fellow prisoners know they were not to be fooled with. Pablo avoided eye contact with them, in fact with most other men beyond the handful he'd come to know. And he was not alone in his isolation. It occurred to him that they were not so different from the hogs back in the valley, snapping at each other in their crowded pens. For an hour each afternoon the convicts milled around in their crowded sty under the blazing Texas sun, moved their legs to keep them from locking up like their minds, tried to stay clear of simmering fights.

When the hour of "exercise" was over, men were herded back to their cells, one group at a time. Until the sun finally set, five hours later, they sat on their bunks, used the toilet when they had to, never at more than arm's length from their cellmates, sometimes raging at each other's vile smells, but mostly sitting in silence and waiting for the minutes, the hours, the days—and in Pablo's case, the years—to go by. If a man rose and stared out the window, what lay beyond the fence was desert that stretched as far as he could see, cactus, mesquite and scrub. Now and then a bird might fly across the fence and light for a moment on the ledge outside the window, ignoring the men caged inside, oblivious to the loss of freedom suffered by creatures on the other side of the bars. Pablo envied the freedom that rested in their wings.

One day it occurred to him that he might be able to attract the birds. Instead of consuming all the unpalatable food the guards brought or sending it back uneaten—or flushing the most disgusting entrees down the toilet—he began to save back crumbs. He collected the scraps in a plastic bag under his mattress where the cockroaches couldn't get them, and when he and his cellmates passed near the window on their way to the exercise pen, if no guard was watching he might cast a handful to fall where the birds would find them and feed. Mostly sparrows or grackles came, but even they were in their own ways beautiful, the subtle variations of gray and brown of the sparrows, the iridescent dark sheen of the grackles. But now and then other birds came, once a brilliant red cardinal, and several times a *sinsonte*, what the *gringos* called a mockingbird, sat on the razor wire and sang. Was he merely oblivious to the blessings of liberty, or was he deliberately mocking their plight, flaunting his freedom in the face of fellow creatures for whom freedom was only a word?

At last the sun went down and the merciful night descended. Gradually the heat seeped from the concrete walls and the cell became less hot. At ten most of the lights were turned out, but darkness never fell. Always the runway lights cast the shadow of steel bars on walls and beds and the faces of men. The guard tower floodlights added their eerie blue-gray glare. That was the one good thing about solitary. In the hole it was closer to dark, but even there darkness never truly came, not the darkness Pablo had known as a child on the farm above Victoria, where the only illumination was from the moon or stars, or on cloudy nights the feeble lights of the distant village. As for light, except for the hour in the searing sun it was never really light in Eden either. The barred window in Pablo's cell was larger and lower than in solitary, but it faced north, a void where the sun's rays never fell.

On Vicente's first night he thanked Pablo for his kindness and stretched out on Pablo's bunk. From then until the sun came up, Pablo's choices were three. He could stretch out on the concrete floor, pass the hours sitting on the toilet, or stand and gaze through the bars at the empty yard, the fence, the floodlights and the pockets of darkness that hid between the lights. Pablo lost himself in that darkness; it was lighter than the darkness in his soul.

The hours until dawn would advance like the pace of a centipede across the vast desert from which the darkness came. Eventually he would lie down on the floor and try to sleep. For now he stood at the window, clutched the unyielding bars and pouring his soul to the darkened wasteland beyond the fence. If only the window faced south he could send some mute message to María, but he faced the other way, toward Dallas, toward Sioux Falls, toward the North Pole.

If only there was some way to contact her, to let her know that he was alive, if in fact his present existence could be called life. He'd learned that making a phone call happened only if a man provided favors for the guards, money, a share of something smuggled in, maybe something overheard from another inmate. But even if he'd had the privilege, nobody he knew had a telephone, and he knew no number to call. There was the public phone at the *farmacia*, but he had no idea what that number might be. Even if he could reach María, what could he tell her, besides that he was alive? He could find out whether Angélica was well and who else in the villages had fallen to the flu, how many had died. He could tell her that there would be no more checks, that he had failed, but she knew that already. He could say to her that he was branded a drug smuggler. That he would not be coming home for a very long time. He could beg her to wait for him, but on many nights he was less than sure that she would, even if she knew.

Self-torture had its limits, even for Pablo. Exerting all of his failing will, he eventually forced his mind from these thoughts by reliving happy times with his family, and especially with María. She was far away, but as tears clouded Pablo's eyes she seemed to come near. He imagined her sweet face, touched the thick black hair that covered her naked shoulders, felt love radiating from her eyes, imagined his hands coursing slowly down her slender firm body to her hips. He could almost taste her lips, the loveliness of her breasts. He relived as he did every night, as he could not have avoided reliving, rolling his body between her legs, the sweetness of her love, the ecstasy they reached together. Pablo felt fire in his groin, needed so badly to release his painful love. But the only things his body produced were sweat and tears.

Chapter Eleven

If only they'd been able to stay on the farm, things would have been different. Their small plot was a scrap of what was once a sprawling *ejido*, which at the uncompromising demand of Emiliano Zapata a century earlier the revolutionary government had stripped from the rich *hacendados* and given back to the *campesinos* who'd always worked the fields. Nobody alive could remember the 1910 revolution of course, though the oldest woman in Victoria told anybody who would listen that she remembered the day the peasants got back their land. As a boy Pablo had heard the stories from an aged blind great-grandfather, a man born the year the ejido was formed. It was to be held in common forever, but many fields had been subdivided each generation until there was little common land left, only *campesinos* working scraps of their ancestral lands. At least they were still working for themselves and their families—until the *gringos* brought the hogs.

There had been enough land for Pablo's grandfather to raise the corn and hay and animals to feed his family well, but Pablo's father had inherited less than two hectares, about four acres in North American terms. Even so, in good years they raised enough vegetables for the kitchen and corn to make tortillas, with plenty left over for the chickens and pigs and a couple of goats. There was hay for the horse and for the cow that supplied the milk they drank and from which his mother made butter and cheese. Skimmed milk went to the chickens, hogs and goats and to the cat that kept the mice from the corn.

Their well was good, a deep well dug and lined with stones by his great-grandfather. In years of drought or grasshoppers times were lean, but even in dry seasons the well had never failed, supplied as it was by groundwater replenished from melting snow.

But that was before the *americanos* came. Pablo's earliest memory—he must have been four or five at the time—was of big semi-trailer trucks rumbling down the highway to the valley, loaded with lumber and steel. It was January of 1994, the time of year when the earth was brown and rain rarely fell.

That same month people came home from church with news that two states south in Chiapas, armed men had emerged from the jungle to take control. The priest said they were protesting something called NAFTA, the North American Free Trade Agreement, something nobody in Victoria had heard about, not even the priest. One villager heard on the radio that the rebels had seized four towns, even the city of San Cristóbal. They called themselves Zapatistas, descendants of Zapata. That was a name every child knew. Zapata's battle cry had been *"tierra y libertad,"* land and liberty, and he refused to stop fighting until the *campesinos* regained their fields. Now the land was gone again, and to Pablo, liberty was only a word.

Even before the corporation came, the villagers and *campesinos* knew that the Mexican government had long forgotten Zapata's dreams, had grown corrupt and indifferent to their poverty, to the lack of roads and schools. They expected nothing from the capital; they had learned to rely on themselves and their neighbors. But the Zapatistas claimed that things were going to get worse, that the so-called "free trade agreement" would let capitalists from the United States in on the game. Victoria hadn't had long to wait.

Suddenly the valley was crawling with North Americans and Mexicans from the city, looking for land. They approached the most prominent landowners first, offering them twice what the land was worth. *Campesinos* with small holdings landlocked by the larger spreads received even more. Some took the money and bought finer houses in town. One sold a coveted strip near the road and bought a small tractor, the first the valley had seen. Threats visited those who refused to sell. A few families left the valley for the cities and did not return.

But most men refused even to consider selling their grandfathers' lands. They had survived thus far, and they had no intention of letting go. Besides tending their animals and working their small plots, most men, like Pablo's father Salvador, had always made extra money during the dry season helping the large landowners haul in their shocks and shell the corn. When money ran low they would slaughter the oldest hens, a goat or a fattened pig and take the meat to the market for sale. Others sold extra eggs, especially in the molting season when eggs were scarce and the price was higher. Unless they were truly desperate, the Reals kept enough of the best for the family. Along with the tortillas his mother patted for the *comal* every morning, the family had plenty of garden produce in season, and in winter months dried beans, eggs, a little meat, and garden vegetables his mother had dried or canned. Their diet was simple, but they ate well. Still, money was always short, so when Salvador heard there were jobs building barns in the valley, he went to work.

Few people in Victoria had seen anybody who didn't look like them, but now the little hotel was full of North

Americans, come to oversee the construction project. The *americanos* brought something the valley had never known, steady jobs. Outsiders came to the valley to work, some from tiny *pueblos* in the mountains, some from the cities. First the men built one long steel barn, then a second and a third and then more, each big enough for a thousand hogs. Would construction never cease? For two years, it did not. Throughout the valley barns were built, twenty here, another twenty up the road. Nobody knew how many, or how many more were to come. Beside each row of barns, bulldozers gouged massive trenches in the earth, longer than Salvador's farm was wide. By the time Pablo started school, there were said to be hundreds of barns spread from Victoria to Perote and beyond.

Before the last of Victoria's barns was finished more trucks arrived, those bringing thousands of pigs. Where they came from nobody seemed to know. When rains returned in the spring, big John Deere tractors followed. Plows that would have taken a herd of horses to pull arrived to work vast plots of land — consolidated from the holdings of many a *campesino* — and larger scraps of *ejido* land the corporation had acquired. Other trucks brought seed, big yellow kernels of corn that were different from what local farmers grew, something called GMO. When the rains fell, the corn leaped from the ground and reached for the sun, amazing growth that nobody had seen. By the end of July the corn was already taller than a man's shoulders. And then the airplane came, flying low over the fields and spraying a fine mist, and the acrid odor drifted across the town. Soon everything that grew in the broad fields was brown, except the corn.

By the third spring all the barns were built and filled. People heard that the valley now housed a million pigs, far more pigs than there were people in all the villages and on all the farms. There were still jobs to be had, but not so many as before. Men who had grown accustomed to a small check every two weeks competed for jobs feeding hogs. For those hired, the pay was less, but at least there were still jobs year around. Every hour of every day the pigs wanted feed, and their excrement had to be washed away into what the company called lagoons.

In the third summer the *campesinos* noticed changes in their corn. It grew oddly, yellow kernels now mixed on a single ear with the blue. It ripened unevenly, making harvest more difficult. Weeds they had never seen began to sprout. Old men bit down on the kernels and scratched their heads. The flavor of the new corn was strange, full of pasty dough. When their daughters made masa or tortillas, the taste was not right.

The following winter Pablo helped his father butcher a fattened pig. They hitched the cart to the horse and loaded the meat to haul it down the hill to the market. First they went to the *carnicería* where they had always sold their meat, but the butcher didn't want to buy, at least not at the price he had usually paid. There were too many pigs now, he said, and not enough people to buy. He offered to pay just over half what he'd paid in previous years. Salvador was outraged. He had known the butcher since they were kids, and had always delivered top quality meat. He stormed out of the shop and took the carcass to *el mercado*.

By evening they had sold most of the pork, but not for the price they expected. The story was the same everywhere.

The butcher had plenty of pork from Granjas Carroll. The pork was soft and juicy, not lean and muscled like the farm-raised hogs. When night fell, Salvador and Pablo headed back up the mountain with what remained. His mother and sisters salted what was left so it wouldn't spoil, and the family ate pork every day for the next two weeks.

And so it went. The next year the well dried up, and theirs was not the only one. The teacher explained that the water had always come from an underground aquifer, fed perennially by Orizaba's streams. But the hog factory's wells were much deeper, and they pumped out millions of gallons every day, so soon the wells dug by grandfathers ran dry. Salvador had no money to dig deeper, and without water the farm was nearly worthless. Now a daily task was guiding the old mare, Corredera, down to the village to haul up enough water to keep the animals and the garden alive.

The less they could produce, the lower the prices for what they grew. Not only were they low on necessary supplies, but the corn Salvador harvested was no good for seed. It was adulterated by what they now knew as Monsanto corn. One *campesino* had a sizable plot higher up the mountain and still had good seed for sale, but everybody needed it so the price was high. In desperation and falling deeper into debt, Salvador borrowed money to buy Monsanto's seed, which the Americans said would produce without much water. But just as the seedlings emerged, a massive rainstorm washed them out. With Pablo in tow, Salvador went to the banker to borrow more money. They waited outside his office while the banker listened to pleas from three other men.

At last Salvador and Pablo were announced and ushered in by the banker's assistant. There were two chairs in front of the desk, but he did not ask them to sit down. He stared for a time at Salvador's ragged poncho, seeming to be in deep thought. "So what do you own as collateral to ensure a larger loan?" he asked at last.

"I have a good two-hectare farm," Salvador began. He started to tell how much his grandfather had owned, but thought better of that. "We have a house with a tight roof and three rooms," he added. "I have a horse, seven pigs and at least two dozen hens. And the well my grandfather dug."

He did not mention that the well had gone dry, but probably the banker guessed as much, since the Real's well was not the only one that had failed.

"*Es todo?*" the banker asked over his spectacles, his forehead wrinkled. "That's all? I'm afraid that's not enough to guarantee a loan."

Salvador put on his hat and led Pablo back into the street. They stopped to see a moneylender that Salvador knew, but he asked for an interest rate that made Salvador's blood boil. "Let's face it," the man said. "You're not the only *campesino* that needs money, and there's not much to go around."

"OK," Salvador said at last, his voice quaking. "I have no choice."

In the fifth year rain came late, and hail when the crop was young. The family was down to three pigs and a dozen chickens. Not even the garden thrived. When the loan came due, Salvador could not pay. He begged for an extension, but the moneylender said no. The family packed their few belongings onto the cart and bumped down the rutted trail to town. Salvador went to the Granjas Carroll office and took a job feeding hogs.

A bolt of lightning flashed through the bars of Pablo's cage and the crack of thunder jolted his mind back to the tiny cell where his body stood. He dropped to the clammy concrete floor and closed his eyes. He searched for answers, for some sign of hope. Except when lightning flashed, he found only darkness.

Chapter Twelve

Lantry kicked off his boots, careful to deposit the now light roll of bills inside. He swallowed more of the cheap fiery drink, stretched out on his back and closed his eyes. The world slowly revolved, but he was accustomed to that; in fact he rather relished this particular phase, which brought a measure of care-free amnesia and made his body feel light, inconsequential, less burdensome than it otherwise did. For a time he slept.

When he opened his eyes again, the dingy ceiling reflected the amber hue of twilight. He sat up on the bed and tried to stand, but stumbled. Holding to the wall, he edged toward the bathroom. He turned on the faucet and brought cupped hands to his face. After half a year he still had to remind himself not to drink, but now his nostrils sensed again the stale ammonia smell, and he remembered the green cesspool and the foamy stream he had crossed. "Probably a particularly bad place to drink the water," he muttered.

But his throat was dry as usual, and his stomach churned. Without warning he wretched. He dropped to the floor and emptied bile and the scant contents of his stomach into the toilet. Feeling even weaker, he dragged himself up again. He washed his face and rinsed his mouth, careful not to swallow. The face in the cracked mirror was drawn, the eyes dark and deep. He recalled that except for the mango and one taco he hadn't eaten since Mexico City. Outside the grimy window, daylight was dying. He eyed the lowered level of his bottle, but resisted its tug. He pulled on his boots and descended the stairs.

Lantry wandered unsteadily toward the dual earth-toned towers of the church, pale yellow and what Linda would have called terracotta. And then she was with him again, but only in his tortured mind. Would he never escape the pain of her loss? He focused on the church. It was modest for a Catholic church in Mexico, but graceful in its way. It loomed above a small tiled plaza skirted by trees—pines, junipers, cypress and a leafy deciduous tree he didn't recognize. But there was something unusual about this place, something he hadn't seen before. Now he realized that not just the churchyard, but the main street was shaded by a boulevard of mature trees, not along the sides, but separating lanes of traffic—if you could call the occasional car and the more frequent trucks "traffic." Peering up streets in every direction he saw that even the paving stoned side street that led from the church toward the mountain—in fact every street he could see—had its line of trees down the middle!

Lantry peeked into the now deserted church. The only reminders of the sad afternoon were the strewn white petals of the flowers mourners had borne. Lantry walked north, soon encountering a small restaurant with the name painted in fancy letters above the door, Restaurante Familiar Doña Lupita, Mrs. Lupita's family restaurant. He stepped over a skinny brown dog sleeping by the door and peered through the screen door from which intoxicating aromas came. But a screen door? Something familiar in parts of Texas, but in all the months in Mexico City he couldn't recall a screen door. It seemed oddly out of place, but then he noticed that the screen was crawling with flies. He brushed one off his face, slid the screen open and entered the dining room.

He was surprised that his entry provoked little surprise, but then he saw that besides a couple of Mexican families and working men there was a table of men speaking English. A teenaged waitress greeted him and he sat at an open table. When he asked for a menu she pointed him to a chalkboard on the wall with the *comida corrida*, the menu of the day. Sadly, after all his time in Mexico he had failed to learn the Spanish words for many common foods. But then he had long ago stopped going to restaurants that offered varied menus—at prices of four or five dollars or more. For months, when he ate at all, he'd eaten mostly street tacos, *exquisitos* and fruits, the foods one can buy for less than a dollar's worth of pesos. This menu offered *pollo, carne* and *chuleta*—chicken, beef and pork chops. He assumed that *barbacoa* was something like Texas barbecue, so he ordered *chuleta a la barbacoa* and a Dos Equis beer.

In less than a minute the waitress brought a big bowl of consume with noodles and vegetables, a basket of fresh-baked rolls and a small pitcher of *agua de melon,* an orange-tinted drink that tasted like cantaloupe. He slurped the soup and listened to the talk at the nearby table. The men were clearly from the United States, and in fact one had an unmistakable Texas accent. He caught enough of their conversation to realize that they were involved with the big hog operation. They were discussing labor unrest and what to do about it. One suggested that the disgruntled workers should simply be fired, but another proposed throwing some sort of bone to head off more trouble. Besides complaints about working conditions, the other reason for the trouble, it seemed, was a flu that was spreading through the community, a sickness people claimed came from the hogs.

Lantry's main course arrived, pork ribs in *salsa verde*, a spicy green sauce made of *chiles* and *tomatillos* that he'd encountered in Dallas, but had come to appreciate in Mexico City. Also a bowl of beans and a basket of hot tortillas. The *barbacoa* wasn't what he expected, but it was delicious, even though the talk at the next table tempered his enjoyment of the pork, which reminded him of the stench he'd ridden through and the putrid cesspool. Nonetheless, he devoured the dinner. He hadn't realized how hungry he had been for real food. Then came the final course, flan, a rich caramel-tasting custard he remembered having once at Café Popular in the city.

Lantry paid his bill, which he calculated set him back less than three American dollars. He felt something like contentment, so much so that in spite of his shrinking resources, he left a generous tip. In fact, a full belly and the rich creamy dessert had altered his frame of mind. Except for the odor of hog manure, the evening felt fine. A new moon and a brilliant planet stood sharply against the darkening western horizon. He crossed to the church and walked toward the now darkening snow-white cone that loomed in the eastern sky.

After a couple of blocks he reached the plaza. He gazed back across the red-tinged valley. The view was lovely, but it held no answer to the recurring question, what was he doing here? Leaving Dallas was somehow inevitable the day he was fired, but his presence in this place and in this moment was anything but. He imagined himself as a scrap of driftwood riding a shifting tide, or perhaps as windborne thistle fleece. Here he was a thousand miles from what he'd thought was home, not a step of the way really premeditated. He hadn't considered north the day he'd left, not because Linda had gone that direction, but because it was winter. He'd quickly dismissed east, because that meant too many people, like Dallas. He had thought about west, maybe New Mexico or Arizona, but at the last moment he'd looked out a window toward the sun and a verdict came. Nothing deliberate, not even at the moment he'd handed over the pickup keys. Yet when he boarded the Laredo-bound bus in Abilene it had somehow seemed right. It was almost amusing, looking back. Nothing more than the sun that bleak February morning had called him south, perhaps a sort of magnet that had drawn what was left of his soul.

Now he had fled a second city, one whose exotic past and present had excited him for a time, but to which he had grown jaded and indifferent. For many months it was mostly alcohol that mattered, he couldn't deny that, but alcohol you can find one place as well as the next. The noise, the pollution and the crowds had played their parts in driving him from the capital, but was the second flight as much toward something as it was an escape? He had longed vaguely for the enchantment he'd felt in the Sierra Madre, the brief stop in Tamazunchale, but now that he was here, standing virtually in the shadow of Orizaba, the next step or the reason for it seemed as distant as ever. Might he recapture something in these mountains, perhaps the power to feel again in ways that he had lost? He found an empty bench and sat. The eastern sky was dark now, all but the profile of the massive snow-capped peak.

His musing was interrupted by the approach of a scrawny old man, a battered guitar clutched in gnarled hands.

"¿Una canción?" the man's raspy voice asked.

"¿Por qué no?" Lantry replied. Why not?

The musician strummed a few notes and began to sing. The guitar was slightly out of tune and the man did not play it well, but the voice conveyed tenderness and pain. In the fading light Lantry saw tears welling in the old man's eyes. The tune seemed vaguely familiar, but he couldn't recognize the lyrics until the chorus came around, then the recurring title line, "*Cielito Lindo*," Lovely sky. "From the Sierra Morena, lovely sky, come down, a pair of dark eyes, lovely sky." Lantry gazed past the singer toward Orizaba. The mountain was barely visible in the new moon's light, and its outline was blurred. There were tears in his own eyes too.

When the song ended Lantry dug a ten peso coin from his pocket, and the singer moved on to a young couple on a secluded bench. An ornate lamp on each corner lighted the plaza, and though it was about as far from Christmas as it ever gets, a string of colored lights still dangled from an arching tree. From a booth selling hotdogs and sodas a radio blared. The plaza was filling now, families strolling across from the church and young couples embracing in the shadows. Sorrow stabbed at Lantry's heart. He could no longer deny the profound loneliness he had so long suppressed. How could he have been such a fool? Linda had been kind to him, even patient. He knew that she had loved him, and he certainly loved her. There was just one problem. He'd loved alcohol more.

No, not loved it, just had to have it. Ever since college it had been that way. He'd done well at Texas State in spite of drinking way too much, and even finished law school. But partying edged out studying for the bar exam, so eventually he applied for a job at the *Dallas Morning News*. The editors recognized his grit, or maybe his craziness, hired him as low

82

man on the totem pole and sent him to the action. Perhaps it was just that he was expendable. As a kid in San Marcos he'd been drawn to detective novels—from Edgar Allan Poe and Agatha Christie to Raymond Chandler and Dashiell Hammett, a propensity that had served him well as an investigative reporter. And indeed his training in the law didn't hurt.

Strangely, he had vaguely thought in the beginning that his ability to drink more than most people and still function was an asset in his work. It took him to places others might choose not to go, and he was better able than fellow reporters to identify with the underside of Dallas that most preferred to ignore or deny. That was before he started getting to work late, skipping appointments, missing deadlines—and before he was fired. Long before admitting to himself that he had a problem, before Linda's impassioned pleas for him to ease up, to look for help, before she packed her suitcase and drove home to her parents in Des Moines.

That should have been a turning point, but he had squandered a last chance. Lantry the fact finder who had prided himself on toughness had avoided facing tough questions about himself. For most of a year now he had lived in an alcoholic haze, his daily routine dragging himself out of bed, downing two or three aspirins to ease the pain, washed down with the very booze that had brought the pain. And now for months he had avoided even serious consideration of what he was doing in Mexico. Yes, he was little more than a scrap of flotsam, sloshed about on a foamy sea.

He recalled how haphazardly he'd thrown a few shirts and jeans, underwear and socks into his backpack, along with the laptop computer he now hadn't turned on in months and a few odds and ends that had appealed to him at the moment,

83

walked out of his apartment in Dallas and headed for Abilene. At least he'd remembered his toothbrush, though he couldn't recall having used it for some time. No question, it was the loss of Linda and of the job that had prompted his flight from Texas. But just as clearly, the alcohol that precipitated those losses had also catapulted him into a well of depression. Perhaps even selling the paid-off pickup worth six or seven grand to the first guy who came along offering five was really an act of self-abnegation, acceptance of diminished self-worth that devalued everything he touched. And until a day ago he had done little to resist the downward spiral.

Lantry stood and strolled around the plaza. Beyond its dim lights the sky was dark now, except for the sinking sliver of moon and emerging stars. He strolled back to the church and wandered in. It was empty now, except for a handful of mostly older women who knelt before their pews as a priest droned on. It must be Saturday evening, late mass. He stood long in the doorway, even thought for a moment of joining the scattered flock at the front. Instead he turned and walked back toward his hotel. He passed two sad bars, the first with relative ease, the second with difficulty. He entered the hotel and climbed the creaking stairs. He took off his clothes and collapsed weeping on the bed.

Chapter Thirteen

Pablo wiped the sweat from his forehead with his shirt. If only they had a fan, like they'd had at the prison in Pearsall. He closed his eyes and longed for summer afternoons in Victoria. At that altitude, what they'd thought of as afternoon heat was more pleasant than the least oppressive night in Eden. Sweet breezes from El Pico de Orizaba brought cooling showers to Victoria most summer afternoons, sometimes even driving the stench away.

The afternoon heat in the cell had grown more unbearable with every passing day. Pablo and his companions shared a corner cell with a window facing the north. But the other wall was west, the thick concrete absorbing the unrelenting summer sun and radiating heat well into the night. There were six of them now, but at least they all spoke the same language. Two were here temporarily, waiting for the ride back to the border. Before Pablo and three others loomed what seemed a lifetime without life. To avoid fights they'd drawn lots for who got the beds for which nights or what parts of a night. Maybe when the short-timers were gone he'd have a bunk to himself, but more likely they'd throw in a couple more to replace them.

Pablo counted his Eden months on his fingers. His second journey north was arrested on Valentine's Day, then a couple of weeks in Pearsall, now five months here. Eighteen months to go—longer than his entire stretch in Sioux Falls. If only he'd stayed there instead of going home for Christmas. If he'd worked another year and continued to send money home he would have had enough to marry María in the church, and maybe even buy back a hectare or two of his father's land. María had promised to wait for him, and he believed her. But at the time neither he nor María could wait any longer. She had sent a letter, begging him to come home, if just for a few weeks. She cried for him every night, the letter said. He too was dying of loneliness, and nothing besides holding her in his arms mattered on the day he caught the bus south to Omaha, another to Dallas and a third to Laredo.

For that matter, why did he leave her in the first place? They could have gone to a city, where surely he could have found some work. If only he could get word to María, to explain everything, maybe it wouldn't be so sorry for either of them now. At least they could make a plan, both find a way to survive the long wait ahead. As it was, there was nothing to do but pass endless afternoons staring at the gray concrete ceiling and fighting to hold thoughts of María and home at bay.

There were no mountains around Sioux Falls, but at least the heat wasn't as terrible as in the Texas desert. In South Dakota he was a guy they called José. He gutted pigs eight hours a day, six days a week, an especially galling job after he became aware that Smithfield, the same corporation that had flooded his homeland with hogs, owned the plant. He worked the night shift, because it paid a few pennies more and because people who'd been there a while wanted the days. The constant roar of machinery and the endless screams of fattened hogs on their way to death drove him nearly insane for the first few weeks, but gradually he grew accustomed to the stench of guts and blood, the burning fat in the rendering wing, the unceasing din. On the farm he had often helped his father kill and butcher a hog, but that was quick and as painless for the animal as it could be. When you feed half a dozen pigs from your hand with scraps from your table every day you come to love them, not as you might a brother or even the cat who kept the mice from the corn, but to love them in a way that made it painful to see them die. In the slaughterhouse it was different—hundreds of hogs coming down the line every shift, watching those ahead drop, screaming with fright until the hammer knocked them senseless.

Some of the men at the packing plant spoke languages from Africa or Asia, but many were from Mexico or farther south. They shouted to each other over the clamor, good-naturedly laughing when somebody took blood or offal in the face. When the shift was finally done they stripped off their bloody coveralls, showered, slipped into t-shirts and jeans and stepped out in time to see a sky full of stars fade into the rising sun. The mayhem of the slaughterhouse gave way to the peaceful rumble of the Big Sioux falls.

On his second day on the job Pablo had been invited to join three other men who shared a small apartment east of the plant, two from Mexico and one from Guatemala. They needed a fourth to help pay the rent. Roaches scurried away when they turned on the lights, but the place had air conditioning, something he'd never experienced or needed in Victoria. That made it easier to sleep afternoons, not just coolness like night, but also the rattle of the little box in the window that helped drown the slaughterhouse screams that haunted his sleep. They sometimes watched silly programs on TV, and gradually Pablo began to understand much of what they said. They walked to a Latino grocery to buy fresh tortillas, and lived mostly on vegetables and beans, though one housemate who dismantled carcasses sometimes risked his job by sneaking scraps of pork from the plant.

On their day off they rested by the river in Falls Park. Sometimes they walked up the east bank to a neighborhood with a little *tienda* carrying their countries' foods, and on payday bought *envíos* to send home all they could spare. One Sunday in June they heard about a celebration in the park, where people from many countries gathered to celebrate their music and food and dance. There was even a Mariachi band, four guys from Jalisco who played songs that Pablo knew. If only María could have been there, not just for that day, but forever. It wasn't a bad place. In fact it was the only place he'd ever known besides the valley of his birth, and now this Texas prison. Maybe he and María could have made a good home in Sioux Falls, though of course it could never have been home. Home was a place protected by the long shadow of Orizaba.

Every day Pablo felt more nervous, closer to the edge. Reliving his months in Sioux Falls was one trick to bring brief distractions, but no memories, not even pleasant ones, could for long hold at bay the opposites that crushed his mind — María and home, and the present living hell. To survive the present and not go mad, he somehow had to stop thinking about her. So day after day he sought other distractions, things to dwell on besides María, besides the sister he'd left fighting the flu, besides the infinity of eighteen months to go. On a particular night he held reality away by reliving in tiny detail his first trip north.

Once they'd cleared the last checkpoint in Texas, the driver turned down narrow backstreets on the south side of San Antonio, then up a trash-choked alley to an unpainted garage. He got out and opened the door and pulled the van in. Along the wall were two ratty couches.

"Wait there," he told the passengers. "I'll be back."

Half an hour later he did return, and with a paper bag full of steaming *tamales* to distribute, two per man.

"There's your table," he said, pointing at a battered door perched on a pair of sawhorses with a big water jug and a stack of paper cups. "I'll be back at dark. Be ready."

And then he was gone again. When he returned, he collected what pesos they had and gave them dollar bills.

"You'll need these sooner or later," he said. "In this country the peso isn't worth a damn."

The trip might have been uneventful if it hadn't been for the tire. Somewhere between Waco and Fort Worth, sometime around midnight, it blew. The driver pulled the rocking van onto the shoulder and crawled under to get the spare. It was nearly flat. He put it on anyway, and they were off again. The van rocked and swayed under its load, especially at any speed above thirty miles an hour. So that was why the highway patrolman followed them for half a mile, then turned on his flashing light. The driver braked hard and the van careened toward the ditch and ground to a stop.

"Run!" he shouted as he tumbled out the door.

The back flew open and the men scattered into the night. There was no moon, which was good, because by the time the police got the spotlight sweeping the area the only thing left to see was the van. It was bad because Pablo ran straight into a barbed wire fence, which tore a gash in his arm. His pack flew over the fence, and in a brief moment he was over it too, groping in the darkness until he found the bag and was off again, running as fast as he could away from the lights.

Pablo tripped and fell headlong in pasture grass. He lay panting, looking back at the officer calling on his phone for help, sweeping the area with his flashlight for people or clues, searching the van. One man had left his bag, which the patrolman searched, then threw into his back seat. Now another patrol car arrived with flashing lights, and soon a wrecker to haul the van away. Pablo tore a strip off the bottom of his shirt and tied it around his wound. What to do now, he wondered?

"*¿Hay alguien?*" he called out when the police were finally gone. Anybody here?

"*Aquí*," a voice answered, then another.

They followed each other's voices in the darkness, and soon they were three. The driver and the others were nowhere to be found. Each offered ideas about what to do next, but none of the plans made sense, least of all remaining here when the sun came up. Far to the north was a glow that must be a town. They climbed back over the fence and began to walk, staying as far from the nearly deserted highway as they could; when a vehicle approached they flattened on the ground until it had passed. And they walked.

At the first hint of dawn they were on the outskirts of a small town. A railroad intersected the highway, and they followed the tracks until they came to a pair of grain elevators and a string of rusting warehouses. They were starving, and their throats parched for water. They came to a gas station and store with a restroom out back. From a dumpster beside the door each retrieved a large soda bottle. They rinsed the bottles and filled them at the faucet. Pablo washed the gash on his arm, which had ceased bleeding and begun to scab. He tore a strip off the other side of his shirt and bound the wound again.

They checked their meager resources, washed their faces and straightened their hair, then entered the store. The clerk had very dark skin, but he was neither Mexican nor black. Pablo understood some English, but couldn't make out anything the man said. Each bought a large hotdog and loaded the bun with as much as it would hold of onions, *chile* and a green sauce that tasted like vinegar. The trio stood behind the store and gobbled the food.

A dilapidated Chevrolet with tinted windows pulled up and a young Mexican man with a tattooed neck and arms and a diamond in his earlobe got out to use the restroom.

"*Buenos días*," he said.

"*Buenos*," Pablo replied.

When the man was inside, Pablo glanced into the car. It was empty.

"Are you going north?" he asked when the man came out.

"*Sí*," the other replied. He looked the three over. "Need a ride?"

Pablo got in the front seat, the others in the back, and the car pulled onto the highway and sped away. The driver rolled his window down, and the leaky muffler made conversation difficult, but Pablo learned that they could ride as far as Fort Worth. Pablo mentioned that their destination was Sioux Falls, South Dakota.

"The hell!" the man bellowed. "I've got a connection up there. And a guy who's heading that way tonight!"

Judging by the driver's looks and demeanor, Pablo was reluctant to inquire about what sort of "connection" this might be; but asked whether he might arrange a ride.

The driver thought for a moment.

"It's a long drive," he said. "Must be eight hundred miles. He might need help driving, cause he won't be stopping anywhere along the way."

"I can drive," said a back seat passenger. "I even drove trucks in Mexico. I can drive anything."

When they got to Fort Worth they drove to a neighborhood of crumbling houses where everybody Pablo saw on the street corners was black or brown. They stopped at a shabby house with a shiny black sport utility vehicle parked in front, the windows nearly as dark as the paint.

"Wait here," the driver said.

He knocked on the door and went inside. He came back out a few minutes later with an older man, a big paunch and glasses so dark they couldn't see his eyes. The pair smelled like marijuana. The fat man leaned into the driver's window and looked the passengers over.

"So you want a ride to Sioux Falls?" he said. "I can take you, but I'll need somebody to drive for a while late tonight. Oh, and there will be no questions, got it?"

"*No preguntas*," Pablo replied, and the others nodded assent.

"And you buy the gas," he added. "That's the deal."

"No problem," Pablo said.

The three had counted their money at the gas station, and between them they had over a hundred dollars, enough to fill the tank a couple of times and have a little change for food.

Plus they still had their work cards, and thanks to the blown out tire they wouldn't have to turn over the first week's pay!

"OK, we leave in an hour," the man said. "I have to say goodbye to my doll."

So the middle of the next morning they rolled into Sioux Falls. The driver dropped them off at the employment office of a slaughterhouse and sped away.

Chapter Fourteen

When Lantry woke the sun was streaming through the dingy window, casting its framed shadow against the door. It looked like a cross, he thought, or perhaps a cage. He lay immobile for some minutes, reliving the strange and unplanned events that had brought him here. What should he do now? He recalled how few hundred-dollar bills were left in his boot. At eleven dollars a day for the room, and maybe that much more for food and drink, he could postpone any decisions for a while longer, but not forever. If he was careful he could hang on in Victoria for a couple more months, but then what?

His most recent half-baked move was to head toward mountains, and he was close, but he wasn't there yet. He'd found things to like about Guadalup Victoria, but what could he do if he stayed here? So far as he could tell, the only jobs here had to do with hogs. Being a *gringo* who spoke English as well as a passing Spanish might get him some sort of management job, especially if labor troubles were on the horizon, but he couldn't see himself working for the types he'd overheard in the restaurant. Anyway he'd fled Mexico City looking for fresh air. He'd chosen Victoria mostly because of the name, and because his map led him to believe it was in the mountains, which turned out not to be the case. Beyond the great dinner and the tree-lined boulevards he'd found few reasons to stay, and better reasons to go. To actually experience the Sierra Madre he'd need to move on.

Maybe there was a bigger town or a small city actually in the mountains where he could find work and support himself. Maybe with a job he could even get his life back together. On the other hand he hadn't really explored Victoria. He decided to give the town one more day, try to stay a little sober and see what the place was about. He threw off the sheet and put on his clothes.

An aged man in a sombrero was sweeping the plaza with a long palm-branch broom. Grackles squawked, but there were singing birds too, some yellow warbler he'd seen in Texas. Shopkeepers were sweeping their sidewalks and school children passed in blue and white uniforms, book bags on their backs. Had it not been for the ever-present aroma, it was a pleasant day in a pleasant enough town. He had coffee, fresh-squeezed orange juice and *huevos rancheros* in a tiny restaurant, then returned to the plaza and to last night's bench to watch the world go by.

Within moments a small boy, maybe eight or nine, arrived with his shoeshine kit. The kid should have been on his way to school like the others, Lantry thought, but there was no question that his boots were dusty and scuffed, so the boy went to work. Suddenly he found himself a magnet for other kids, some selling Chiclets, others begging for a peso. What all had in common were grimy faces and ragged clothes. Apparently the pigs hadn't made everybody rich. Against his better judgment, and since he was probably leaving town anyway, Lantry doled out pesos from his heavy load of pocket change. Before the waifs could recruit more friends he stood to go, but he couldn't leave behind a sadness for kids who lacked the opportunities he'd had—and mostly squandered.

The sun had now cleared El Pico de Orizaba, glinting off the pinnacle of ice. He walked east toward the summit, past the last stone-paved street with its tree-lined boulevard. Only when he'd left the last of the shade and emerged in full sun did he stop to look back. What an amazing thing. Instead of a painted centerline, almost every street in town had its shading row of trees. What visionary planner had long ago made this happen? Did the people of Victoria, some of whom had perhaps never left the valley, appreciate the pleasantness that decision had produced?

Still contemplating that question, Lantry turned his newly polished boots east again and trudged upward, past where the gravel ended, past where colorful cement houses gave way to a muddy, trash-strewn track between rusting tin roofs and abandoned vehicles, guarded by dogs that barked when they saw him because they recognized that he did not belong. He had entered a zone where those with a better place to live had no reason to go.

Half a mile later he passed the last abode, and then the wagon track became a path that ended at a rusting barbed wire fence. Beyond that a few tiny structures climbed a deserty hill toward the Sierra Madre. Lantry sat down on the protruding roots of a last pine and gazed toward the snow-capped peak. How far it was he couldn't guess, and his map offered little help. Too far to walk, that was sure, several miles south and at least that far east, just to where the real assent would begin.

He rose and strolled back toward town, walked until he came to a little *cantina* with swinging half doors. He opened the doors on the cave-like interior, his narrowed pupils registering little detail. He stepped inside. In a corner three men sat at a rickety table with three bottles of beer. They glanced up, and conversation ceased. Now Lantry could see that the establishment consisted of four tables, the others unoccupied. He sat at the one farthest from the group. When a short, stout woman appeared he asked for a beer.

Conversation resumed, but in hushed tones, occasional glances tossed his way. He did make out specific hard to miss words—*gringo, granja de cerdos, huelga*. Gradually he pieced together enough to ascertain that the three were speaking in low but agitated tones about the hog farms outside town. He remembered that "*huelga*" meant strike.

Lantry finished his beer and stepped to the bar for another. It occurred to him that beyond brief and superficial conversations with bartenders, waitresses, children and drunks, he hadn't had a real conversation for perhaps months. Without forethought, he asked the men if he might sit down.

They were clearly reluctant, but not impolite. One pulled the fourth chair out and Lantry sat.

"*¿Qué pasa en Victoria?*" Lantry asked, the only thing he could think of to say.

"*Mucha gente enferma,*" the oldest of the men replied, a man old enough to be Lantry's father.

"*Un muchacho ha muerto, mucha de la gente está enferma,*" another added.

Lantry knew about the dead boy; he'd seen the funeral. But many others were sick.

"*¿De qué?*" he asked. From what?

"*No estoy seguro,*" a younger man replied, "*pero pienso que es la gripe. La llaman influenza porcina.*"

Porcina, that was pigs, Lantry recalled, so swine flu.

"*Hay muchos cerdos muertos,*" the younger man added, "*y muchos de los trabajadores están enfermos, también.*"

Lantry had now heard the same story twice. Hogs were dying and so were kids, but also workers at the pig farms were falling ill. And now the older man uttered another phrase, with the inflection of a curse.

"*Los cerdos de la corporación americana, Smithfield Foods.*"

"*¿Y la huelga?*" Lantry asked.

He wanted to know about the strike. Now the men were silent, exchanging guarded glances. As a North American he was obviously suspect, a *gringo*, maybe a spy or an agent of the foreigners that had flooded the valley with hogs. Lantry searched for the Spanish words and tried to explain that he had nothing to do with the swine, that in fact he hadn't even known they were here. He wasn't sure that the men were convinced. Lantry finished his beer, thanked them for sharing their table, and stood to go out. Standing in the doorway he saw that the rain had resumed, and so did the muted conversation at the table.

Chapter Fifteen

María was a *campesina* kid like Pablo. If anything, her family had less than his. She was born on her father's scrap of *ejido* handed down from the land redistribution of the 1920s. Her father's land was rocky soil, higher up the mountain slope than Pablo's, even beyond a tiny settlement at the end of a rutted road above La Gloria. Generation after generation it had been parceled up and handed down, until the scrap that was left could barely feed a family in a good year, let alone produce extra to sell.

That was why her father went north the year María started fifth grade. María was the only child, and he wanted her to have an education. How he knew that was important wasn't clear, because few people in the villages finished high school, and most country kids never even got there. But he saw the world changing around him, most of the people they knew losing their land, most of the men left with four choices: do seasonal agricultural work on the bigger farms, feed pigs for the corporation, head for Mexico City and a very uncertain future, or go north. He mixed concrete for the foundations of the first set of barns, and for a year or so fed pigs, until the pay was cut.

He crossed the river in the first year of the new millennium and never returned. For a couple of years he sent money, but that gradually became less regular, and even before the money stopped, María and her mother heard that he had taken up with another woman and started a new family.

Eventually María and her mother accepted the idea that he wasn't coming home. Her mother kept the two of them fed and clothed by cleaning houses for two Granjas Carroll managers in Victoria, until she developed a lump in her breast. She died when María was sixteen. María moved in with a family on the better side of town, where she cleaned and cooked for room and board.

Pablo and María had met as children, it must have been in fourth grade, before Pablo stopped going to school to help his father wield the hoe, care for the animals and harvest the corn and hay. Living in Victoria with her mother allowed María to finish elementary school. Evenings she peddled Chiclets in the plaza to help pay for books and supplies. She was even able to attend two years of high school before her mother died.

María's and Pablo's paths rarely crossed until his family lost the farm and they moved to town. Then they saw each other every Sunday at church. One Sunday he overcame his shyness and asked her to meet him on the plaza after mass. Soon they knew they were in love. Evening found them amongst the teenagers at the plaza, holding hands and hiding away in the shadows when night fell.

When he turned sixteen Pablo began seasonal work in the Granjas Carroll fields, growing corn for the hogs, moving irrigation pipes to water the plots of carrots and onions that grew bigger than anybody had ever seen, harvesting the crops and bringing them in. He had expected to eventually join Salvador at Carroll Farm, as they were told to call it. His father smelled like pig manure when he came home, and the pay was low, but it was more than Pablo earned, there were no other jobs to be had, and gradually people paid less attention

100

to the stench. María was in love with Pablo, and he wouldn't smell much worse than the air in town. For years she lamented that if her father had stayed he could have worked there too, but gradually she had divorced him from her mind. Yet each night before bed she still whispered things to the mother she powerfully missed, and often fell asleep on a pillow wet with tears.

Carroll Farm wasn't really a farm, not by any stretch of the imagination. But the local men—and the handful of women who joined them—were familiar with livestock and accustomed to hard work. The odor inside the barns took some getting used to. Half the time the fans that were supposed to bring in fresh air didn't run, and even when they did, they circulated fouled air from the sewage lagoons.

Before long, many workers went home not only stinking like hog manure, but with a cough. A couple of men thought they should organize and demand better conditions, at least have face masks to protect their lungs. The pair whispered to other men. Everybody agreed, but only a handful were willing to risk their livelihood by speaking up. Three were chosen to ask the managers for a meeting to ask for improvements in the working environment. The managers listened in stony silence, but on the second night after the meeting, the house of one of the leaders caught fire and the family barely escaped. Everybody got the message, and nothing changed.

The million pigs and all the waste they produced had to go somewhere. The company pumped it from the open sewers beside the barns and spread it by irrigation on the hundreds of hectares of former *ejido* lands they had acquired, simultaneously watering and fertilizing the genetically modified Monsanto corn. Unlike on communal lands and the small farms, there were no jobs chopping weeds. The first airplane most of the villagers had ever seen up close delivered Monsanto's Roundup, which killed every plant except the corn. That of course included most of the scrawny trees that had survived many long dry seasons in the valley.

Toward the end of Salvador's second year, a new manager arrived in Victoria from the U.S. He called the workers together and told them that the company needed to cut expenses, and eliminate some positions. When Salvador picked up his next paycheck, he learned that this would be his last. The manager told Salvador he had received reports that his work was not satisfactory. Salvador was shocked, humiliated and outraged. He had worked hard, as always. And even though he had often awakened feeling ill and coughing up yellow phlegm, he'd always gone to work anyway, and done what was asked of him. Few men knew more about hogs than he. His father and his grandfather had always raised hogs. Salvador knew that hogs had died in some other barns, but not in his.

"I have a wife, a son and three daughters to feed," he said when he had controlled his anger enough to speak. "I have to have a job."

Finally the manager agreed to let him stay on, but his pay would be cut to that received by entry-level workers who cleaned the barns. Salvador swallowed his anger and walked out. He went to the bank to cash his check, then straight to the bar.

It didn't take long to learn that he was not alone. Most every man there had the same story.

"But what can we do," one lamented. "Low pay is better than no job."

102

"Those hogs have to be fed every day," Salvador said. "The barns have to be cleaned. If none of us showed up for work, they would have no idea what to do. The *gringos* know nothing about caring for pigs, and even if they did, there aren't enough of them to do the job. We can't let them treat us like this."

Some men were afraid, saying they simply couldn't live without the paychecks, regardless of how low, but others nodded in agreement when Salvador spoke. By the second beer they had begun to make a plan. Each man would go back to his neighborhood and talk to the others, and after church on Sunday they would gather in the plaza to organize.

When Pablo came home from the field he learned what had happened to his father. The whole family was afraid. Most every job in town was on the line, and there were no other jobs to be had. They couldn't go back to the land, because that was long gone. And his father's cough worried Pablo most. Salvador was not an old man, not yet fifty, but even before they left the farm he had developed trouble breathing. They couldn't spare the money to see a doctor, and anyway, Salvador had assumed the cough would go away. But inhaling the caustic air inside the barns had made the condition worse, and after two years his strength had waned. For a time they'd all tried to ignore the cough, but that was no longer possible.

Pablo had never disagreed with his father, at least he hadn't said so if he did, but now he wasn't so sure.

"Maybe we should just go to the city," he said. "Surely there would be other jobs there, jobs that wouldn't make us sick, that wouldn't make us stink like pigs."

Salvador leveled a menacing look at his son. He slowly shook his head.

"No," he said flatly. "You were born here. I was born here. My father and his father were born here. The Revolution freed us from the *hacendados*, and I'm not about to be driven from my ancestors' homeland by another group of *hacendados*, especially not bosses from Estados Unidos. No, I will live and I will die here, like all of my ancestors, but first I will fight."

Pablo hung his head. There was nothing to say. His father was clearly right. He feared what might lay ahead, but he knew that what his father had said was true. There was only one thing to do.

After church on Sunday, Pablo and his family walked to the plaza. They joined a small group that had gathered, and waited for the others to come. Half an hour passed and only a few trickled in, most glancing about in fear. Then a big SUV rolled to a stop and half a dozen men got out. One had a camera and began taking pictures of the crowd. The manager stepped forward and faced the huddled group.

"You are all fired immediately," he said. "We know who your leaders are, and they are all out of jobs, regardless of whether they are here. We have your names, and none of you will find work here again."

The men got back in the vehicle and drove away.

"Sons of whores!" one man shouted after them. "We'll burn their barns down! We'll roast their damned hogs in the barns!"

"I'm not sure that would solve anything," Salvador said. "They would just throw us all in jail."

Then he collapsed in a coughing fit that wouldn't stop. One man pounded him on the back until he could breathe again, then he and Pablo each took an arm and they walked him home.

By the next morning Salvador was too weak to pull himself out of bed. Pablo helped him up, then rushed off to his job in the field. But Salvador was a broken man, not only his lungs, but his heart. He lived a few more months, but Pablo and Salvador's friends carried his casket to the cemetery before Pablo headed north. He went north because he saw no other choice. It was well known by now that GCM had what was called a *lista negra*, a blacklist. After his father stood up, Pablo's name was surely on the list.

Chapter Sixteen

On the second morning in Victoria Lantry woke before sunrise, troubled by the stale, humid air in the cramped room. He threw open the window, but instead of fresh air, a northwest wind brought the choking stench. He slammed the window shut, but too late. He'd had only two beers the previous evening, and he'd opened his eyes feeling a little better than usual, but now he thought that he would gag. He suppressed the urge but headed for the bathroom.

Sitting on the toilet, he studied the map and considered his options. Staying in Victoria was not among them, he decided. The map showed the small cities of Perote and Xalapa to the north and east, Orizaba and Córdoba to the south. There were no population figures, but judging by the size of the print, probably any of the four would be big enough that he might find some work, maybe even as a journalist. The one thing he had accomplished in half a year in Mexico was that his Spanish had improved enough to get by day-to-day. Whether he could translate that into a job was another question. He knew he had the skills, but the path was strewn with unknowns. Not just language, but ignorance about most of what was important here, most of what went on. The giant hog operation for example. He'd stumbled into the midst of an environmental disaster, widespread sickness and talk of a labor strike, all of it perpetrated at least in part by a huge American corporation, and he'd known absolutely nothing about any of it.

But he could learn. He'd finished law school, he reminded himself. Yes, he'd failed the bar exam twice, too much drinking to buckle down and study. Nevertheless he'd found ways to use what he'd learned in the investigative reporter job, and could surely learn what he needed to know here. That is if he could persuade somebody to hire him, and then if he could stay sober enough to hang on to the job.

The new awareness that Smithfield hogs had flooded this remote valley raised other issues Lantry had mainly ignored, things like NAFTA and its effect on immigration. He recalled covering a couple of trials of Mexican immigrants in Dallas, one busted for drug smuggling, the other for some sort of robbery. But that wasn't his beat, and he'd found it easy to accept the notion that illegal immigrants ought to be rounded up and thrown back where they came from. Whether they might have had good reasons to cross the border had been of little interest to him. In the detective stories he'd grown up with, Mexico was where crooks sometimes came from or where they fled to when things got hot. Yes, making a go of it as a journalist—if he could get a job somewhere—would mean not only staying sober, but opening his eyes to things he hadn't even known he didn't know.

Lantry got dressed and went to the little restaurant a couple of doors down the street for breakfast. Waiting for his food, he studied the calendar on the wall that pictured the cathedral in Mexico City. If mass was Saturday night, this must be Monday, August 17. He calculated how long he'd been in Mexico. He'd crossed the Rio Grande on February 14, so that was six months and three days. Then it hit him like a lightning bolt. If he remembered right, the visa issued at the border was for ninety days. He pawed through the contents of his wallet and dragged out the tattered card. His visa had expired three months ago! He was in the country illegally, what Texans generally called an illegal alien.

So what now? Probably he could cross the Rio Grande again without consequence and start over, but that was hundreds of miles away. Besides, in the soul-searching of the last couple of days he'd essentially ruled Dallas out. That part of a decision was enhanced when breakfast came, *huevos rancheros, frijoles* and coffee. And of course hot, freshly-made tortillas. He polished off the eggs and beans and wiped his plate clean with the last tortilla, had a second cup of café *americano* and paid his bill. Minus the smell and with a job, Victoria might be a good place to stay, he concluded, but the odor was inescapable and there was no job he'd want to do. It was time to move on. He pulled the ragged map from his hip pocket. The Sierra Madre range was long, and again he studied the names and locations of cities north and south. To the south, in a valley circled by steep mountains lay the city of Orizaba. It took its name from the great dormant volcano, so maybe it shared something of the aura of the peak. The road south would also take him closer to the mountain. Orizaba it would be.

Lantry walked to *El Mercado* and bought three oranges for a peso. On the way to his hotel he stopped at a small tienda and added a roll and an avocado. Back at the room he threw his few possessions into his backpack. He asked the woman at the desk how to get to Orizaba. She told him the proper name was *Citlaltépetl*, mountain of the star, and that it would be a very long walk.

"I mean Orizaba the city," Lantry clarified.

"There are no buses to Orizaba," the woman said, "only the van."

She directed him to a street corner a few blocks away where he could catch the van heading south. It was already mid-morning, and the clouds were breaking up and floating west. The magnificent glacial peak loomed above him, looking almost close enough to touch.

Chapter Seventeen

Pablo tossed and turned on his bunk, but sleep wouldn't come. Among the things that bothered him most was that he got no real exercise. He felt his flexed bicep, then his calves and thighs. Flabby and limp. He longed for work, not just to pass the hours, but to keep his body strong and his muscles taut.

Work had been his life. It had been the life of everybody he had known. Perhaps the hardest, and certainly the least enjoyable work he had done was at the slaughter plant in Sioux Falls. But from childhood until he first left Victoria at seventeen, most of his waking hours had been devoted to physical work on his family's farm or in neighboring fields. He couldn't remember a time before now when he'd had no job.

One of his first jobs was carrying buckets of kitchen waste and excess skim milk to the hogs. He must have been about six years old. He could barely raise the four-liter pails above the trough to dump the disgusting mix that made the pigs crazy. There were six of them that year if he remembered right, plus the sow that had given them birth. One pail he dumped into the sow's feeder, then the other into the lower trough where her offspring impatiently squealed. Pablo had loved to watch them eat, slopping the mess all over their snouts and each other, shoving each other aside for more until the last corn shuck or scrap of potato peal was gone and the wooden bottom slicked clean. Then they trotted off to dig for grubs, roll in the mud if it was rainy season, stretch out in the sun in winter or grunt contentedly in their little thatched hut if a cold rain fell.

When the pigs were two months old, Pablo's father, Salvador, hustled one into a burlap bag, slung the squealing pig over his shoulder, and the two of them herded the sow up the hill to the Lopez place, where the old man kept a boar. They came home with an empty bag, but a few days later went back up the hill and guided the sow home, already at work on another litter of pigs.

When a few more months had passed—or when the lard bucket behind the door where cured meat was kept ran low—Salvador chose the fattest of the pigs, put a rope around its back feet, knocked its head with a hammer, slit its throat with a sharp skinning knife and hoisted it from a tree limb to bleed. Pablo and his sisters watched as his father dunked the carcass in a tub of boiling water to loosen and scrape the hairs, then slid the knife down the belly, down the legs and around the throat, and tugged until the thick fat skin slipped free. Salvador sliced off the hams, severed the head and systematically disassembled the carcass. Pablo's mother, Rosalia, received each hunk of meat, plunged it into a barrel of salt, wrapped it in cloth and bore it to the house for curing and storage.

Not all the meat went into the larder. Early next morning Pablo and Salvador—or Rosalia and the girls if Salvador and Pablo had fieldwork to do—loaded the meat on the cart. Corredera, the aging nag upon which Salvador had bequeathed the name when she was young and could truly run, pulled them and the load to the market street in Victoria. When the pork was gone they made the rounds of the market, buying the few things they didn't raise on their two-hectare farm. There wasn't much to buy, because their garden produced most of the vegetables and the various *chiles* they needed, their little field the corn, the Jersey cow the milk, their chickens the eggs. But Rosalia needed flour and oil, and the coffee that grew higher in the mountains. Sometimes Salvador also brought home bottles of beer or a small bottle of mescal.

By the time he was eight, Pablo had become Salvador's right-hand man. The rains returned in May, and by late June the corn and *chiles* and vegetables were up and reaching for the sun that followed afternoon showers. Salvador sharpened an old hoe and cut a dried sapling for a handle the boy's size, and they went off in the cool mornings to chop the weeds that threatened the growing corn and vegetables and to till the soil when it dried sufficiently after rain. By late summer the corn stood far above Pablo's head, and the ears were succulent and sweet. Before the kernels began to harden, they ate fresh *elotes* with their beans and vegetables and pork and eggs. Then the rains wound down, and the stalks grew brittle and brown. Salvador and Pablo walked the little field, pulling off an ear here and there to test the hardness of the kernels. When the grains were too hard to crush with his teeth, Salvador declared harvest time. Pablo and his parents made their way down the rows, plucking off ears and collecting them in the shoulder bags Rosalia had sewn. They deposited the bounty at the end of each row, and at the end of the day carted them to the lean-to beside the house.

When all the ears were harvested, the family returned to the field with machetes and chopped the brittle plants down. Even Pablo's little sisters could help now, dragging the dried stalks together into piles. They stood thirty together in teepee fashion and bound them with scraps of twine. The shocks would shed any late rains so the fodder would not rot and could be hauled in as needed through the long dry months ahead.

When the season's work was done, Pablo and his oldest sister, Angélica, walked down the hill to the village for school each morning. Pablo learned the skills he would need, beyond those his mother and father taught. He learned to read and write and to calculate the numbers he would need for success in the marketplace. The classroom window faced east, toward the snow-capped peak. Most of the older people called it *Citlaltépetl*, but the younger generations knew it as Orizaba. The teacher explained to the students that neither name was a Spanish word; both came from their ancient language, Nahuatl, which lots of people in the mountain valleys still spoke. Citlaltépetl meant mountain of the star, she said, delighting them with the legend that the white peak was the body of the hero Quetzalcóatl. She told them that Orizaba means the valley of happy waters. She tried to impress upon them the great good fortune they had inherited here—protected by the tallest mountain in Mexico, an ancient volcano that had spawned the fertile soil that grew their crops and that faithfully supplied the rain upon which their lives depended, and in the dry season the pure waters from melting snow.

But by the time Pablo started school, the changes in the valley and the villagers had already begun. The teacher explained that politicians in the capital and in the United States had agreed on a plan they called NAFTA, which officials said would make both countries rich. The priest looked around his flock of poor parishioners, and imagined them with money in their pockets, not only money to spend, but money to help replace the church's leaking roof. The teacher wasn't so sure. How exactly would it work, she asked the few people in the village who paid attention to such affairs. "Free trade" sounded good, but wasn't that what they already had? Everybody in the village and the valley had a niche in a system that, as long as weather didn't interfere, seemed to meet the basic needs of every family that was willing to work.

There was not a man, woman or child in the village or the valley who did not know the story of the *hacendados* that long ruled here, of the revolution that had thrown them out and had taken back the land three generations earlier, of the *ejido* system that had allowed *campesinos* to grow their own animals and crops, and to eat—or freely trade—the things they grew. But the teacher also talked about more than just Mexican history, which she saw as replete with cautionary tales about previous interventions by the colossal neighbor to the north and beyond. First came the long-gone Spanish, who of course left behind their language, their religion and their blood. She told them about the French, who had finally been driven from power, in large part by the people of these very mountains and valleys. And then there were the Americans, who took half of Mexico's land, then supported the dictator that oppressed them. Could you really trust an agreement that was made by rich people and corporations on both sides of the border, she asked, trust that it would look out for the welfare of the *campesinos* and the *pueblo*?

When a corporation called Granjas Carroll de Mexico began buying up land across the valley in 1993, not even the *alcalde* or the priest had been told why. There seemed to be a new rumor every day. A couple of regulars at the bar claimed

114

they had overheard talk about a huge plant that Ford Motor Company was going to build there, with lots of high-paying jobs. That and other rumors finally gave way to word that instead of cars, it was hogs the valley would produce, but they still had no idea that there would be a million hogs, or that they would be owned by people who had never seen the valley. How many was a million, anyway? The most affluent *campesino* had a herd of maybe twenty-five.

But whatever was coming, there would be lots of jobs with high pay, year-around work. And who in the valley knew anything about building cars anyway? There were two Nissan taxis and a handful of rattling pickup trucks in town, all of them built in a place called Japan. But if there was anything the local men did know about, it was raising hogs and the corn to feed them. Most were convinced that this might be just what the valley needed to bring prosperity. No more living from harvest to harvest, from one butchered pig to the next. No more living half the year without work. Now there would be a paycheck every two weeks.

One day a carload of government officials and *gringos* showed up, dressed in suits and shiny shoes. They called a meeting in the town plaza to announce that the company was ready to hire. Men who could write filled out a sheet of paper, those who couldn't made their mark. Soon dozens of men were showing up each morning at a job site north of town and were put to work building row after row of long, low steel barns. Once the barns were finished, there would be more jobs, feeding the hogs and spreading their waste.

Pablo's reminiscence of the town before the pigs was vague, but memories of his family's life were vivid. And so was his memory of the steady unraveling of threads that had bound the community in a sustainable web for generations. Men Pablo's father had known all his life seemed somehow changed when they came home from the pig barns. Then came the gradual decline of demand for everything the Real family grew, and the money they received. Life-sustaining vegetable gardens ceased to thrive, sometimes growing exuberantly in spring as they always had, only to wither when chemicals from spray planes drifted across the land. People grew accustomed to the stench that wafted across the valley when the north wind blew, then a July deluge burst the dam at a GCM lagoon and turned the pure waters of an Orizaba stream a nasty brown.

But the one broken thread that was impossible to reweave was the loss of land. When the Reals and many others lost their meager plots, the birthright to which they had always clung, no good choices remained. Men who didn't take a job with GCM were forced to uproot their families or leave them behind in the valley of their birth. Some caught a bus for Mexican City or Puebla, where there were vague rumors of jobs. Others headed north, crossing the Rio Grande to look for work in the United States. Among those who remained, the men gathered in the bars and the women in the marketplace and complained to each other, but there was nothing they could do. There were no laws to protect them, even if they'd had money for a lawyer and some idea where to begin.

Chapter Eighteen

"*Buenos días*," rang several voices as Lantry climbed into the van.

It was nearly full and ready to roll, but a woman with a baby in her arms scooted tighter into the corner to make room. He was the only North American in the van, and all eyes followed him as he took a seat.

The van was an aging Ford, a model that had come with two bench seats and luggage space behind. Somebody had removed the seats and replaced them with a homemade bench that spanned all four walls. Besides the mother and baby were three men who looked like farm workers, a pair of adolescents in school uniforms, one man dressed like an office worker and an elderly woman with a cane and a tub of potatoes. The van appeared close to capacity, nine plus the baby and the driver, but before it left the outskirts of Victoria they picked up half a dozen more, a couple of whom squeezed into the already full benches, the rest steadying themselves on bumps and turns by clinging to a bar that spanned the roof. Lantry's covert count was fifteen, seventeen counting the baby and the driver, when the bus rumbled out of town and headed south on a narrow blacktop road.

From his seat at the back Lantry watched the country unfold. To his west, vast fields of irrigated corn broke now and then for tiny plots of shorter corn, squash, onions, tomatoes, melons, and other crops he didn't recognize. The van slowed when they approached a *campesino* in a broad sombrero, herding a flock of goats beside the road. Much of the flatter land to the west was irrigated, the large fields by sprinklers, some of the small plots by hand-dug ditches. To the east the land rose steadily, then precipitously toward the Sierra Madre. There the fields looked drier, except for meandering strips of green where an occasional watercourse snaked down from the mountains. Small islands of green surrounded tiny homes. Beyond the farmed land rose the foothills, the cacti and scrubby trees a pale green, and above that a belt of darker green, most likely pines and perhaps oaks, Lantry guessed. Above that zone lay a wide ring of earth and stone that soared high above the horizon before yielding to the vast white cone that marked Orizaba's peak.

The van pulled off the road onto a gravel shoulder and two more climbed in, men with machetes dangling from rope belts. As usual, passengers greeted the newcomers. Did everybody in the van know each other, Lantry wondered. But they had greeted him as well, a *gringo* none of them had ever seen. So now there were nineteen. Every few kilometers they slowed for another dusty *pueblo*. At each stop people got off or on, and at one point passengers numbered twenty. No question now, the van was definitely full, rocking and swaying, bottoming out on the axle with every bump. But did "definitely full" mean they would not stop for more? Apparently there was no such thing as a full bus. Each time a new person got in, the population shifted, somehow making room.

Between two heads Lantry maintained a narrow view to the east. As they drew nearer the great mountain his attraction grew, a magnet tugging his soul. It was a strange and unsettling sensation, something he could not recall experiencing for a very long time, perhaps never before. At last he spoke to the schoolboy beside him, expressing his amazement at the mountain. The boy smiled, possibly embarrassed, perhaps delighted to be tutoring an emissary from another world. He told Lantry that Orizaba was a dormant volcano, but that he needn't worry. The mountain had not erupted for hundreds of years. The boy's teacher had impressed her students with their local history and geography. The boy explained that the wide green swath on the map Lantry had unfolded was a national park, established by the government of Lázaro Cárdenes in 1936.

Lantry half listened to his informant, his concentration focused on the mountain. Wasn't this what he'd imagined during all those months in Mexico City, at least in those rare moments when he had emerged from the fog of alcohol and depression long enough to dream? That patch of mountain green, that towering peak. The question now forming in his mind, was it possible to go there? How, and from where?

The van from Guadalupe Victoria stopped at every village in the valley, plus at muddy trails that led to homes and ejidos, any and every place where somebody wanted to board or leave the bus. The first *pueblo* was Guadalupe Libertad, which like Victoria and many another community honored Mexico's patron saint, the Virgin of Guadalupe. But also, he was realizing, names that celebrated long ago battles for independence, victories that liberated the *campesinos* and their countrymen from Spain, France, and the United States. And the 1910 Revolution that freed them from home-grown dictator, Porfirio Díaz, the decade-long struggle that after nearly four centuries of serfdom bestowed ancestral lands upon the people who worked them, the establishment of communal lands.

They were inching ever closer to the alluring peak, and when the bus stopped in Libertad to release the pair of young scholars, Lantry was tempted to get off. But he was too slow. While he contemplated the move, the door slid shut and they were off again. But when it squealed to a stop at the tiny *pueblo* of Emancipación Quetzalapa, Lantry was ready. An aged man waited to board. Without further consideration Lantry grabbed his pack and stepped down. He helped the man up and handed the driver his fifteen peso fare, and the bus groaned back onto the road. Lantry gazed after the van as it grew smaller in the distance. What now? Was he insane? He obviously had no plan, other than that he was drawn to the startling peak, which now loomed higher than ever to his southeast, but how far away? It looked so near, but he knew that mountains always appear closer than they are. Certainly several miles. After all, they had already ridden half an hour, and the mountain had looked close from Victoria.

Would it be possible to hike there and back down before dark? Not likely, but he determined to try. No sooner had he begun to walk toward the village when a rattling Toyota pickup pulled over.

"¿*Quieres paseo?*" the man asked.

"*Sí, muchas gracias,*" Lantry replied.

He threw his pack in the pickup bed, which was littered with bark and twigs and topped by a well-honed ax, and climbed in.

"¿*A donde va?*" the driver asked.

He was a man of middle age with a coarsened face and gnarled hands.

120

"*A la montaña,*" Lantry replied.

The driver put the truck in gear and they rattled away in a cloud of smoke. The man concentrated on dodging the worst of the potholes, but threw furtive glances Lantry's way. He was clearly curious about his passenger. Other foreigners had come through his village on their way to climb the mountain, and he had hauled others as far as his town, he said. But those who came to climb Orizaba always had special gear, heavy boots, warm jackets, backpacks full of water and food. This man wore cowboy boots and carried only a light pack.

"*¿Por qué?*" the driver asked at last. For what?

Lantry contemplated the question, a good question, for a long moment.

"Because it is tall and beautiful, and I have to go there," he said, knowing that the answer was unsatisfactory to either his benefactor or to himself. Then he added, "I need to go to a higher place."

That was the best he could do by way of explanation, but perhaps it was enough.

The two rode in silence except for the roar of the engine, which had climbed to the mountain village too many times. The muffler was shot, and something loose under the hood rattled with every bump. Finally the man could contain other questions no longer.

"You are going on foot?" he asked. "With just that?" he added, pointing a thumb toward Lantry's pack in the bed. "And you should expect rain," he added.

"*Sí,*" Lantry replied.

And then they were silent, until at last they reached the tiny *pueblo* of Oyamecalco el Cajón.

"*Vivo aquí*," the driver said. "I've lived here all my life."

He explained that he once fed hogs for Granjas Carroll, but he developed breathing problems and now he made a meager living cutting firewood on the mountain slope and selling it in Tlachichuca and other valley towns. He had never climbed higher than necessary to get wood, he said. Feeding his family took all the hours in the day. Besides, he could see the peak well enough from his house.

He braked to a stop at a crossroads.

"*No hay hoteles en* Oyamecalco," he said, but he welcomed Lantry to sleep the night at his home.

"*Muchas gracias*," Lantry replied, genuinely moved by the man's generosity. "But I will sleep on the mountain."

The man's eyes squinted for a better look. Clearly he considered the plan unwise, and Lantry a *gringo* without good sense.

"*Hace mucho frío en la noche*," he said. It will be freezing. "And they say that sometimes jaguars come."

Lantry got out, retrieved his pack and extended his hand.

"*Me llamo* Lantry," he said. "*Muchas gracias*."

"*Yo soy* Antonio," the driver said. "*Cuidado*," he added. "*Y buena suerte*." Be careful, and good luck.

Lantry squinted toward the sun, then back across the broad plain from which he had come. It was nearing noon in August, but he could feel that it was already cooler at this altitude. According to infrequent elevation markers on his map he judged that the village must be something like two miles above sea level. Clouds were building in the mountains. He pulled the jacket out of his pack and began to walk. At first there was a narrow dirt road, probably the one Antonio took to the wooded slope. He crossed a rushing mountain stream on a rickety bridge, then followed the rutted road, which rose higher and steeper, then dwindled to a pair of vehicle ruts.

At last the desert plants gave way to scattered trees, and another hour later Lantry was in a deep pine forest. He saw evidence of woodcutting where the two tracks ended. At the far edge of the clearing he found a primitive trail that followed the path of least resistance between ever-thicker boulders and trees. Human tracks were obscured by those of other animals. The trail grew steadily steeper, and he became aware of how starving he was, and thirsty. More than once he stumbled on a rock or other obstruction he should have seen. The peak seemed no closer, and breath was coming hard. He stopped and looked back toward the village, barely visible now, several miles behind. He knew the rational thing would be to turn back, perhaps wait for another day. But instead he plunged stubbornly on, even as the sun sank lower in the western sky.

When he felt he could walk no longer he stopped in a little clearing, collapsed onto a fallen trunk and pulled off his pack. He examined the contents again, and wished he'd made better plans. Besides the laptop computer he hadn't turned on in months, he found a couple of changes of clothing, a small bag of peanuts he'd forgotten about, the roll, a now somewhat squashed avocado, the oranges, less than half liter of water and half a bottle of tequila. He munched the end of the roll and washed it down with water. It was now more like evening than afternoon, and he remembered that he'd had no alcohol all day. He pulled out the bottle and eyed the level. He unscrewed the cap and raised the bottle to his nose. The sharp aroma burned his nostrils but also excited his senses. He

123

put the rim to his lips, tasted the sharp sweet fire that curled his tongue and stirred the powerful desire. With head tilted back to drink he glimpsed the tremendous white peak, now magnified even beyond its true proportions by the curvature of the glass. Abruptly he lowered the bottle, the alcohol unswallowed, and replaced the cap. Instead, though the level in his water bottle was alarmingly low, he gulped water that cleansed his pallet of the acrid drink.

A sudden clap of thunder announced a boiling surge of clouds that now raced across the peak to meet him. He stuffed his things back in the pack and rose to go. Rain began to fall, first big drops splashing on the pine needles at his feet, then quickly a deluge that blurred all that lay beyond the little clearing where he stood. He grabbed his pack and raced to the downwind side to an arching Mexican pine.

The thundershower ended as abruptly as it had begun, and within minutes the sky was almost clear again. Lantry was still very far from the peak, even from the beginning of snow, but he could see the point at which the pines grew small, dwarfed by the prevailing wind, and then gave way to rocky terrain.

He wondered how high he had come. He'd been told that the elevation of Victoria was about 8,000 feet, and he and Antonio had climbed steadily to Oyamecalco, so that town must have been more than 10,000 feet. Antonio had told him that pine trees grew at a higher elevation here than anywhere else on Earth. He wondered if that might be true. The trail had climbed and dipped, climbed and dipped, but even his breathing told him he had gained significant elevation. He guessed that he was perhaps 3,000 feet above the village, so if he was at 13,000 feet, the pinnacle had to be at least a mile higher yet. That would probably put the snow line about half a mile above him. Clearly he would not make it to the top today, maybe not even to the timberline. In fact, thinking realistically, he knew that without equipment, experience or a guide, he probably couldn't reach the summit in another day, if ever. Like most of what he had done for the past half year, he had begun the assent without a plan. Once underway, his goal had gradually been downgraded from reaching the peak to at least reaching snow. The sun was now just two palms above the horizon. He admitted to himself that not even the snowline could be reached this day. On the other hand, it was also too late to turn back and to reach Oyamecalco before dark, probably less than an hour away. It was too late to accept Antonio's hospitality.

Suddenly Lantry's body shivered with cold. As the sun sank lower, the temperature plunged, and his clothes were damp from the shower. It was August, but he was two and a half miles above sea level and the air was thin. An intensifying breeze from the mountain brought the chill from ice and snow. He pulled out his warmest shirt, a long-sleeved flannel, and put it on between the shirt he wore and the jacket. Probably he should look for a more sheltered spot for the night. He shouldered his pack and trudged on. He had gone only a few feet before he stumbled over a tree root, but caught his fall on hands and knees. The few bites of bread had not alleviated his hunger, and his head felt light, even dizzy now, not just from elevation, fatigue and hunger, but no doubt from the lack of alcohol, the medicine that dulled whatever pain might come.

Lantry stumbled on in gathering darkness until he reached another clearing where splinters of fading light streamed feebly between the trees. The western sky was fading from gold to red. In another ten minutes it would be too dark to navigate the now trackless slope. He stopped dead still and searched the darkening perimeters of the clearing for some semblance of shelter. Except for the breeze that rustled the pine needles above, the evening had reached the moment of calm between the sounds of day and those of night. Straining his ears, it seemed he heard the murmur of water. He plunged blindly toward the whisper, down a little slope and around a huge volcanic boulder. There the barely discernible babble gave way to the music of a gushing stream! He dropped to his knees and dipped a trembling hand into the water. It was cold as ice, recently descended from the glacier above. He cupped his hands and drank. The water was as sweet as it was cold. He emptied the contents of his plastic bottle and refilled it, drank and filled it again.

There was no moon, only a fading glow above the plain, and above that, emerging stars. He dropped his pack and stumbled through dusky dark, breaking off dead pine branches kept dry from the rain by foliage overhead. Finally he had gathered a pile he thought might see him through the night. He dug deep in pine needles until he found dry kindling, stacked a teepee of tiny twigs in a dry place beside the boulder and struck a match. Thank God he'd thought of that at least! In moments he had a meager fire.

Lantry stood close above the little fire, shivering despite its growing warmth. He had walked for hours, and since breakfast he'd eaten only a small taco, a bite of bread and a bit of fruit. He stomped his feet and swung his arms until the shivering eased, opened his pack and wolfed down half his remaining food. He tipped the bottle for another long drink from Orizaba's peak. He fed the fire with more wood from his pile and stretched out on pine needles in the narrow space between the boulder and the flame. Distant thunder again rolled down from above. If the rain returned there would be no shelter, no way to keep the fire alive.

When he closed his eyes his head began to spin, a feeling he knew well, though now accented by fatigue and thin atmosphere. And by lack of the tonic that lessened whatever hurt. A partial remedy lay in the bottom of his pack, the last of the tequila. He unzipped the pack and pulled the liquor out. He held the bottle to the firelight, the bottom half a beautiful translucent amber. He held the bottle in trembling hands and studied the label, which identified the local maker of the drink. His desire was profound, and he unscrewed the cap. Again he raised the elixir to his lips. But again it came to him that he had now consumed no alcohol for a complete day and more. The first day in how long? It must be years. Long he stared at the bottle before his trembling hands restored the cap and set it aside. He stretched as close as he dared by the fire and closed his eyes.

Chapter Nineteen

It was completely unjust that Pablo had been thrown in the hole again, but here he was. No way was he a leader of what the local newspaper called a riot. Of course his eyes and ears were open, and yes, he had known what was about to come down. Yes, his shirt was smeared with food, but that was somebody else's doing. He'd tried to stay clear of the fight.

Those who passed the word in the exercise yard were mostly the toughs, men who made no effort to hide their violent past, and in fact relished repeating tales that set Pablo's teeth on edge. Some were doing hard time, others had been in this or other joints before. They were men with no wife waiting for them, no particular home to go back to, men who saw nothing to lose. If somebody died in the fight, that was a price worth paying, even if the somebody was them.

Pablo had no weapons, and in his two decades of life had not been involved in so much as a fistfight. Before he knocked the robber off the train, he had never engaged in an act of violence toward any man. The only thing that drove him now was that he had to get out, and he had seen a vague chance. He hadn't even touched a guard. His only goal was to be near the front when the surge of men pushed toward the door. But certain guards seemed to have their eyes on him. One in particular, a pudgy punk named Travis, delighted in threatening to send him back to the hole. His eyes were narrow slits in a pock-marked face, always a stubble of beard. Spit flew when he talked. Pablo detested the guard, but would have gladly walked away from him and never given him another thought. Yet he couldn't help wondering whether he could kill the man if it came to that. He had killed one already, maybe an evil man. He knew that one was one too many, but if another killing was the price of fresh air—he couldn't be sure what he might do.

There was no way to know how many they had rounded up. He didn't know how many cells the solitary block contained, but more than he'd been able to count as he was herded past the long string of doors in the dark runway, and anyway he'd been in no mood to count. What he did know was that he'd seen the corridor twice before, once going in and once coming out. The first lockup they'd claimed was because there wasn't another cell for him, and now after the food fight. One thing seemed sure; they had caged as many men as they had holes to put them in, but maybe others were waiting their turn. Perhaps this time it would be less than two weeks. Or it might be more. They didn't tell you such things.

How long he'd been asleep when he woke to screaming he didn't know. It could have been before midnight or it might have been near sunrise, because every hour of darkness was the same. The only way to gauge the time of night was that at some point the curses and wails and banging from other cells diminished, followed by longer periods of relative calm, though calm rarely lasted long enough for an uninterrupted hour of sleep. Now Pablo was wide awake, searching for the source of the latest outburst. The scream had erupted from the throat of a man who lay bathed in sweat, his own hands gripping his throat. Slowly he realized that that man was him. And María was not really here. She was in a bed, but not her bed. It was a bed in a strange place. The scream had escaped from Pablo's throat, but it was María's scream, the pain of childbirth. The strangling hands were about her throat, choking her life!

Pablo swung his legs off the pallet and struggled to stand. He was drenched with sweat, but his face was also wet with tears. He stood on the bed and strained toward the tiny window, gasping for breath. If only it would open to the night air. No doubt it was another stifling Texas night, but at least it would be air, not the foul, fetid atmosphere of his body, buried in this tomb. "*Tumba*," he muttered aloud. Yes, this was his tomb, the place of the dead. And by merely uttering the word he found himself face to face with a question he had never before allowed himself to think.

Many hours, both waking and sleeping hours, had been haunted by the man he'd killed on the train, hours examining his crime, if that was what it was, and by speculation about whether he could kill again, and if so for what reason. But never before had it occurred to him that he might be better off dead. Now it seemed he would never get out of Eden alive, and if he did, inside he might already be dead. He eyed the threadbare sheet that lay crumpled at the foot of his cot. Of the two things the prison provided in solitary, the toilet was a necessity; the sheet on stiffly Texas nights was not.

Pablo pulled the sheet from its moorings and mopped the sweat from his body. He grabbed a section in each hand and gave it a mighty jerk. The sheet did not rip. He eyed the bars on the tiny window, half a dozen inch-thick bars covering a window not much more than a foot wide. A tall man might have peered out the window from the far side of the cell, but for Pablo the square of not quite dark began at the top of his reach. He could tie one end of the sheet to a bar, stand on the mattress, wrap the other end around his neck and simply step off. It would be easy, even quick. He wondered if that was what he should do.

He grasped a corner of the sheet, and standing on the bunk, tied it securely around a bar. The other end he wrapped around his neck. It felt comforting, smooth, cool to his sweating flesh. But how did one tie the knot? That he had never contemplated. He recalled the knots his father had taught him, one for binding a shock of corn stocks, another for leading a horse or a cow. Then there was the slipknot, the one you made if you wanted to drag a heavy load, but then easily set it free. Surely the slipknot would do. He fashioned such a knot and arranged the loop around his neck.

From where he stood on the mattress, one star penetrated the dingy little glass. If he moved his head slightly, it disappeared behind a bar. Move his head again and the far away light reappeared. Darkness and light, even if the light was very dim, very far away. Staring at the tiny point of light, he for a moment forgot his mission. It seemed the light was directed at him, that it could penetrate his soul. Were other human beings in other places drawn at this moment to this faraway sign, or did it exist only to communicate something to Pablo's troubled mind? He moved his head again and the star disappeared. Utter darkness, or vague distant light, those seemed to be the choices. Long he stood on the bed, stood until the sweat on his body dried to a slimy scum. He took one long breath and removed the noose. He raised on tiptoes and untied the other end of the sheet and pulled it down. He again mopped his body with the cloth, then collapsed on the bed and wept.

But he could not shake himself free of María's scream, of her body writhing in pain on that strange bed, of the baby that in his dream had emerged from her wonderful womb. He stretched on his back and maneuvered until he found another far away star. He breathed deeply until he had calmed himself. What if María was really pregnant? If she was, then that new life would have begun on one of their far-too-few nights of love-making in January, or possibly from the promise and the gift of her soul and her body on Christmas eve. He couldn't be sure, but he thought August had turned to September. He counted the months, and yes, September was the ninth month. But if there was a baby, and if his dream had communicated what was real, then the baby would have come early, and that in itself would be reason to worry. Then he remembered that he himself had been born on the first day of September. If this was September, he must have turned twenty. "Great birthday party," he mumbled. To his surprise, his throat produced a scornful chuckle.

But the strange bed, where was María now? Was she alright? And if in fact she had given birth, was he the father of a daughter or of a son? He lay until morning, ever moving his head on the mattress this way or that to maintain contact with whatever wayward star might swim across his narrow view. When the fuller light of morning had begun to rise, Pablo had grown certain of two things. They took the form of resolutions, which he swore to God and to María that he would not forget. First, he would not take his own life. If he were to die at twenty, it would be at the hands of those who would bury him in this Texas hell. Second, he would not remain here for the lifetime of another eighteen months. He would get out, one way or another. If he had to die trying, it would not be at his own hand. If he had to kill to be free, perhaps he could do that too. He felt certain that María had a daughter or a son, and he would be with them soon.

Meanwhile, no more interminable nights of longing for María. No more self pity, he promised himself. No more doubts about the events that had brought him here, or of the one great crime that only he or God could punish—and he vowed it would not be him. No, from this moment on, one thing would occupy his mind, animate his soul, guide his actions—to make and execute a plan of escape. He would escape to life, not to death.

When the darkness subsided, Pablo swung his bare feet to the cement floor. They splashed in liquid. Was it urine, or just water? It wasn't the first time somebody had plugged a toilet and flooded not only his own cell, but the runway and all the cells nearby. Pablo took a closer look, and saw that the liquid was not yellow, but red. Somebody had cut himself. By the amount of blood, somebody had to be dead.

He jerked his feet up, plunged them into the toilet to wash them, dried them with toilet paper. He would remain on the bunk until somebody finally came to mop. A roar of voices began to build up and down the runway, accompanied by banging on windows and steel doors, curses and howls that escalated to a blood-curdling crescendo. He was not the only man baptized in urine and blood.

As he waited, Pablo concentrated on seeking the threads of a plan. He could outlive any dreams of escape at the end of a bed sheet noose, and he could survive another two weeks in the hole, or whatever they threw at him, if only he could stay focused on a plan. But this time he had to act smarter. He was pretty sure that he was smarter than most of the guards, and who knew, perhaps even God was on his side. With that thought, he realized that he had not been in a church since he and María had made their private commitment to each other beneath the brown and yellow towers. Nor had he spoken to a priest. But without intending to do so, he found himself in prayer. As morning broke he gazed out the little window at the fading stars and asked God to show him a way out.

Chapter Twenty

A lightning bolt jerked Lantry from sleep. The crash of thunder was almost immediate, so the strike must have been near. It ricocheted off the rocks and was still rolling down the mountain when it was answered by a blood-curdling cry. Lantry's wide eyes stared into the blackness, searching for the source of the wail. Was it real, an animal, from the thunder, part of an interrupted dream? How long he had slept he didn't know, but in spite of his hungers and the cold, he felt rested and alive. The fire still burned, so he must have roused at least once to add wood.

Lightning flashed again, but its light revealed nothing. It must have come from below his altitude, he decided, or perhaps from a place his boulder hid. He felt sure now that what he had heard was not a dream, and he tried to reshape the sound. If the cry was real, was it a coyote, or perhaps a wolf? He didn't know what creatures might prowl the mountain. But it was not so much a howl, he decided, more like a scream. Huddled against the boulder, he breathed deeply of the cold mountain air. He pulled his jacket close to his chest. He listened intently, but heard only the music of the stream. His head felt clear of its usual haze, and the sky was ablaze with stars. Far above all sources of pollution or even dust, they were the most brilliant he'd ever seen. He picked out the big dipper and followed the cup's lip to Polaris, the North Star.

Lantry averted his eyes from the firmament to search nearby, but he could see little beyond his fire's small circle of light. He had no idea what time it was, except that the dippers hung low in the northwestern sky, so several hours must have passed. Perhaps dawn was near. He raked scattered embers toward the flames, then settled another stick on the fire. When the sparks died away, he lay back on his pine needle bed and closed his eyes.

When the scream came again he was still awake. This time there was no question that it was real. Whatever creature had produced it must be big—and not far away. But what? He was pretty sure it was some kind of cat. Did mountain lions roam Orizaba's forest? He recalled that Antonio had mentioned jaguars. He hoped he would not find out. He was sure that he would sleep no more. He could only wait and hope that daylight would come soon. But minutes became an hour, his tension eased, his eyes grew heavy, and again he must have drifted off to sleep.

When Lantry again rose to consciousness, it was to the whisper of an intermittent gentle wind. He stirred and opened his eyes again on the blackness of the sky, pierced by the million points of light. The new sound that had roused him was guttural, a low rhythmic rumble. He rolled his head toward the fire. Beyond the now flickering flame two other fires burned through the blackness, two blazing yellow orbs— fire reflected from the eyes of a huge tawny cat!

Now the creature moved. Squatting low on its haunches, it slinked one step toward the fire. The nostrils flared and sniffed. The upper lip curled, and out came a breathy snarl. Then the mouth opened wide, baring a bevy of flesh-tearing teeth. Lantry felt frozen to the earth, flat on his back between

136

the boulder and the fire, the cat not more than ten feet away.

The face was yellowish brown, white on the mouth, dark on the long-whiskered cheeks. The cougar crouched low, surveying the prone man and the fire. It crept another step closer, its wide pink tongue lolling between its teeth. Its bared claws were curved and long. Lantry realized that he was not breathing. He inhaled deeply, then his hand crept slowly toward the fire and gripped the end of a burning stick. With deliberation that an observer might have described as calm, he raised the burning limb slowly above his head. Then he threw his body up with a mighty yell and lunged toward the cat, jabbing the torch with all his might toward the hungry eyes. Now he was on his feet, swinging the faggot as the cat screamed once more and leaped many times its body length and disappeared into the underbrush.

For how long he stood with the burning stick in his hand Lantry could not have told, but finally he became aware that the ember, his arm, his very body, all were shaking beyond control, and his mind had lost all focus. He dropped to his knees by the fire and shoved the remaining fuel onto the flames. The fire rose to consume the new offering.

When he had calmed himself a bit, he stood and carried the blazing stick before him as a light and a shield and broke off more dead branches that had sheltered from the rain. He built the fire to a roaring blaze, and for the first time since the sun went down he became truly warm. Satisfied that the fire would last until morning, he stretched out once more, as near to the fire as he dared, and in spite of all intentions, drifted back to sleep.

When Lantry next woke, the sun had risen. He lay without moving and stared beyond his boulder toward

Orizaba's crown. The sun had not cleared the glistening peak, but had encircled it with a halo of pink. Chilling images of the night replayed in his mind. At last he stretched his back, sore and stiff from sleeping on cold, lumpy earth. He rolled to his elbows and gazed through a break in the forest, out toward the plain. Down the path he had come, splinters of light danced amongst the trees and underbrush before dissolving into a vast sea of clouds that spread as far as he could see. The entire world below was calmed and smooth and white. Only he and the mountain peak stood in sunshine above the fog.

His fire was nearly dead now, only smoldering embers and wisps of smoke. His pack lay beside him, undisturbed. In fact all seemed peaceful, secure. He rose to his knees and crawled beyond the fire to search the forest floor where the big cat had crouched. The thick bed of needles appeared undisturbed. Like an archaeologist searching for clues to the past, he carefully brushed the needles aside. He could discern no tracks. Surely there would have been something, he thought, if nothing else some disturbance where the cat had leaped away. He found no clues. Could the whole thing have been a dream? Surely not. If so, it had undoubtedly been the most vivid of his life, and a dream not induced by alcohol. But perhaps there would have been no tracks. The needles on which he had slept were a good inch thick.

Lantry walked to the stream and stripped off his clothes. Shivering in the cold mountain air, he washed his face and then his body in the icy water, then pulled on clean clothes from his pack. He fell to his knees and drank the sweet water of Orizaba, then in a manner that had eluded him for a very long time, gave thanks. He found that his stomach was collapsing with hunger. He went back to his pack, emptied the last few peanuts from the bag and wolfed them down, down to the salty dust. He peeled and ate the last orange, drank again from the bottle that held the cold elixir from above.

The dwarfed pines overhead had been cleansed of dust by the evening rain, the water in the stream was crystal clear, and the snowy peak stood in stunning relief against the blue blue sky. Everything in Lantry's purview was vibrant and clean. He realized that his mind, too, seemed clearer than it had been in months, maybe years. He was weak from hunger and still shaky with shock at what he had experienced, but it was morning and his head did not throb! He recapped with amazement the many miles hiked up the slope of the sleeping volcano. He had slept well by a distilling fire, and had fended off a hungry lion. But most remarkably, he had slept without alcohol and had awakened rested. He searched his memory for his last full day and night without a drink, not to mention several too many. Was it before college? For as far as he could reach back, alcohol had been essential to his life.

Lantry opened his pack and lifted the half bottle of tequila free. He twisted off the cap and sniffed the contents. He brought it to his lips to taste the bittersweet flavor dried on the rim. The urge to pour the liquid fire into his mouth was still there, still powerful as ever. In spite of how good he felt in the freshness of morning on the mountain, he wanted this drink as much as he ever had. He clinched the bottle in his fist and held it away. He raised it to the rising sun. Through the pale liquor and the curvature of the glass the colors of a rainbow appeared. And then he was aware that the mirage was both softened and enhanced by tears. In a single motion he flung the liquid into the coals. The fire flared for an instant, then died back to its warming tone.

Lantry raked the pine needles away from the coals and snuffed the embers with his boot. He went back to the stream, rinsed the bottle three times and filled it with melted snow. He drank the bottle empty, refilled it to douse the last dying embers, then filled it again. He shouldered his pack and gazed long at the snow-covered peak, unattainably far above. At last he turned his feet down the trail he had come, a path that in morning light seemed new.

Chapter Twenty-one

Pablo's case was not unique. Every man had a story, and except for the few career criminals, the stories had common themes. Poverty and hopelessness. No jobs back home. Families left behind. Kids to clothe and feed. Their fears were also common, and their desperation. Somewhere in every mind was the dream, and in some a half-formed hope of breaking out. The daily hour in the blazing sun seethed with covert grumblings, most in Spanish, never in earshot of a guard who might know the language. Other men simply stood dazed beneath the razor wire and gazed toward the distant mirage.

Nobody knew how many solitary cells Eden hid. Every man Pablo knew had done time there, though few had endured burials almost back to back. One inmate had a lawyer who told him that the prison corporation was paid by the head, so it was essential to keep every cell full. Overfull was better. The contract even required that ten percent of the convicts be in isolation at any given time, the lawyer claimed. Inmates routinely began their time in the hole as Pablo had, at least theoretically because there wasn't another bed. But there was the side benefit of breaking the man, making him more compliant with the arbitrary orders of sometimes-malicious guards. Pablo had heard plenty of stories about what went on in Mexican prisons, but most Mexicans assumed that being locked up north of the border wasn't so bad. They hadn't been in Eden.

Out of solitary at last again, Pablo reached accommodation with his new cellmates, and even found most days and nights close to tolerable, partly because he'd come to think of his confinement as temporary. He didn't yet have a plan, but he invested most of his waking hours grasping for threads he might somehow weave together to build a scenario that would put him on the other side of the fence. He didn't question whether once outside they would find him and drag him back, as they had most of the few men who had escaped. Once he was gone he would be gone. Yet, there was a problem. He stood by the fence of the exercise pen and squinted out across the scrub country that stretched to the horizon, cacti and brush that stood starkly like dried corn stalks after harvest, and he saw no place to hide. Finding a way to conceal himself until night fell would have to be part of any plan. Unless of course he escaped under cover of darkness, which would make things less complicated.

It was Pablo's first day in the sun in two weeks. Even though his skin was dark, his arms and face felt as if they would blister. His unaccustomed eyes squinted at the intensity of its rays, and it was difficult to focus on anything beyond the chain-link fence. The desert sands, the mesquite, the few scraggly trees, was any of it real, or all just illusion? What was very real was that in the two weeks since the uprising that put him back into solitary, anger had not subsided; it had continued to build. Most of the grumblings were about rising up, taking control, exacting revenge, breaking out. Some inmates bragged openly about what would happen to certain detested guards if they ever lost control. Apparently there were homemade weapons hidden in places difficult to find, knives aimed to gouge out eyes, cut off balls, put sadists in the graves that they deserved.

Such talk made Pablo nervous, but he listened intently, gathering every scrap he could of the rage, the bravado, the half-baked plans. What he put together was that another uprising was brewing, a riot that would make the food fight look like a game. One man swore openly that he would take out a particular guard or die trying. Pablo had no desire to kill another man, not even the guard who called him a filthy wetback drug runner and shoved him around at every opportunity. And he did not want another two weeks in solitary. He remembered his father's indignation at the abuse inflicted at the pig farm, the firing, his father's futile efforts to organize fellow workers, his courage. But also his defeat and his death. His father's courage inspired him, but he had to find a smarter way.

On Pablo's second day out of solitary, a new man showed up in the exercise yard, a man who looked familiar. He knew the guy, but from where? Their eyes met, and the other man's mouth fell open.

"Pablo!" the new inmate called. "It's Fernando." He advanced and the two embraced.

"Fernando!" Pablo said. "Of course I remember you. We went to school together for a couple of years. From La Gloria, right?"

"That's me," Fernando said. He held Pablo away for a closer look. "So what are you here for?"

Pablo told his story as briefly as could, then demanded the same from Fernando.

"Caught at the border," Fernando said. "It's getting harder every day. They usually just dump you back in Mexico, but this was my second time so I'm here for a while, maybe a month or two before they send me back."

"There was another guy here from La Gloria, Vicente," Pablo said. "He's gone now, but you must know him."

"Sure, I know Vicente. Haven't seen him for ages."

"Do you know María, my girlfriend in Victoria?" Pablo asked hopefully. "Actually now she's my wife. I went back to Victoria at Christmas time and we got married. God, how I wish I'd stayed. Leaving again was the stupidest thing I ever did."

"The María you hung out with in the plaza every evening? Sure, how could a guy forget a girl like María? And you say she's your wife, you're married! I guess you know she's pregnant."

"What, María pregnant?" Pablo cried. "O my God, are you sure, Fernando, the same María?"

Fernando laughed. "Pablo my friend, there might be lots of Marías, but no other like your María. Yes, I swear to God, I saw her not long before I left. She wasn't huge pregnant, but she's going to have a baby."

"O my God," Pablo said again. "I have to get out of here, Fernando. I don't know how, but somehow I've got to get out. I will get out!" he added. "Listen," he said in a low voice after a pause for the news to sink in, "Will you go back to the valley when you get out?"

"Definitely," Fernando said. "I've had enough of this crap. I'd rather starve to death in the shadow of Orizaba than live in this hell hole."

"OK, listen Fernando, I want you to swear that when you get back to the valley you'll go straight to Victoria. Promise me you'll find María. Tell her where I am, and that I'm coming home. I'm supposed to be here for another year and a half, but I swear to God," Pablo said, raising his right hand, "if there's any way possible, it won't be that long. I'm getting out of this joint, Fernando. I have to get out!"

"I swear," Fernando said, also raising his hand. "I'll go straight to María and tell her."

Pablo could tell by his face that Fernando thought he was probably crazy. After all, how many men had Pablo seen break out in the months he'd been here. Maybe three, but at least two that actually made it off the grounds were caught and brought back, another year tacked to their sentences for escape. Every man who tried and failed also did long stretches in the hole.

"I will do it," Pablo said again. "I swear I'll find a way. Tell María that I will come. I will come soon."

Chapter Twenty-two

It was the week before María moved in with Pablo that the first people in La Gloria got sick. La Gloria was a few kilometers from Guadalupe Victoria, but several men from Victoria worked at Granjas Carroll barns there, and they brought the news. It was some sort of flu, people said, something that likely would soon go away. But just before Pablo left, the flu arrived in Victoria. His oldest sister, Angélica, was among the first to fall ill.

The news Fernando brought was terrible. In March a four-year-old boy died in La Gloria, and two more children died in April. The doctor said it was pneumonia, but the children were healthy one day, and could hardly breathe the next. Within weeks half the town of La Gloria was sick, and so were many residents of Victoria.

Some thought the hogs caused the sickness, maybe spread by dry season dust or by the swarms of flies from the putrid lagoons and the piles of decomposing pigs, or by polluted water, maybe all of these. Officials of the corporation denied any connection. It couldn't be, they said, since they routinely administered antibiotics to the hogs. There was no way the sickness could be a mutated strain of H1N1, swine flu transferred to humans, the corporation insisted; that had never happened before. Government officials were eager to agree with the corporation, at least at first. After all, GCM had brought lots of money to the valley, and steady jobs.

But not everybody was convinced. There was no denying the pile of rotting hogs, and suspicion spread like the contagion. The Victoria teacher who had taken it upon herself to study animal confinement issues shared a Mexico City newspaper story that said feeder hogs produce four times the waste of humans. If that was true, then the hog manure produced in the valley equaled the waste generated by a city of four million people, and eighty percent of that waste went untreated. The hog manure and urine also bore the hormones and antibiotics routinely fed to the swine, the paper said, which meant that antibiotics given to sick people might not work, even for people who could afford the medicine.

Whether the contagion really started in La Gloria could not be determined for sure. In fact something similar was happening about the same time in San Louis Potosi, north of Mexico City. But whatever the circumstances, panic spread throughout the valley after the three healthy children died, and as family after family was laid low by the epidemic.

Pablo had already determined to go back north for work before the flu hit. He had kept enough money for the bus to the border, but at the last minute he'd left most of what he'd saved to pay Angélica's doctor bill and to buy medicine. He assured María and his mother that he could make it just fine on the train. And that was the last anybody had heard.

April had turned to May, and the outbreak continued to spread. María was now four months pregnant, a fact that had become difficult to hide. Fearing the worst for her unborn child, she decided that she must flee. She had left the valley only once before, when she rode the bus with her mother to Perote to sell a dozen worn out hens in the market. But there were hog farms all around Perote too. If it was true that there

147

were now a million pigs spread across the Perote valley, then going north would make no sense. If she were to find safety, she would need to go another direction, and someplace farther away.

There was nobody she could turn to for help, certainly not for money, not even for good advice. Her father had gone to the US long ago to work and did not return, and her mother was dead. She awoke from a nightmare in the bed of the little hovel she and Pablo had rented, and immediately the obstacles she faced rose to meet her. She lay staring at the sheet-iron roof, trying to decide what to do. She knew that the municipal capital of Orizaba lay south beyond the big mountain, in a valley separated from hers by the Sierra Madre. Perhaps there she and the baby in her womb could be safe. Finally she rose, packed her meager belongings and what food she could carry into two market bags, and walked to the intersection where the van departed Victoria for Serdán. The driver told her that in Serdán she could catch a second-class bus across the mountains to Orizaba.

The bus pulled into Orizaba in early afternoon. María sat with her bags in the bus terminal and munched on the food she had brought. What now? She had enough pesos to buy food for a few days, but certainly no money for a hotel. When she wandered outside she heard the murmur of a river nearby. Beside the river bridge a stone path led down to the water. She ventured down the river trail, and to her astonishment came upon cages and pens that held amazing animals she had never seen. She had of course seen coyotes, a few of the birds and the deer, but others she had seen only in pictures, or not at all. She passed a black bear, a pair of camels, even a huge tiger. At last she came to the monkeys. She sat on a bench and watched them. They were confined to a cage, but soon a keeper arrived and brought them food. It occurred to her that her situation was not so different, except that nobody was going to bring her food. Not knowing what else to do, at dusk she retraced her steps to the bus terminal. She ate more tortillas and beans, then found a bench in the least-populated corner where she hoped she might sleep.

Night fell and she stretched out on the bench, looping her arm through the handles of the plastic bags, but sleep wouldn't come. She had never been in a place where lights remained on through the night, and every time she began to drift off, a bus would pull in, or the loudspeaker would announce a departure. And always there was the milling of passengers. Crying babies brought back to her the reason she had fled the valley of her birth. And then there were the men, who sensed a vulnerable young woman and in various crude ways would not let her be.

Finally she fell asleep, but not for long. It was still dark outside when the loudspeaker blared that the bus to Granada would be leaving in five minutes. She opened her eyes on the strange place and glanced at the clock over the ticket window. It was nearly five o'clock. There were no bags on her arm. She jerked from the prone position and found the bags still at her feet. Her few possessions were still there, her clothing and a pair of tortillas wrapped around beans. Her back felt kinked from sleeping on the narrow bench. Her stomach rumbled. She had something to eat for breakfast, but nothing to drink. Water was for sale in bottles, but she would need the meager contents of her purse for more important things. Looping her bags on her arm she went to the toilet, washed her face and combed her hair. She drank from the sink faucet. She walked to the river again, stopping at the first bench she found. She ate one of the tortillas and waited for some plan to come. Two things she had to find before the sun went down again—a place to sleep, and some kind of job.

María stood straight and smoothed her dress. Summoning all the meager courage she felt, she crossed the river and walked toward the rising sun. She hadn't walked far when she came upon a large robust woman who was washing the sidewalk in front of a little hotel with a bucket of water and a broom. The woman whistled as she worked.

"*Buenos días,*" the woman called as María approached. For some reason the very homely sign of friendliness touched María deeply, and she began to sob.

"*Pobrecita,*" the woman said. "You poor little thing. Whatever is so wrong?"

And then the woman's eyes dropped to María's belly. Probably most men would not have known, and María had told herself she could still keep her secret of a four-month baby in her womb, but the woman knew.

María didn't know where to begin. What was not wrong? Pablo was gone, and she had not heard a word. She was pregnant and in fear for her unborn child. All she had between herself and destitution was one bean-filled tortilla and the few pesos in her purse. She burst into tears and could hardly speak. The big woman propped her broom against the wall and gathered María in her arms.

"*Pobrecita,*" she said again, hugging the trembling girl close.

When her sobbing subsided, María told her story.

"*Ah, tenemos suerte,*" the other woman said. "We are in luck." Not "you," she had said, but "we."

María was not completely alone. The woman told María that just now the hotel manager was looking for a maid, and that if she was hired, there was a tiny room in back where she might sleep.

"*Me llamo Esmeralda,*" the woman said. "*¿Y tú?*"

"*Yo soy María,*" María said.

Esmeralda took María by the arm and led her to a little kitchen in back, where a big-bellied man in shorts and flip-flops sat at a table eating a plate of tortillas, *chorizo* and eggs. The man asked María if she could clean and do laundry. She assured him that she had experience and could do the job very well. The man told Esmeralda to show María the room out back where she could stay. She could eat her meals in the kitchen, and she would be paid two hundred pesos a week. It was all María could do to fight off the return of tears.

"*Sí,*" she said. "*Sí. Muchas gracias.*"

Esmeralda showed María to the lean-to room on the back wall. The room contained a narrow cot, a little table and a chair. María could use the bathroom in back of the hotel. Esmeralda told her to take a few moments to unpack and get settled, and then there would be work to do. María sat on the bed and breathed deeply. Two hundred pesos was not a large salary, to be sure. The men at the hog farms made that much in a day, that is if they could stand the conditions and keep their jobs. But with food and shelter provided, she could save most of her earnings. How far two hundred pesos would go toward supporting a baby she didn't know, not to mention the possible costs of bringing a baby into the world.

Chapter Twenty-three

It was well past noon when Lantry dragged his blistered feet back into Oyamecalco. What a fool to think you could hike up a mountain in cowboy boots, especially in boots with the soles worn thin. The water from Orizaba's peak was long gone and his eyes blurred from dehydration. He stopped at the first tiny restaurant he came to and collapsed on a plastic chair.

"*Necesito agua,*" he croaked, surprised at how unlike himself his parched voice sounded. "*Y comida.*"

The cook left her stove to bring him a *jarro de agua de jamaica,* a pitcher of ice-cold, magenta-colored tea made from the flowers of a common Mexican tree. Lantry drank the first glass without setting it down, refilled from the pitcher and swallowed that too.

"*Tienes mucha sed,*" the woman said, amused.

"*Sí,*" Lantry replied.

In fact he couldn't recall having been so thirsty before. And now the first course of the comida corrida arrived, a steaming bowl of chicken broth with scraps of carrot, *chile* and squash. He sipped the juice as fast as its heat would permit, then devoured the vegetables. And then came the chicken, a hind quarter simmering in creamy red salsa and rice. He made quick work of that too, which was followed by pineapple gelatin.

When he had finished the meal, which he realized he must have consumed in not much more than five minutes, he leaned back in the chair and sipped the last glass of *jamaica*. He paid his bill, two dollars in Texas money, left a tip half that much, thanked the woman and went back out to the muddy street. Again he hadn't walked far when a pickup truck stopped and offered him a ride. There were four men in front, so he threw his pack in the back and climbed in with it. The truck mostly coasted down the slope to Emancipación, as though it knew its destination had freed it from work.

Lantry walked toward the intersection where the van had let him off. He glanced back toward the peak and saw that it was now obscured with roiling clouds. A clap of thunder rolled down the mountain and it began to rain. He took shelter from the storm in the doorway of a tiny tienda, where he bought a bottle of water and waited with other would-be passengers for transportation to arrive.

The same van from yesterday groaned around the corner, sitting low on springs compromised by the heavy load of humanity. Two got out and he and three others got in. There were no seats available, so Lantry and other latecomers clung to the roof bar as the van rumbled on south.

When they reached Lázaro Cárdenas, several people got off and plunged into what had become a persistent downpour, and Lantry got a seat. Turning the name of the *pueblo* over in his mind, a pair of vague memories coalesced. Lázaro Cárdenas was not only the Mexican president who had created the national park on Orizaba; he was also the president Lantry had learned about in a high school history class, the one who nationalized Mexico's oil, something Texans with oil investments still talked about, and not favorably. The van rolled on, through the towns of Tlachichuca, San Miguel Ocotenco, Ahuatepec del Camino. The countryside was green with corn and other vegetable crops, farmed by horses, harvested by men, women and children working the rows by hand. When he had begun to think that every tiny town required an at-least-two-word name, they arrived at Texmalaca, and finally at the small city of Serdán, the end of the line for the tired van. There he bought a ticket for a second-class bus, a big bus that had seen better days, but where he had an assigned seat. That bus stopped for more passengers in Esperanza, another inspiring name that meant hope, then climbed steadily from the valley to the heights of the forested Sierra Madre. For half an hour they climbed and twisted, climbed and twisted, and finally began the long descent to the valley where the city of Orizaba lay.

The bus came to a stop at last at the terminal beside Rio Orizaba. Lantry ask for directions to El Centro, but near the river he passed a small hotel. He admitted to himself how exhausted he was and how badly his blistered feet needed rest. He asked for a room. The man behind the desk told him no rooms were ready, but he could deposit his pack in a room and return in a couple of hours. Outside his window, the mountain stream gurgled over the rocks, crystal water from the same melting snow that had sustained him that morning on the mountain's other side. He opened the window to the afternoon air, sweet with flowers and refreshed by a recent shower. He pulled off his boots, rinsed and massaged his feet and collapsed on the unmade bed. He had no intention of doing so, but soon he fell into a deep sleep.

When some time had passed he was roused by a knock, and the door opened. A young woman in a white dress and sandals was there to clean the room and make his bed.

"*Dispénseme,*" the woman said, then seeing that he was likely a North American she added in English, "Excuse me. I come back later."

"No, no, it's OK," Lantry said. "I'm sorry. I just laid down to rest a moment. I didn't intend to fall asleep. Please come in." He sat up on the bed, pulled on his socks and boots and moved his pack into a corner. "I'll take a look at the river and come back after you've finished," he said.

He tucked in his shirt and went to the door. She entered, set clean sheets and a towel on the chair and proceeded to strip the bed. Lantry lingered in the doorway. He couldn't help watching as she worked. It appeared that she might be pregnant, but even so her figure was nice, he thought, legs creamy brown to above the knees when she bent over the bed. Long black braids were bound together in back.

Lantry knew he should go, that staring at this stranger at work was impolite, but he couldn't pull himself away. He realized, in fact, that he was feeling sensations he had not experienced in a very long time. He did not want to go. When she turned to pick up new sheets, Lantry saw in her profile that in fact she was quite pregnant. She met his eyes, and he thought she smiled tentatively, then returned to her work. And now he felt embarrassed for watching her. She was the woman of some other man, and he knew he had no right to the feelings that had risen in his body and his mind.

He smiled an embarrassed smile, and added awkwardly, "Excuse me for interrupting your work. I'm going now. I need to go."

Lantry was really going, but then he turned back.

"You spoke to me in English," he said. "How do you know the language?"

155

Now he saw pain in her eyes.

"I have a few words from my husband," she said. "He worked in the United States, and now he's gone back. But" — she averted her eyes to the floor—"I haven't heard from him for so long. Maybe he's in jail or in trouble somewhere, I don't know."

When she glanced back up, her face revealed embarrassment, maybe shame. She had weakly and unintentionally revealed secrets and fears to a stranger, a foreigner at that.

Lantry didn't know what to say. He wanted to go to her, comfort her, hold her. But of course he could not.

"I'm sorry," was all he could say.

He dug in his pocket and pulled out a twenty peso bill.

"Here, this is for you," he said. "Thank you for cleaning my room and making my bed."

"*Muchas Gracias*," the woman muttered embarrassedly, taking the bill, and then he darted out the door and hobbled away.

But her face went with him. It was a very pleasing face, a slight blush in her cheeks, maybe because of his watching, or maybe because she was carrying a child. In his line of work as an investigative reporter he had habitually studied the faces and movements of others for clues about their thoughts and their lives, but there was something about this woman that provoked more than curiosity.

When he had crossed Rio Orizaba from the bus terminal he had noticed that a stone path followed its course on both sides. He found steps leading to the water and began to walk, gingerly because of the blister on his heel. And then for the second time that day, and again over the murmur of a

156

mountain stream, he heard the roar of a mighty cat. He stopped dead in his tracks. Was he going insane? He hadn't had a drink of alcohol for nearly two days. Was this what reality was going to be like? Perhaps this was the delirium tremors he'd heard drunks talk about and had once experienced. He felt the need for a drink profoundly. At the first street crossing with a staircase he ascended to the street and walked toward the city center, searching for a bar. But then came the roar again, behind him this time. He stopped abruptly, holding his breath. What kind of coward had he become, that he couldn't look reality in the face without hiding behind alcohol? Long he stood, immobilized, then turned back toward the river.

A gaggle of avian voices drew him to a large netted enclosure with birds of many feathers. Amazed, he walked on, past a pen full of ostriches, past a black bear, a pair of camels, and finally to the source of the roar, a large female tiger. Unlike the mountain lion that bared its teeth in his face, if in fact that had really happened, the tiger now sprawled lazily against a tree. Its mouth opened wide, but only with a sleepy yawn. Staring at the cat, Lantry began to laugh, first at himself, and then at life, or at least at the marvels he had experienced in the three short-long days since Mexico City. Especially in two days without tequila, even without beer. He sat on a bench beside the river, and tears filled his eyes. At first he tried to stop, wiping his eyes on his sleeve, fighting to retain composure. But night was falling, and there was no one to see, no one except a tiger, two camels and a brown bear, and Lantry wept.

When the sobbing stopped, he dried his eyes. It was the second time in as many days that he had cried, he realized. Looking up he saw that, as if in accord, the sky had grown dark. Clouds rolled down from the mountain and thunder clapped. A light rain began to fall, but quickly the clouds opened and released a torrent. He trotted as fast as his pained feet would permit, back up the river trail, up the steps to the street and to the hotel. His only clean shirt and pants were soaked when he arrived, but the air was warm, and he didn't care. He turned the key, flipped on the light, and took off his clothes. He lay down a second time on the bed, now smoothed by the pregnant woman's hands, and closed his eyes.

In his year and a half alone, Lantry had mostly succeeded in getting Linda out of his head, but now she was back, or was it the young Mexican who had cleaned his room? His longing for a woman, for intimacy, for love, was suddenly profound. In his long stupor and depression he had hardly looked at or thought about a woman for months, and now a passion he hadn't felt in a very long time was rising in his body and in his soul.

For the first time in a long while he allowed himself to really remember Linda, to picture her naked body and her face. What was she doing now? Did she have another man, a husband perhaps? If she didn't, and if he could stay sober, might she possibly take him back? But he had decided just moments ago to confront reality head-on, and he knew that was not likely to happen. She was a beautiful woman, smart, with everything to offer to a man who would be good to her. He knew he had to put her out of his head and move on. As he drifted off to sleep, her blonde image somehow fused with that of the dark young hotel maid. The maid had a husband she said, but he had disappeared, and who knew? Might he not return?

He woke from his second nap of the day thinking of the woman whose name he didn't even know. With her swollen belly, it frankly hadn't struck him to want her for sex. But he found himself wanting her, nonetheless. Newly-committed realist that he was, he knew it was perhaps mostly the drag of loneliness, or perhaps that she was vulnerable, in need of help, perhaps in need of a man. He got up, wrung the water from his wet clothes and hung them in the shower to dry. He put on his cleanest dirty clothes and went out to find food.

Chapter Twenty-four

A month had passed since Fernando was hauled back to the border, and Pablo hadn't heard a thing, not from Fernando, not from María. Did Fernando make it home, Pablo wondered. It was easy to imagine all sorts of calamities. Did he find María? If so, why hadn't there been a letter or a call? Maybe something bad had happened to her too.

The guards seemed to be watching him constantly now, so maybe a letter had come for him and they didn't hand it over. Or maybe María thought he had deserted her as her father had. Perhaps she had even found another man. That thought stabbed at his heart. Of course he couldn't blame her if she had. After all, unless Fernando found her and delivered his message, she had no way of knowing where he was, that he was alive, that he loved her and would never leave her. Yet, she had to eat somehow, and if the baby hadn't come yet, it would come soon. Was it a girl or a boy? If it was a boy, would she name it for him? Anxiety was driving him mad; yet he still didn't have a plan. He had been praying toward the tiny window every night, but God had not showed him a way.

Pablo had had nothing to do with the riot, no more than what had happened in the cafeteria. In fact he hadn't even seen it coming until he saw an iron bar swing, saw it connect with the back of the guard's neck and saw him go down. Yes, he had rushed the door like anybody else with good sense, mostly for a chance at freedom, but also to escape the tear gas. And yes, he came closer to making it than most, but he was among a surge of dozens. So why did they grab him for another trip to the hole?

The wall was thick as his forearm was long and the opening so small that there was never a panorama, only the occasional floating cloud by day or by night that moment's star or handful of stars beyond the bars. Though Pablo never actually saw the moon, he knew when it was waxing. On clear nights the full moon cast a comforting yellow hue that softened the harsh blue glare of the floodlights from the guard tower. Even on the darkest nights those lights illuminated the gray walls, the steel door, and the bars that carved the tiny square into a grid of narrow rectangles. It was never too dark to see his hands, even the deep scar on his forearm that he'd carried since a badly-aimed stroke of a machete had opened it wide when he was a child. Day or night, natural light was never complete and full, and darkness was the same, never complete—except in his soul.

María haunted his mind through the long sleepless hours of night. Nearly nine months had passed since he'd seen her in the flesh, held her in his arms. He tried to focus on other things, but that wasn't easy in a solitary cell. Thinking of anything he cared about brought mostly pain. The only future to contemplate was escaping the hole, and then the prison. Looking for some diversion, any diversion, Pablo's mind ranged back across the days and months since he'd caught the train in Orizaba. Terrible as that journey was, the memory brought scraps of relief, imagining the boxcar to which he had clung, rocking and careening through the valley toward the city and beyond, the wind in his face. The roar of the locomotive, the rush of air, the *campesinos* gathering their crops beside the tracks. But reliving that journey brought its own perils. The image of the man he'd thrown from the train emerged from the shadows as it always did.

Who was that man, he wondered. Was he a country kid like Pablo, but one who had somehow taken a wrong path? Was he like the handful of boys from the valley who had fallen in with drug gangs, thugs who gave them top quality marijuana and then stronger drugs, lured them into a web from which there was no escape? Their stories had drifted back to Victoria. Sometimes young men, boys really, were required to kill members of rival gangs, and if they refused, they themselves would die. Was the man he'd thrown to his death such a man, or had something else beyond mere need driven him to brutality, to robbery and violence as a way of life?

Even though their encounter was brief, a few seconds at most, the man's face was etched in Pablo's mind, never to be erased. He was a young man, maybe a few years older than Pablo, and of slight build like him. His hair was black of course, long and tangled, his facial hair sparse. The hand that held the gun was tattooed with a girl's name. In the moment that must have been less than a second Pablo had read the name. Sonya. But the eyes—what was it in those eyes? They glared with such fierceness—was it hate, fear, or madness? Such questions, Pablo had come to recognize, were mostly diversions from the larger question he could not escape. He himself would emerge from a third term in solitary, perhaps today if his count was right, and if they chose to keep their word. Then back to the cell with three or more other men to rot until his time was finally up and he could cross the river one last time—or until he escaped. At the first hint of morning light, it would be easier to believe the day of release might come.

But for the other man there would be no release. He would cross no rivers. What was his name, Pablo wondered. Did Sonya love him, and did he love her? Surely not, or he could not have lived by hurting others. One thing was sure. That man would never go home, wherever and whatever that might have been. If Sonya was waiting somewhere for him, her wait would be forever. Pablo relived again, could not avoid reliving in slow motion the thing that must have lasted no more than two or three seconds, the body spinning from the strike of his backpack, the struggle to regain footing, the momentum of the train in the man's favor but not enough to match the ferocity of Pablo's blow. Over he went, backward, headfirst, the eyes meeting Pablo's in the split second he disappeared, then nothing but a final scream of terror. Pablo had dropped to hands and knees at the head of the rumbling car in time to see the contorted body bounce off the car, hit the rails, and then the heavy steel wheels slicing him in half and the body disappearing in a blur of blood.

Sometimes Pablo thought he remembered a bump, sometimes not. But the heavy load clung so efficiently to the steel rails that surely a few pounds of human flesh could be chewed up and spit out and the machine that was the Beast would register no reaction. And what then? Did coyotes come for the mangled corpse that very night? Did a caracara light next morning to pluck out those awful mad eyes? One thing that troubled Pablo was the fear that his mind would never be free of the man as long as he might live, that in some terrible way the man would live on through him, and yet he would never know a thing about the life the man had lived before

163

the moment he was struck in the back by a pack holding two changes of clothing, a bottle of water and cans of beans.

Pablo shook the images from his mind and focused on the small patch of still gray but growing light. He was in prison for the crimes of crossing a river and carrying a bag of marijuana he didn't own and had no intention to consume or sell. His only real remorse was that he had been caught. But this other crime, that was something else. On Sundays a priest came to Eden to talk to the men and to offer them communion, but Pablo had not gone. Maybe if he could confess his real crime, some of the pain would go away, but that he could not do. First, it would be dangerous to tell this story to a *gringo* priest who, who knows, might turn him in. And second, he wasn't even sure that killing the man had been a crime, or even a sin, and if so, what kind?

The pale light of morning now softened the harsh blue glare. Another night was coming to an end. He always watched this moment to see what was in store. Sometimes the morning glow was pink, but today it was gray, the light of a clouded sun. This must be late September, so the equinox was near. For the next three months each night would be longer than the night before.

As for days, except for variations in light, one day was indistinguishable from all the others in the hole. The bland pasty food, the snarling guard who delivered the meals, the toilet stench, the itching fungus that grew between his toes. They had finally given him a tube of something, but so far it hadn't made a difference. Maybe the toes were just the beginning. Maybe the rot would spread up his legs, eventually consuming his entire body, not to mention his soul.

When it was light enough to see, Pablo lifted the corner of the thin stained mattress to check the marks his fingernail had scratched. He counted them out, thirteen, then added another. He stood and paced three steps to the steel door, three paces back, three paces, three paces. He stretched to touch the concrete floor. He reached on tiptoes toward the light. Morning must be breaking in Victoria too, though the sun would not clear the mountain for a couple of hours.

The thud of two pairs of heavy boots rang down the runway, coming to a stop at his cell. A key turned and the door slid open.

"Time's up," one guard said.

Each gripped an arm and guided Pablo down the dim hallway and around the corner to cell block C. They stopped before a cell, slid open the bars and pushed Pablo through.

When they had gone, Pablo raised his head. Only three men. He would have a bed, and now a cell that faced east! Morning light streamed in, gray, but almost blinding after the darkness of two weeks in the hole.

"I'm Pablo," he said weakly, and collapsed on a bunk.

"That would be my bed," one said. "Yours is up there," pointing to an upper bunk.

Pablo dragged his body up and gazed out at the morning light. Finally he turned back to face his new companions. All Mexicans, none with glaring eyes. He felt something like happiness, or at least relief.

"So we know why you were in the hole," another man said. "And we don't want to go there, so if you try any more of that funny business, leave us out. We're all doing short time here, and we want to go home. If you want to protest the stinking food or demand some kind of rights, you'll just go

165

back to solitary," the man added, "and we don't want to go with you."

"Better just keep your mouth shut and do your time like the rest of us," said another. "If you do that, there won't be any trouble. *Comprende?*"

Chapter Twenty-five

Lantry awoke refreshed. There was a certain uneasiness in his belly, but he couldn't remember when his head had felt so clear. He pulled on his jeans and stepped outside. The sky was bright too, as was the river that tumbled down from Orizaba. From here he couldn't see the peak itself; lower mountains hid it from view. He looked up and down the street, wondering whether and when the young maid might appear. He wanted to see the maid again, to know her name and more about her. He stepped back inside and put on his cleanest dry shirt. Sometime today he'd take the others someplace to have them washed. He searched the sky, but saw no sign of rain.

He set out toward the rising sun, looking for coffee and breakfast. At a little cafe he found strong mountain coffee, and when the eggs came they were so fresh that the bright yellow yokes stood erect. The hand-made tortillas were hot and the beans had a touch of *chile* that curled the tongue. He had just begun to eat when the man at the next table rose to leave.

"*Buen provecho,*" he said as he passed Lantry's table. Like the French *bon appétit,* enjoy your meal.

Lantry felt cheered to be among people so friendly that when they departed after enjoying a meal they invariably wished a total stranger the same.

What should he do today, he asked himself. He wanted to explore the city, but he also needed to find work. If he didn't find something here, and soon, he'd need to go back home. "Home?" he muttered under his breath, forgetting there were other diners near. But in the hours since he'd arrived in Orizaba, somehow it was starting to feel like it could be home. The hotel was comfortable and quiet, the air and the mountain river were fresh, everything he'd seen of the town was in fact alluring. And the woman; if only she could be part of home.

The condition for surviving here, or anywhere, was finding a job. There had to be a newspaper of some kind, but would they pay him for what he could do? Would they hire him with his limited ability in Spanish? If they did, could he deliver? And then there was his legal status. He wished he'd realized before he left Mexico City that his tourist card had expired so he could have tried to get it renewed. But even if he had a valid visa, that might not permit him to work legally, or anybody to legally hire him even if they wanted to.

Lantry recalled with some chagrin an investigative piece he'd done in Dallas about undocumented workers. It had all seemed pretty simple then. If you want to go to another country, do it legally. If you want a work permit, follow the rules. That was the American way, whether you were a citizen or not. But that didn't stop undocumented Mexicans from working in Texas or anyplace else. There was always somebody happy to look the other way or pretend fake papers were real if they could hire workers at a low enough wage. Now the shoe was on the other foot, and maybe things weren't so different here. He knew well that even if everything was in order, any job he could get here would pay far less than north of the border, but on the other hand he was paying twelve dollars a day for a hotel room, and he could eat well for far less than that. If he could stay off booze, he could probably get by on twenty bucks a day. He determined that he would find a job, any kind of job, regardless of what it paid.

He finished breakfast and headed back to his room for a close shave, to make himself as presentable as possible. When he arrived the door was open, and as in the previous afternoon the young woman was bent over his bed, tucking in the sheet. He watched quietly for a moment, then knocked.

"*Buenos días*," he called.

The woman whirled around to face him, and returned his greeting. The morning sun lighted her face, and she smiled.

"*Pasa*," she said. "Come in. I'm almost done."

"I just came back to clean up," Lantry said, "but I'll wait outside until you're finished."

"It's OK, you can come in," she said. "I just have to gather my things."

Lantry stepped into her presence.

"My name is Lantry," he said, extending his hand.

"*Me llamo María*," she said. She took his hand, and her hand was warm and firm. Not soft, because her life was not soft, but warm and strong. He held her hand for longer than he should have, not wanting to let it go.

Now she turned, embarrassed, and began gathering her cleaning equipment.

"Would you go with me for dinner tonight?" Lantry blurted out.

The question surprised him as much as it probably did her.

"*Gracias*, but I get food here," she said. "It's part of my pay."

"Maybe you could show me a bit of the town?" he added. "I really don't know my way around."

"And neither do I," she said. "I go only to the river to see the animals. I have no money for the town."

"Then let's walk together down the river to the plaza tonight," he persisted. "We could at least have ice cream."

María paused, perhaps trying to figure what to think of this foreigner, whether he might mean her harm.

"OK," she said at last. "I can go after six." Then she grabbed her gear and was gone.

Lantry sat down on the just-made bed, imagining the stroke of the hands that had smoothed the sheets. He took off his shirt, turned on the bathroom light, and carefully shaved. Tonight he would be with a woman for the first time in well over a year, and he hoped he would be able to tell her that he had a job.

When he felt presentable, Lantry went in search of a newspaper. At a newsstand just off the plaza he found that Orizaba actually had two papers. He bought a copy of each and sat down on a bench to read. The papers looked rather lightweight compared to the *Morning News* where he'd worked, but after all Orizaba was not a large city. Come to think of it, he couldn't think of any city this size in the US that still had two dailies. He noted the addresses, both within a few blocks of where he sat, wrote down the names of the publishers and editors, allowed a *lustrador* to shine his boots and set out to get a job.

At the first paper the editor was busy and spoke no English, but at the second he was invited to sit down and visit. As it happened the publisher was looking for somebody skilled in layout, but who also spoke both Spanish and English, partly to edit international news, but also to cover stories with North American content or angles. Lantry described his educational background and experience, trying to find the middle ground between boastful and modest. He admitted that he was not really fluent in Spanish, but apparently the part of the interview that was conducted in that language satisfied the editor, Octavio. He agreed to give Lantry a try. Octavio apologized for the low salary, but Lantry figured that whatever he could earn would be that much more than he was earning now, so he agreed. But then Octavio asked to see Lantry's work permit, which of course he did not have. Even his tourist visa was expired.

The editor explained that if Lantry could get his visa renewed, then the newspaper could facilitate the process of converting that to a work permit. But since Lantry had already overstayed his visa, there might be problems. In the meantime, they could try Lantry out as a stringer, writing under a pseudonym. The pay would of course be even less. But in the meantime the process of renewing his visa and obtaining a valid work permit could be pursued. The situation was far from satisfactory to Lantry, but after all, his illegal status was nobody's fault but his own. He saw no good alternatives, so he agreed to the arrangement. Lantry's first assignments would be local stories, and if that went well, the editor promised to send him up the Orizaba valley for a bigger story they'd been working on.

Lantry had no idea whether he could get the work permit, whether the job would be long-term and satisfactory, or whether he could live on the meager salary. But he did have a job, he had gone more than two days without alcohol, and he would spend the evening with a pretty woman. He strode back toward the hotel with a smile on his face and a spring to his gait.

Chapter Twenty-six

"¡Rojas!" the guard roared. "Get your ass out of bed and get dressed. You're going for a ride."

Fernando opened his eyes to a flashlight in his face. He struggled out of bed and found his orange pants and t-shirt. "Not those," the guard said, thrusting a plastic bag at Fernando. The bag held the jeans and ragged shirt he had worn the day they took him in. Asking no questions, he pulled on his clothes and sneakers and stood. The door rolled open with its loud clang and Fernando stepped through. He was hustled to the waiting room, where a dozen or so other men rubbed sleep from their eyes.

"Here's your last free meal," another guard said, distributing brown paper sacks with grease stains seeping through. "Now line up and get on the bus."

The sun had not reached its zenith when the bus rolled into Laredo. It stopped at the border and another guard came on board. He handed out clipboards with papers and pens and instructed the men where to sign.

One man raised his hand and asked meekly, "What about our possessions? I had thirty dollars and my grandfather's watch when they took me in."

"Possessions?" the guard sneered. "You're lucky to cross the river alive. I don't know anything about your so-called possessions."

He exited the bus and it rumbled on across the border, coming to a stop at the bus station in Nuevo Laredo. There the men were sternly warned that if they crossed the border again they would do hard time. They were issued tokens to purchase tickets back to their claimed points of origin.

All afternoon Fernando's bus rolled south, through Monterrey and Saltillo, through the high desert country to San Luis Potosi and Queretaro. He eyed each city they passed, wondering whether it might hold prospects for him. He thought about getting off the bus more than once and wondering the city streets to see what he might find. But he kept his seat, and finally, as darkness fell they arrived at Terminal Norte in Mexico City. He knew there were just two options back in the valley, work in some capacity for the hog factories, or starve. Surely there was something better for him someplace else, maybe here in the capital.

He checked the departure board and found that a second-class bus was departing for Guadalupe Victoria within the hour. His ticket was good for that last leg. He hung around the terminal for a while, but finally decided that for at least the evening he would explore the city he knew only from stories he had heard. He asked directions to El Centro and began to walk.

The splendor of the city was overwhelming, the lights, the ever-present roar, the street musicians, the vast throngs of people, the aromas, and of course the magnificent architecture that overwhelmed his senses, amazing him that men could have built such things. He stumbled through the streets, gawking at the tall ornate buildings, taking it all in. But finally he could no longer ignore how hungry he was. He had not eaten since the sausage and egg biscuit, his parting gift from Eden. He inhaled the aromas of tacos al pastor, offered from tiny street-front shops everywhere he looked. His stomach churned with desire, but his pocket was empty.

In spite of that fact, he found himself joining the line before the slowly revolving *trompo* where thin-sliced pork roasted before an open flame. When his turn came the cook glanced up from his work of slicing scraps of meat and pineapple onto hot tortillas.

"*¿Cuánto?*" he asked. How many.

"*No tengo dinero,*" Fernando meekly explained. "I just got off the bus, deported from the US."

He didn't know what to expect. He had never begged for anything before, not even food. The cook stood straight from his work and sized Fernando up. Then he filled a tortilla with meat, tomato, onion, avocado and salsa and handed it over.

"*Buen provecho,*" he said.

Fernando felt tears welling in his eyes.

"*Muchas gracias,*" was all he could say. He cradled the taco in his hands and demolished it in a few quick bites. But now what? The capital was clearly a miraculous place, and there must be many good people here. But it was not his home, and he was pretty sure it could not be. He had no money, no job, he knew nobody in the city. And then he remembered Pablo and the promise he had made. He retraced his steps to the terminal and turned in his voucher for a ticket to Victoria.

The sun's first rays were silhouetting El Pico de Orizaba when the bus squealed to a stop in front of the church. Fernando got off and began to walk, at last a route so familiar he could have done it with his eyes closed. In half an hour he had climbed past the edge of town and was knocking at his mother's door. When she opened the door and the aroma of *tamales* rushed to his nostrils, Fernando knew that he was home. Why had he ever left in the first place? For a brief moment his mother was frozen in shock, then she wrapped her arms around him and called out,

"Fernando, Fernando is home!"

In a moment Fernando's brothers were there too, the oldest encircling him in his arms, the younger ones clinging to his legs.

It was a day of celebration. The little house was filled with good food and love. Word spread down the street that Fernando had returned, and soon neighbors were at the door. He told his story again and again, but in fact his arrest and brief incarceration in Texas were but vague memories now, almost amusing in a way, the sort of tale he could tell forever and perhaps embellish with the passage of time. Of course his story was nothing new to most of the neighbors. They had heard it all before, and some had lived it. In the fifteen years since Smithfield had arrived, many a man had made the journey north. A few had never returned. Most had worked for months or even years and had faithfully sent remittances to keep their families alive before one day returning to the valley of their birth. Fernando personally knew three families who lived in modest new homes in the neighborhood, built by money earned in the United States. And then there were those like Fernando, who hadn't made it far past the border. Instead of work they'd found jail.

When night fell Fernando's brothers doubled up in their beds and left a whole bed for him. He lay down to rest, a happy man, yet sleep was slow to come. There was the question of tomorrow, what he would do to earn money. The harvest was underway, so for a few days or weeks he could likely find work in the fields, but what after that? Realistically the choices were the same as those he'd left behind when he walked out the door two months earlier, he reminded himself. Work for the hog factories or look for something someplace else. The former was no more attractive to him now than it had been before, so he knew that at some point he'd have to move on. Two months in Eden had convinced him that crossing the river again was a risk he didn't want to take. That meant going to some city to see what he could find.

When he woke the next morning, Pablo was on Fernando's mind. He had taken a solemn oath to find María and tell her where Pablo was, and that had to be the first order of business. He knew that María's father was long gone and that her mother was dead, and he knew of no other relatives with whom she might be harboring. At breakfast he asked his mother and brothers if they remembered María, the María who had taken up with his friend Pablo, and where he might find her.

"Yes, of course I remember María," his mother said. "She always came to mass, but I haven't seen her since, well, I don't know when. It's been a long time."

"Didn't she leave town when the flu came?" one of Fernando's brothers asked. "Many people left then, and once the flu died down, some have not returned."

So Fernando set out to search for María. First he checked the tiny shack where Pablo and María had briefly lived, but it was empty. He asked around until he found the home of Pablo's mother and his sisters, but nobody was home. He hoped the girls might be in school, and maybe the mother had gone to the market. He scrawled a note on the back of his bus ticket telling them that Pablo was in prison in Texas, and

176

that he promised to come home. Fernando went to the market, where he found a few people who knew María, but nobody who could say where she had gone. He woke the priest from his siesta, but he groggily replied that he hadn't seen María for months, had no idea where she had gone. When evening came Pablo returned to his mother's house, his mission unfulfilled. He had looked everywhere he could think to look, had inquired of everybody who might have known María. It seemed she had simply disappeared. It occurred to Fernando that she might have succumbed to the swine flu, but if that had been the case, surely the priest would have known.

Fernando went to bed that night with a great sense of unease. He knew how important it was to both Pablo and María that he find her and tell her that Pablo would come. But was there anything else he could do, any rock he hadn't looked under? He turned the question over in his mind until finally he drifted off to sleep, unsatisfied.

When morning came he had no new ideas, so he decided to devote himself to the other pressing need, finding work, either here in the valley or someplace else. He had seen how little food was in his mother's kitchen, and how ragged his younger brothers were. He had left the valley in the first place because he detested feeding hogs and hosing down manure, and his two-month absence had not made those jobs more attractive. If he got work in the harvest, that might last a few weeks, but then what? He drifted around town for a second day, inquiring about work, but found nothing. By nightfall he had reached the conclusion that he would have to leave Victoria again, either now or soon. Maybe he could find work in Perote or Orizaba, small cities that lay to the north and the south. Before he slept he mumbled a promise to Pablo that wherever he went and whatever he did, he would not forget about María, that he would continue to search.

Chapter Twenty-seven

With the promise of a job, Lantry's inclination and habit dictated stopping at a bar to celebrate. But there was nobody to celebrate with, and more importantly, a single morning's good fortune of a job and a promised evening with a woman renewed his resolve to keep walking past every bar on his route to the hotel.

Back at his room he sorted through the pile of dirty clothes. Besides what he had on, only one pair of pants and two shirts would do for his new job. The few shirts and jeans he'd brought from Texas had grown threadbare, and some had stains that would never wash out. Maybe in a paycheck or two he could buy some new things. For now he rolled all his dirty clothes into a ball and carried them to a laundry he'd noticed along the way.

When María finished work at six, Lantry was waiting for her on the folding chair outside his room. She excused herself and went to wash up and change from her work dress to something else. When she emerged a few minutes later it was in a faded flowery dress that flowed around her swollen belly. She was stunning, Lantry thought, somehow blending the raw beauty of a simple peasant girl with the stately maturity of a mother. How old was she, he wondered, possibly in her twenties, but judging by the innocence of her eyes, maybe younger.

She stepped tentatively toward him, and he reached to take her hand.

"You look beautiful," he said.

She thanked him, but quickly withdrew her hand and stared in apparent embarrassment at the ground.

"Shall we walk down the river?" he asked, taking her arm and turning her that way.

They crossed the river, and again he took her arm as they descended the steps to the stone path that followed the river's curves. The gurgle of water and the rush when it cascaded over rocks filled what might have been an awkward silence. They stopped by the fence to watch deer munching hay, strolled past the cage where three coyotes paced a well-worn path inside the fence, obviously wishing for the freedom of the other side, past the netted enclosure where raptors eyed sparrows that had entered the danger zone. Besides comments about the animals, neither spoke.

Just beyond a swinging suspension bridge they came to the monkey cage, the end of the west-side path. The river was a bit wider there, and calmer. They watched spider monkeys climb, swing and leap, pursuing their lifeways in what Lantry imagined was an uninhibited display of joy. Then high on a limb overhead, a male reached his long spidery arm around a female and drew her close. Lantry took the cue, pulling María's warm young body to his side.

"No," she murmured. "I can't. I'm Pablo's wife, and I know he will return."

Lantry saw both pain and longing in her upturned eyes.

"Yes, I'm sorry," he said. "I had no right."

Yet the look in her eyes told him she wanted, or at least needed his embrace, though perhaps the closeness of any other human being might have served as well, anyone who could share her anxiety and pain. He had released her, but his body tingled from the electric warmth of momentary contact. He found himself strangely and powerfully attracted to her, needing her as he'd needed nothing else, besides alcohol, for a very long time.

The pair turned and retraced their steps to the hanging bridge that spanned the river. With every step the bridge dipped and swayed, and María's heavy belly made balance difficult. She almost lost her equilibrium, and instinctively she grasped his hand.

When they had crossed she withdrew her hand, and they strolled side by side toward the center of town until they reached a pedestrian-only street. The route took them past the newspaper office Lantry had visited that morning. In fading evening light and with María at his side it was no longer a place of anxiety, but a place of hope. He stopped before the door.

"I have something to tell you," he said. "I got a job today. Not a very good job, but maybe something I can do to make some money. In the United States I worked for a newspaper, and the editor of this paper agreed to give me a try. I hope my Spanish is good enough to do the job."

"¡*Bueno!*" María said. "I am glad."

They strolled up Madero, the no-traffic street that led to Parque Castillo, which Lantry had discovered that morning. A ragged young man juggled four bowling pins for tips. A group of teenagers took turns breakdancing, one spinning like a top on his head. Vendors hawked ice cream, *tamales* and nuts. People gathered at tiny restaurants for *tacos al pastor*. Lantry's adopted habit would have been to stop for a delicious two-dollar meal, but this was no ordinary night. True, the roll of bills in his boot had grown thin, so thin he was hardly aware of its bulge against his ankle. But the prospect of a job was comforting, even a job that paid a tiny fraction of what he'd earned in Dallas. But even if he had only enough cash for one sumptuous meal with María, he thought, he would gladly spend his last peso.

Well before they arrived at the park they heard the music of a Mariachi band. A small crowd circled the gazebo where the musicians played and sang. The pair stood on the fringes and listened, and again Lantry could not help taking María's hand. This time she did not resist. A warm current flowed to Lantry from her body, but then the band stopped playing and the trumpet player worked his way through the crowd with a small plastic bucket. Lantry reached in his pocket and withdrew all the coins and tossed them in.

"Shall we have dinner?" he asked.

"*Sí*," María replied with a laugh. "*Tengo mucha hambre*," then trying her English, "I very hungry."

Lantry led María past the street vendors and taco stands, across the park and past the cathedral, then across another street to the small park that fronted the Palacio de Hierro, the "iron palace," the nineteenth-century building he'd discovered that morning. It was designed and built by an architect in France, then disassembled and shipped across the Atlantic to Veracruz, he'd learned, hauled across the mountains to this valley and reassembled here.

Everything about the place was lovely, the exotically-designed palace itself, the little plaza, the carefully manicured flower beds in full bloom. Lovers cuddled on the park benches that surrounded a pair of fountains. Lantry guided María past the couples and up the steps to the outdoor patio. A waiter in a neatly pressed white jacket ushered them to a table overlooking the plaza. Lantry ordered a seafood platter to share, and in the intoxication of the moment and with too little thought, two glasses of red wine. Immediately he wondered if that was a mistake. He hadn't drunk alcohol for three days now. Two days had passed since he'd flung the last of the tequila into the fire. Too late now. On the other hand, he rationalized to himself, now might be a better time than most to test whether he could drink one glass of wine and then stop. The attractive young woman who sat across from him was the most powerful incentive he'd experienced in such a long time, and now he even had a chance to rebuild his crumbled career. He hoped, without evidence, that never again would he fall into alcohol's powerful snare. He told himself that he would exert whatever will was necessary to avoid backsliding to his old ways.

The wine came, and Lantry raised his glass to María with the traditional toast.

"*¡Salud!*" To your health.

It was not only to María's health, he realized, but also to his own precarious health, and to the health of the baby in María's womb. The thought came that the wish should also extend to María's husband Pablo, wherever he might be, but he suppressed that idea and the mass of contradictions it raised.

María copied Lantry's gesture. Their glasses touched and he brought the wine to his lips. She did as he did, but the taste brought a noticeable squint to her eyes, a wrinkle to her forehead.

"I've never tasted wine before," she explained after an awkward swallow. "At a friend's wedding I drank mescal, but only a little. I didn't like the taste, but the wine is not as bad."

183

"Not bad at all," Lantry responded with an amused chuckle.

He took another sip, which warmed his body and calmed his agitated mind. But try as he might, he couldn't entirely suppress from the lovely evening the image of the missing Pablo, an image he had invented in his mind, since he'd never seen the man or even heard him described. Was he tall, or short like most of his countrymen? No doubt his skin was dark, and his hair and eyes. Was he María's age, or an "older man," like Lantry? He must be handsome to attract a woman like María, or perhaps she simply had few choices. The elation he felt at this moment, sitting in a fine restaurant overlooking a lovely park, across from a woman blushing with the beauty of motherhood, sipping a glass of good wine and awaiting the first fine meal he'd had in months, all of that was somehow eclipsed by the shadow of a man whose right to this woman he was betraying, as perhaps she was too. But a man who hadn't been heard from for months, and for all anybody knew, might be dead. He honestly didn't want that to be true, but he couldn't deny the selfish hope that Pablo would not return.

The meal came, a large ceramic platter filled with fish filets, shrimp and octopus, along with a colorful array of vegetables and a basket of bread. Lantry served a portion to María and then to himself, and they began to eat, he carefully moderating the savage satisfaction of his hunger by a modicum of civility, she shyly watching his manner and following suit.

Fortunately the pitcher of *agua de jamaica* that accompanied the meal helped Lantry temper his craving to guzzle the wine. More than any alcoholic drink he'd had in ages, he savored the flavor, consciously sipping very slowly and only occasionally, depending for intoxication upon the pleasing circumstances of the evening. When he had swallowed the last bite of his food and wiped his mouth, there was one small sip left, as there was in María's glass. He waited for her to finish her dinner, trying not to stare at the lovely face or the long glossy hair or even at the reddened and work-worn fingers that lifted her fork. When she too was finished, he raised his wine to hers and together they tipped their glasses back.

Lantry paid the *cuenta*. By Texas standards the meal cost very little, but it did require one of his larger bills. He was glad he'd had the forethought to transfer it from his boot to his wallet. Even with his new job and the pay it offered, he wouldn't be able to afford many such extravagant evenings, at least not for a while. But at the moment neither that nor anything else mattered. Except for the specter of the missing man who seemed to peer over his shoulder, Lantry felt completely satisfied, utterly happy. Happier than he could remember. He left a much greater than expected *propina*, which the waiter acknowledged with a broad smile and a restrained nod.

Lantry rose and pulled back María's chair. He took her arm as she stood, then found her hand and guided her down the steps and back through darkened streets toward the hotel where they both had waiting beds. Lantry wished more than anything he'd wished for in years that María could share his bed. Yes, she would be delivering a baby before long, by the looks of things within a month or so. It wasn't even sex he especially desired. Just holding her warm naked body in his arms would be enough, at least for now. But of course this could not be, and there was a tinge of guilt in even imagining what should not be.

Yet, when they arrived at the hotel's back door where María would go to the little lean-to and to a bed that Lantry had never seen, he wheeled her around, took her in his arms and kissed her lips. At first she resisted, but then for a moment surrendered to the kiss before pulling herself free and plunging toward her door, throwing a conflicted "*Buenas noches*" over her shoulder.

Lantry turned the key in his door and entered the small lonely room. He took off his clothes, carefully turned back the cover and stretched his body on the cooling sheets. Again he stroked the cloth smoothed by María's hands. He fell asleep with nothing but her in his mind.

Chapter Twenty-eight

One of the men in Pablo's new cell had a calendar. He was a short-timer, with a six-month sentence and just two weeks to go. He had marked off every day with a fingernailed X, so for the first time in months Pablo knew the exact date, October 1. He'd been here even longer than he'd thought. Almost certainly María's baby had been born by now, and still Pablo had no plan. He had learned the hard way that simply being in the middle of a riot surging toward the door would not work. The guards had pepper spray and tear gas for that, and if necessary billy clubs and rubber bullets.

On his second day out of solitary, Pablo overheard guards talking about two inmates being released who had worked in the prison laundry.

"Sir, I worked in a laundry in Mexico," he lied. "I'd like to volunteer."

The guard looked him up and down.

"So you're one of the guys that just got out of the hole, right?" he asked. "I'll talk to the man. But one tiny infraction and you'll go straight back to segregation."

"Yes sir," Pablo replied. "I've learned my lesson. I just want to stay out of trouble and do my time. There'll be no problems, I promise."

Pablo's shift ran eight hours, and the work was hard. Even in west Texas the summer heat was finally easing, but the heat and steam produced by the washing machines and driers made the atmosphere almost unbreathable. By evening

Pablo and his clothes were drenched in sweat. The good thing was that the laundry had its own shower room. He could clean up and put on fresh clothing before being escorted back to his cell. He determined the first day that he would be the hardest worker in the room. It was easy outworking the locals who ran the place. They were eager to shift all the work they could to the inmates. But Pablo also outpaced the other two prisoners who shared the work. He did all that was asked of him and more. It felt good to be using his muscles again, muscles that had grown soft and flabby in his seven months in Eden.

He did miss the hour outside each afternoon, but his cellmates always discussed any news in hushed tones. Pablo feigned indifference, but in fact he eagerly gathered, sorted and evaluated each new rumor, especially any that might serve his purpose. From what he gathered, it sounded as if a widespread uprising might be brewing that would make the food fight and the last feeble rebellions look like child's play. The food was uniformly bad, now and then rancid, but usually simply overcooked and void of seasonings other than too much salt. Hadn't the cooks ever heard of *chiles*? Overcrowding had grown even worse, and now he knew that was by design. But the more rats you confine in a cage, the more fights you get, the more rage. One of Pablo's cellmates claimed to have seen weapons exposed in the exercise yard, knives, scraps of iron pipe, razor blades. Pablo absorbed the news, but didn't comment. His evolving plan involved no weapons, only stealth.

After Salvador died, Pablo's mother, Rosalia, had fed the girls by cleaning houses and mending clothing. She had of course taught those skills to Pablo's sisters, but fortunately to him as well.

"You never know when you might need to stitch up a shirt or a gunny sack or something else that without attention at the right time would be quickly ruined," she often said.

In his second week he informed the boss that his mother had taught him to sew. He asked to be assigned to sorting and repairing torn or worn clothing. The orange cotton pants and t-shirts the inmates wore were easy to sew up, and the supervisor soon saw that Pablo was quick and efficient with a needle and thread.

The prison managers were able to increase profits by using inmate clothing until it was threadbare. But the laundry also washed and maintained the guard uniforms, which were a bit more complicated. For one thing, most of the guards were overweight, some severely obese, and splitting seams were common. For mending jobs more complicated than simply patching a hole, the prison shop had machines. Before long Pablo had mastered the sewing machine, and he was mending the trousers and shirts worn by the guards.

But after so many times through a washing machine, even the uniforms reached the point of no return. Pablo demonstrated his ability to squeeze just one more use out of a monkey suit or a uniform, but when they were no longer usable, they were tossed into the recycling bin. Before the uniforms were hauled away they ran through a machine that shredded them into three-inch strips. The first time he performed this task under the watchful eye of the supervisor, Pablo dutifully dumped all remnants into the recycling bin. Next time, the supervisor was busy instructing a new inmate, and after surveying the room to be sure nobody was watching, he stuffed as many scraps as would fit inside his underwear. There were plenty of needles and spools of olive drab thread, so he was pretty sure those would not be missed. He showered, transferred his scraps to his clean underwear, and was escorted back to his cell.

All three of Pablo's new cellmates were Mexicans, like him convicted under various provisions of the Criminal Alien Requirement. Before long he felt a sort of friendship with two, but about the third he wasn't sure. José was distant and uncommunicative. He sometimes said things that made the other three reluctant to speak openly about anything that mattered, so Pablo determined that he would share his plan with nobody. When the lights were out and all three cellmates were snoring, Pablo dragged out his material, needle and thread, and went to work by the dim light from the guard tower. Seven months in Eden had produced in Pablo's mind a very clear image of what a guard uniform looked like, so it would be a matter of time until he could collect the pieces and reconstruct what in the midst of chaos, and hopefully under the cover of darkness, might pass for an official uniform. By midnight of the first night he had assembled that day's scraps into the back of a guard's shirt, the simple part. He ripped a hole in a bottom corner of his mattress cover and carefully arranged what he had pieced together inside. Not bad for one night's work.

After eight hours in the laundry and two hours of reconstruction that began when others were asleep, Pablo was very tired. He slept well until the horn blast thundered down the runway at six. After breakfast in the mess hall, it was back to work. On the third day he was able to salvage a collar. And so it went for the next two weeks, until Pablo's clandestine work was almost done. He had produced a pair of trousers that looked like the real thing, and the shirt was complete except for the hard part. By now he had so ingratiated himself to the shop manager that he was frequently left alone at the shredding machine. The manager was happy to take an extended break while Pablo did the work. Pablo very carefully fed a worn out shirt to the shredder in such a way that the strip with buttons remained intact. Then he shredded off the corresponding strip with buttonholes.

According to rumors his cellmates brought, the promised fracas might begin at any moment, though the day and time of day was anybody's guess. The flaws in his uniform would be less apparent in the darkness of night, but such timing wasn't likely, since most men would be locked in their cells. Gambling that the riot would instead begin during his workday, Pablo donned his newly-minted guard uniform before his cellmates were awake, turned the collar under so it wouldn't show and camouflaged the olive green under orange. After he was delivered to the laundry room, he feigned a diarrhea attack, excused himself and rushed to the toilet. He removed the uniform, rolled it tight, and when nobody was looking stuffed it beneath and behind a stack of inmate garb—along with a safety razor, a pair of dark glasses a guard had left in a shirt pocket, and a flowery shirt and a pair of ragged jeans a civilian supervisor had left amongst the rags.

With no more physical preparations to make, Pablo thought he would get more sleep. Instead his nights brought countless sleepless hours, living and reliving every possible scenario his imagination might produce. He felt as ready as he could be; now he simply had to wait. Another week passed, and nothing happened. No doubt the guards had overheard the stirrings. Watchfulness and repression had mounted, and the air was heavy with apprehension. The place was about to blow.

Chapter Twenty-nine

Darkness had long since fallen when Lantry's bus pulled back into Orizaba. He was very tired from eight hours of travel and five hours in Victoria, but he crept to María's door to tell her he was back, and to wish her a good night. He knocked gently, then louder, but she did not answer. He tried the latch, and it was not locked. He opened the door and peeked in. María was not there.

The night manager told him that in mid-morning María's labor had begun, and that Esmeralda had taken her to a midwife's house. Who knew, by now her baby might have come. Or maybe not. What should he do? Was there anything he could do? He had no idea where the midwife lived, nor did the manager, and even if he had known, Lantry could find no reason or right for him to show up there. He certainly could do nothing to assist the birth, and anyway, the baby was the child of another man.

Lantry went to bed in his room, but he couldn't turn off his mind and fall asleep. He couldn't stop thinking about María and the possible scenarios that might be unfolding, including the possibility that things were going wrong. But he was also too exhausted by his long day to sleep. The day wouldn't seem to end. He'd been with the newspaper for several weeks now, and apparently had proven himself satisfactory. Octavio had given him the most ambitious assignment yet. He'd sent Lantry up the valley to investigate the continuing epidemic of swine flu. Besides the dead children, the flu had already sickened hundreds when Lantry had arrived in Guadalupe Victoria a few weeks earlier, though at the time he was mostly oblivious to the catastrophe. After nearly two months, the influenza had not released its grip. By now both *pueblo* residents and government officials had connected the unrelenting plague to the million pigs that surrounded the villages.

It was fortuitous that he had already visited Victoria and had seen the CAFOs—the concentrated animal feeding operations—for himself, even witnessed the funeral of a child that residents believed had died of swine flu. Octavio was impressed with the in-person information Lantry was able to provide, and wanted him to dig deeper. So very early that morning Lantry had walked to the terminal and taken the first bus out. It was the second day of October, so days had grown much shorter, and daylight was just breaking when he got off in Serdán. He had coffee, a *tamal* and a banana in the just-opening market, then caught the van to Guadalupe Victoria, reversing the journey that had brought him to Orizaba. He was also reversing course by going to investigate what had driven him from Victoria, the pigs.

The sky still emptied itself at least briefly most days, but the rainy season was winding down. The overloaded van bounced from *pueblo* to *pueblo*, and the heavy clouds that shrouded the valley began to part, revealing again the magical peak of Orizaba. Lantry gazed at the ivory pinnacle, and images from his amazing night on its slope resurfaced. He saw again the mountain lion, crouched ready to spring. He relived the long wait for dawn, saw the fire flare as he flung the last of his liquor away, remembered his tears and felt again how the encounter had purified his soul. Maybe it was mostly the woman that had captivated his mind, but whatever the

194

case, he felt growing confidence that he had beaten back the demon that had ruled his life, perhaps even the demons that had driven him to its refuge. When the van screeched to a stop in Emancipación Quetzalapa, the little village where his trek toward emancipation had begun, the sun was just clearing the snow-capped peak. Lantry whispered a prayer of thanks.

The next stop was Guadalupe Libertad, and finally Guadalupe Victoria. The sky was clear now, and in the morning light the little town seemed a charmed place, everything from flower gardens to trees and bushes in full bloom, an artist's pallet of color. Rain had washed the streets and buildings clean and had invigorated every living thing. Yet the first breath when he stepped from the van told a different story, the story that had driven Lantry from the village and now had brought him back.

He had witnessed the funeral in August, but to most else he had been oblivious. He knew now that the child's death was but a chapter in a story the Mexican and international media had followed for months. He had breathed the polluted air, seen the flies on the restaurant's screen door and heard the stories in the bar, but he had failed to comprehend that in seeking refuge from the chaos and pollution of the capital, he'd stepped into ground zero of an epidemic that had gained attention around the world. At the time Lantry had been a lost and drifting soul, disconnected from the journalist he had been. He had brought little to his Victoria experience beyond idle curiosity, dulled by drink. Now he was back, not just in body, but in mind. Now he knew María's story, and he had felt the fear that forced her to flee. He knew why Pablo and many other men had left the valley of their birth to seek work north of the Rio Grande. On today's visit he had seen things through the opened eyes of a journalist, seeking to methodically assemble pieces of a disturbing puzzle. But also through the eyes of fellow humans who had felt the pain that racked the valley and the town.

He'd felt the apprehension and anger among men whose livelihood depended upon feeding hogs and working the filth they produced. He had talked with mothers in the market who lived in fear for their husbands and their children. On the long ride back to Orizaba he had pieced together his notes, including what research had taught him of the changes factory farms had brought. Now villagers knew that Granjas Carroll was a front for the world's largest swine producer. They were angry about the secret deals that opened the door for Smithfield Foods. Some had heard that Smithfield's US operations were also under fire for environmental pollution and worker abuse. Many were furious that they had been used, pawns in a game over which they had little control. They understood that Mexico itself had been unprepared, lacking local, regional and federal laws to regulate the size, concentration, location or operation of factory farms.

If Lantry had been sober enough to read newspapers in Mexico City, much of what he now knew would not have been news. By the time María had fled the valley in May, half the residents of La Gloria had fallen ill. The capital city paper *La Jornada* had reported that "clouds of flies emanate from the lagoons where Granjas Carroll discharges the fecal waste from its hog barns—as well as air pollution that has already caused an epidemic of respiratory infections." Agents of the Mexican Social Security Institute had concluded that "the vector of this outbreak are the clouds of flies that come out of the hog barns, and the waste lagoons into which the Mexican-US company spews tons of excrement."

Officials had sided with the corporation for as long as possible, but by May the government's health minister had stated that the virus had "mutated from pigs, and then at some point was transmitted to humans." The state legislature had demanded that the Smithfield subsidiary turn over all documents and environmental certifications on three massive waste lagoons. The chairman of the environmental committee had called the factory farms breeding grounds of potential infection for cities beyond the valley, including Orizaba. The outbreak had emerged at the height of the dry season, and even the US Centers for Disease Control had stated that people could be sickened by the virus, borne by dust. There was still no absolute proof that the illness had emerged from the hog confinements, but Lantry found few people who believed otherwise.

By mid-afternoon he had spent four hours traveling and five hours interviewing villagers, but he had not yet found time to eat. As a journalist he wanted the response of corporate officials, but he doubted that the persons he needed to interview would be found in Victoria. He'd likely need to do that from Orizaba by phone. But hunger had finally asserted itself as a higher priority than completing his work, so he walked to Restaurante Familiar Doña Lupita for the comida corrida he had so enjoyed during his earlier visit.

While he ate, four men came through the screen door. Two were Mexicans, the other two, if he could judge by their accents, were from a southern US state. They were not dressed in the attire of the attendants of hogs. As it happened, they took a table next to his and ordered drinks. The topic of conversation was H1N1, and the tenor was how to tamp down growing speculation that GCM hogs were somehow to blame. Lantry grabbed a napkin and began to take notes.

He finished his meal and paid his bill, but he sipped slowly on the sweet *agua* until the other men pushed back their chairs and rose to leave. He followed them out the door.

"Excuse me," he said to the man who appeared to be in charge. "My name is Lantry Martin," he said, giving the altered last name he'd adopted for his newspaper work. "I'm with the newspaper in Orizaba. I wonder if I could take a moment of your time." He held out his hand.

The man turned a cold eye on Lantry, ignoring his hand. He was obviously aware that Lantry had been eavesdropping, that he had overheard the conversation that had just ensued.

"I've got no time for interviews," he said, "especially not for newspaper spies that generally already have their minds made up. And just in case you think you have some kind of First Amendment right, let me remind you that this is Mexico."

He turned to go.

"If I could just follow up on a couple of things I overheard," Lantry said, touching the man's jacket sleeve. "I'd like to be sure I heard everything correctly. And by the way, let me remind you that Mexico is also a free country."

"Get out of my face," the man barked. "You said your name is Lantry Martin, from the Orizaba paper?"

He turned to the other American. "Write down that name and check this guy out," he said. "He sounds like a Texan to me. I'm sick of dealing with his type. Let's find out who he is and what he's doing in Mexico."

The four turned and strode to a waiting pickup truck.

Lantry watched them speed away. Was there anything else to be done here? He hailed a taxi, and the driver took him out to the hog complex a couple of miles northwest of town. They bounced on truck-rutted roads around long rows of low, shabbily-constructed steel-clad barns, skirted by the stinking manure lagoon. He stopped the driver and took photos, the cesspool in the foreground, then the barns, then the *pueblo* of Victoria, and in the distance, the peak of Orizaba, glistening in the afternoon sun. The taxi driver drove him back to town, to the intersection where he could catch the van and begin the four-hour journey home.

"By the way," he asked the driver before he opened the door, "Do you by chance know a young man named Pablo? He went to the US for work in February."

"Pablo, I know of a couple of Pablos," the driver said. "Yes, I knew the one that went north in January. He left right after his father died from breathing hogs. He hasn't been heard from since."

Chapter Thirty

Lantry woke well before dawn, dreaming of María writhing in the pain of childbirth. She was crying out for help, but all alone. Rain pounded on the roof, and somewhere water was dripping through. He threw off the covers and checked his watch. It was not yet six o'clock. He showered and shaved and dressed for work, though he wasn't sure he would show up at the newspaper office. The higher priority was finding María.

When he emerged, Esmeralda had just arrived for work. She stood by the front door, thrashing her raincoat to fling off as much water as possible before she entered. Lantry went straight to her and asked for news, and where he might find María. Esmeralda was a big and strong woman, seemingly afraid of nothing or nobody. Lantry had come to know her stolid stare, the unflinching, piercing eyes that seemed to look straight through the eyes of another and into his soul. It had seemed to Lantry that she had gradually come to grudgingly respect the American guest, but at the same time she had remained distant and suspicious. She of course knew María's story, knew from the very first day that María was married and that she had arrived carrying her husband's child. She was clearly reluctant to tell Lantry where he could find her. No doubt she feared he might take advantage of María; yet she herself was in no position to help. It was obvious that María could not continue to work, at least for a while, and that she would need some kind of support.

Esmeralda had lived long enough to know that in a far-from-perfect world, people had to do what they had to do to survive. She recognized that Lantry and María had grown close, and who knew whether Pablo would ever return? If he did not, he would certainly not be the first young husband and father who had gone north never to return, or perhaps never to be heard from again. If that was the case, then María would need a man, somebody to take care of her, and now to help support her child. At last, without a flinch in her stare, she spoke. "Go three blocks north of the bus terminal," she said. In the middle of the block west is a small tienda. The midwife lives behind the store. You can find María there."

"Have you seen her?" Lantry asked. "Is she all right? Has her baby come?"

"Just go," Esmeralda said, and she turned her back.

Lantry went back to his room for a poncho and cap and plunged into the pouring rain. It was early October, and the rainy season was supposed to be nearly over, but not today. He sloshed through puddles and crossed the now-raging river to the bus terminal, then followed Esmeralda's directions until he found the tienda. It was the typical tiny neighborhood store where through a barred window the proprietor sold junk foods and local vegetables and fruits, drinks ranging from cola and manzanilla to beer and mescal, and basics like toilet paper and aspirin. The window was closed. Lantry stood in the rain and banged on the window, gently at first, then as hard as he thought safe without breaking the glass. Nobody came. He tried the door beside the shop, but it was locked. At last he circled the block and found an alley that he thought might correspond with the address, and entered. He came upon a tiny courtyard that opened upon another door, presumably to a residence. He knocked on the door and called out María's name.

When the door opened, a stooped old woman stood in the frame.

"*¿Qué quieres?*" she asked. What do you want?

"I'm looking for María," he said. "Is she here?"

"*Y quién es usted?*" she asked. Who are you?

"*Me llamo Lantry,*" he replied. "*Soy un amigo de María.*"

"*Momento,*" the woman said, and she closed the door.

Lantry stood dripping under the slight roof overhang, until a few moments later the door opened again.

"*María dice que te vayas,*" she said. María said go away.

"But I must see her," Lantry insisted.

He took the old woman's arm and gently moved her aside and entered the room. From another room farther back came sobbing sounds. He went toward the weeping, opened the door from which they came, and found María. She lay on a narrow cot, a baby in her arms. Long he stood in the doorway, immobilized by the scene, until finally the gaunt prone figure turned her head toward him and their eyes met. He stepped into the room and fell to his knees beside the bed. One hand went to her tousled hair, the other to the blanket that covered the tiny sleeping form in her arms.

"I have come," he said to María. "I am here to help you and the baby. I will do anything you need, anything you ask."

María did not speak, but tears trickled down her cheeks. Her eyes softened from what looked like fear to something like relief mingled with sadness, Lantry thought, and maybe a glimmer of affection. Finally her free hand crept from under the blanket and covered his.

"*Sí,*" she said. "*Gracias.*"

Lantry bent and kissed her pale cheek.

"Today I will find a place for you and the baby," he said, then added, "for us."

And then he remembered that in his complete focus on María he had almost forgotten the baby that slept on her bosom.

"And the baby," he said, "is it a boy or a girl? Is it OK? Are you OK?"

"His name is Ángel," María said. "He is magnificent. And I am well."

"I have to go now," he said. "I have work to do, but also I must find us a home. I'll be back for you."

He kissed her cheek again and rose to go. The old woman waited outside María's door to see him out. Now there was a hint of smile on her face.

When Lantry passed the hotel on the way to the office he stopped to tell the clerk and Esmeralda that he would be checking out, that he'd be back later to collect his things, as soon as he'd found a place to rent. Then he sloshed through the unrelenting rain to the newspaper office. He met with Octavio and reported on the events of the previous day, including the threat that the American was going to look into Lantry and what he was doing in Mexico. He spent a few minutes at the computer roughing out his story, then asked permission to go look for a place to live, promising that he'd return as soon as possible to finish his work.

"I might know a place for you," the editor said. "My brother-in-law has a small house you could probably rent. The tenants moved out last month and he's looking for somebody."

Lantry got the address and went to find the house and the brother-in-law. It was a tiny house, three small rooms.

The kitchen was best, a good stove, a small refrigerator and a table with four chairs. The cramped bedroom had a slightly lumpy double bed, a *cama matrimonial* it was called, and the third room held a couch and a couple of chairs. The place was reasonably tight and clean, and the rent just two thousand pesos a month, about a hundred fifty American dollars, considerably less than Lantry was paying for the hotel room. He paid a month's rent and got the key.

Back at the office Lantry worked like a demon to finish his story about sickness in the valley of pigs and of the Americans who denied there was any link to their operation. But concentrate as he might, María was never far from his mind. He finished before the office closed and was hustled out by Octavio and told not to come back to work the next day, but to take care of the baby and María.

Heavy clouds still hung over the Orizaba valley, but the rain had ceased. He stopped at the hotel and packed his few things, then went to the midwife's house. The young woman at the tienda had been instructed to admit him, and soon he was at María's side. The baby was at her breast, and a smile lighted María's face.

"I found a place for you and the baby," he said, "for us if I can be with you."

"*Sí*," she said again. "*Gracias*."

When little Ángel was satisfied, she pushed back the covers and handed him to Lantry.

"You can hold him while I get dressed," she said, "but hold him very carefully."

Lantry awkwardly cradled the infant in his arms and turned his back so María could dress. The baby boy was tiny. Everything about him was dark, his skin, his eyes, the tuft of

204

glossy hair. Was this the first newborn baby he'd ever held? Memory provided no experience in his thirty years that might compare. Ángel was beautiful, he decided, just as his name implied. He found with great surprise that he felt love for the tiny offspring of another man.

When María was ready, Lantry paid the midwife what he could. María still felt unsteady, so he went out to find a taxi. He helped her into the back seat and they rode across town to the little house. He unlocked the door and they stepped in. María stood in the doorway, and her eyes filled with tears.

"Thank you," she said again. "It's wonderful."

"You and Ángel can have the bed," he said. "I'll sleep on the couch."

She said nothing and did not resist, but Lantry thought he saw disappointment in her eyes, mingled with joy.

Chapter Thirty-one

Most of a year had passed since Pablo had left, and still no word had come. Little by little María had begun to assume the worst, that Pablo had abandoned her, perhaps had found another woman in the north, or worse yet, that he might be dead. Neither idea was easy to contemplate, indeed not the idea that the man who had been her friend and then her lover, who in desperation to support her and his mother and sisters had left them all to go north for a job, might have abandoned them for another life. But the other possibility, the possibility she had experienced again and again in her dreams, and even in many waking moments—that Pablo was dead—that was even worse. Did he even make it to the border, and if so to safety beyond? Far too many stories had filtered back to the villages about those who had died along the way, sliced by the wheels of La Bestia, robbed and shot by gangsters, drowned in the river, dead of dehydration in the desert. If Pablo survived the journey, then what? She knew that prisons also awaited those who were caught, but if that were the case, certainly she should have heard by now.

If Pablo was not coming home, a conclusion María had gradually come to accept, she would have to look out for herself, and now for little Ángel. At the very least she owed it to Pablo to take care of his son. She knew she couldn't do that by cleaning rooms and making beds at the hotel. For the time being she couldn't even keep that job, even if it had paid enough to sustain her and Ángel. She felt gratitude to the

American who had provided them with safety and a home, and now that she could not work, with food. But it was more than gratitude, she had come to admit. Ever since Lantry had showed up at the hotel several weeks earlier, especially since the night they had walked down the river together and dined at El Palacio de Hierro, since she first held his hand and even kissed his lips, she knew she felt more. Out of loyalty to Pablo she had tried her best to deny those feelings, and she had never given up hope that Pablo would return.

But she couldn't live in this limbo forever. She did not doubt that Lantry cared for her, and even for her son, the child of another man. He even sometimes changed the baby's diaper, which she'd never seen a man do. Every day he came straight home after work, except that he walked to the market on the way home and brought fresh fruits and vegetables, sometimes meats or fish, occasionally special treats. And another thing she'd never seen a man do, he sometimes cooked their meals. She couldn't help smiling when he burned something or took something off the stove half raw, but there was no question he was doing all he could to please her.

Since their first walk down the river María's growing affection had been mixed with guilt, the feeling that she was betraying Pablo by merely allowing another man to be with her, to hold her hand, to buy her food. But gradually the affection she felt for Lantry had grown to the point that she wondered whether the better word was love. Perhaps the time had come to admit to herself that Pablo was not coming back. Ángel was thriving, and she felt her strength returning after giving him life. So on a chilly night in October, two weeks after they had moved into the little house, María made a bed for Ángel in a cardboard box on the dresser top and asked Lantry to share her bed.

Lantry was overwhelmed. Tears filled his eyes. There was absolutely nothing he wanted more, in fact he could recall nothing in his life that he had ever wanted as he now wanted María. He too had come to believe that Pablo would not return, though he could not be certain that his conclusion was based strictly on logic and what was known, or whether his desire overpowered his rational powers. But on this night he did not second guess. He asked no questions. He simply took María in his arms.

"Yes, yes," he said. *"Te amo. Te amo tanto."* I love you, I love you very much.

He had not spoken the words before, had not dared even to think them, but when he spoke them he knew they were true.

For reply, María unbuttoned Lantry's shirt and her hands crept around his back and held him close. She gazed with desire into his eyes, and their lips met, not a kiss on the cheek as had become their way, but a kiss that fully expressed the passion both felt. And then the buttons of her dress were flying open and their clothing crumpled to the floor and they were in the bed, locked in a hot embrace that Lantry hoped would never end.

When their passion was spent they collapsed panting on their backs, Lantry's arm around María's neck, her leg looped across his. When his breathing returned almost to normal, Lantry turned to María's face. A tear rolled down her cheek. He reached to wipe it away.

"Was it wrong?" María asked. "I loved Pablo, but he's not coming home, is he?"

Lantry held his breath. What should he say?

"Probably not," he said at last. "I don't think he is. If he's not, and if you love me like I love you, then this is right. This is what I want more than I've ever wanted anything before. You make me happy. I want to spend my life right here, even in this bed, with you. And I love Ángel your son. I hope one day he can be my son too. I want you María. You have become my life."

"*Yo te amo*," María said at last. "I love you. I had given up my life, and you have given it back."

And so, Lantry and María and Ángel became a family. Lantry grew supremely confident that alcohol would not regain its grip. He even promised himself that he would not tempt what could have been fate by repeating the single glass of wine. This love, and this life, it was more than he had imagined life could be. He had loved Linda, but now that seemed so conventional, almost an expected thing. Yes, they'd had great sex at first, and yes, his drinking had poisoned what might have lasted a lifetime. But lying in María's arms, he was for the first time not sorry at the turns his life had brought. In Mexico he had reached bottom, but on the mountain he had found himself, saved his life, found reason to go on living. With María life had reached a pinnacle he had never imagined, a crest higher than Orizaba, a life that was so much more than a reason to go on living, that held promises of which he had never dreamed. Lying in each other's arms, Lantry and María drifted off to sleep.

Chapter Thirty-two

The season of almost daily rain had tapered to occasional small showers and most days of sun. Orizaba was in its glory. Five months of abundant, sometimes unrelenting precipitation had greened every leaf, nurtured every flower, cleaned every stone and concrete wall, even sidewalks and streets. The plaza was a garden of exotic delights, and often María rolled little Ángel there in late afternoon in the stroller Lantry had brought home from the market. His route from the office to their home passed through the plaza, and María would watch for him there. In the lovely evenings they might walk home together or sometimes join other lovers and families in strolls along the Rio Orizaba paths. Nearing the end of his second month, Ángel seemed to watch the animals intently, and perhaps it was María's imagination, but he sometimes seemed to coo at the monkeys in their tree.

Lantry's work was going well. Both he and his employer had, without further discussion, allowed the question of his legal status to go unaddressed. At work and in print he remained Lantry Martin, but after several weeks of proving himself he was employed full time and his salary had increased. It was still a fraction of his pay in Dallas, but their monthly rent was cheap and the market provided the freshest, most delicious produce Lantry had ever seen at prices Texans could not have imagined. The family had settled into a comfortable routine, and all was well. Except of course that neither Lantry nor María could completely put Pablo out of their minds. It was something they didn't discuss, but more than once when he came home, Lantry found María's eyes red from crying. He took her in his arms and gently held her. There was no doubt she still mourned the man she'd known as husband for only a few days, the man who would always be the father of Ángel. The pain was still there, not just loss, but no doubt worry and guilt.

For his part, Lantry could not deny certain facts. Neither he nor María knew what had happened to Pablo, whether he had abandoned María, whether he was thriving north of the Rio Grande, whether he was alive or dead. Lantry had convinced himself that Pablo would not return, that the new and wonderful life he had with María and Ángel was not only right, but maybe even gallant on his part. He gave them all he could, but in fact he had gained far more than he was able to give. His new life not only brought him happiness, it had enabled him to remain free of the noose of drink. But he also knew about the various nooses that could have snared Pablo on his journey north.

Lantry had no more idea than María whether Pablo might return, but he knew that death or unfaithfulness were just two of many possibilities. He had not told her all he knew about The Beast, about stories he'd read in the US, and even the movie he'd seen that exposed the brutal violence that befell many a traveler on the train, everything from terrible injuries to robbery to death. As a reporter he'd learned more than he'd wanted to know at the time about the tribulations and the fates of many who made it across the border without papers, victimization by drug gangs, arrest, brutal treatment by law enforcement, death in the long walk across the forbiddingly arid south Texas landscape to avoid checkpoints.

From all he had learned and felt from María, Pablo sounded like an honorable young man, a man who had risked all to care for a family because he saw no other way but to cross the border. If that was true, how could he possibly have abandoned a woman like María? Yet Lantry had mostly succeeded in convincing himself that if Pablo were alive, surely after all this time he would have found a way to contact her.

It was a lovely Friday afternoon, and María was feeling strong and well. She had fully recovered from childbirth and regained her strength. She had appreciated Lantry's efforts in the kitchen, but in fact he lacked the skills her mother had imparted to her. Lantry knew about the few *chiles* that he told her were commonly used in Mexican cooking in Texas, but there were so many subtle flavors he didn't know. He didn't know how to choose avocados in their prime, nor how to turn them into guacamole without making a big mess. Plus, being a *gringo*, he always paid too much in the fish market or even for such things as mangos and pineapple. María determined that she should resume her rightful role as a woman in *el mercado* and *en la cocina*. She wrapped Ángel into her shawl, looped her woven bag across her shoulder and headed for the market behind the cathedral.

She was dickering over the price of a kilo of tomatoes when over the shoulder of the market woman she saw a face that looked familiar. She squinted for a better look. Yes, she knew the man. It was Fernando from Victoria, pushing a dolly loaded with melons down the crowded isle. He rounded the corner and came straight toward her. Only when he glanced up to navigate around her did their eyes meet.

"Fernando!" María gasped.

"María, is that you?" Fernando asked, incredulous. "I looked for you all over La Gloria and Victoria," he said. "I couldn't find you, and nobody seemed to know where you'd gone. All they could say was that one day they saw you and the next day you had disappeared. Have you been here the whole time?"

"Yes," María said, "ever since the flu came to Victoria. And you?"

"I looked for you," Fernando said again. "They told me you had gone, but nobody seemed to know where."

Then Fernando's eyes fell on Ángel, whose sleeping face barely protruded from María's shawl.

"And this…this is your baby," he said, and she saw that he was calculating, recalling the months since Pablo had gone. "This is Pablo's child?"

"Yes," she said, tears filling her eyes. "I've had no word from Pablo since he left."

"But that's why I looked for you," Fernando said. "I wanted to tell you about Pablo, to give you the message he sent."

María's bag of tomatoes dropped to the cement floor.

"Pablo…Pablo is alive?" she stammered.

"Yes, alive, but in prison in Texas," Fernando said. "I was with him there. He wanted you to know."

And now María's legs went limp and she could not stand. Fernando caught her and wrapped his arms around her and around Pablo's child and kept them from falling.

"Oh, Pablo," María cried, and she began to sob.

Fernando left the bag of smashed tomatoes and his cart in the isle and guided María to a chair at a nearby lunch counter and set her down.

"And the baby," he asked. "Is it a boy or a girl?"

"It's a boy," María said. "His name is Ángel." She peeled back the shawl to reveal Angel's face.

The baby's eyes opened, and he began to cry. María unbuttoned the top of her dress and guided him to a nipple and he grew calm and satisfied.

"Pablo has a son," Fernando mused. "If only he knew. It might give him hope."

Then Fernando remembered the dolly of melons he'd left behind.

"I need to get my cart out of the way," he said. "I'll come back."

Fernando wheeled his load of big yellow fruits to a corner beside the counter and took the seat next to María. She had dried her tears, but her face was agitated by shock, by fear, by emotions Fernando could not have read. While her baby nursed, Fernando told her how he too had gone north, that the border patrol had apprehended him near San Antonio, and sent him to the prison in Eden. His only crime was a second illegal entry, so he was sentenced to just two months. To his great surprise he found Pablo there, his childhood friend from Victoria.

"I told him that you were pregnant," Fernando said. "That made Pablo almost crazy with fear. Before I got out Pablo made me swear to go straight back to Victoria and tell you where he was, and that he would come."

María gripped Ángel with one hand and held to the lunch counter with the other. Her face was pale and she did not speak. Fernando told her how he was bussed back across the border and then made his way home to Victoria. When he got there he'd asked everybody he could think to ask, but nobody seemed to know where she had gone. He had come to Orizaba looking for work and had found a job in the market, unloading produce and delivering it to vendor stalls.

"But when is Pablo coming home?" María demanded at last, impatient with the long narrative that failed to get to the one piece of information that mattered to her.

"*No sé*," Fernando said, his eyes on the nursing infant. I don't know. He explained that Pablo's sentence was two years, which meant he still had over a year to go. "But I don't think he'll stay that long," Fernando said encouragingly. "Pablo told me to tell you that he will find a way out, he'll find a way to escape. I can't tell you when, but he said to tell you he will come home."

Now María was silent, tears welling again in her eyes. The baby began to fret at her breast. Then a voice yelled Fernando's name, demanding to know why he wasn't delivering the melons as he was told.

"I have to go," he said. "You can find me here if you need help."

"*Gracias*," María said. She wiped her tears and tried to smile.

Fernando looked behind him to see that the man behind the voice was retreating, then slipped a melon into a fold in María's shawl. He leaned forward and kissed her lightly on the cheek, then wheeled his cart away. María rose and tested her knees. She found that she could stand. She retraced her steps to where her market bag had fallen. The vendor had picked it up, cleaned out the worst of the smashed tomatoes and refilled it.

"*Estos son gratis*," the woman said, handing the bag to María. There is no charge.

María made her way down the narrow isle between racks and piles of vegetables and fruits, *chiles* of many hues, big burlap bags filled with seeds and grains, past chickens hung by their necks and slabs of pork, past the isle full of bouquets and vases of flowers, and finally into the open air beside the cathedral. She stared across the sun-drenched plaza, then entered the cathedral doors, tentatively like a tourist, gazing up at the magnificent pillars, at the effigies of the slain savior, at the painted stations of the cross. She took it all in, as if for the first time. After all, she had been in Orizaba for half a year, and she had entered the church only once. What would her mother think if she were alive and knew? The confession booth stood empty by the wall. Even if the priest were present, what would she say? What exactly were her sins? Living with Lantry, no doubt about that. She was an adulterer, the kind of woman that the Bible said might be stoned. But she also recalled the words of *El Señor*, "Let him who is without sin cast the first stone."

María dropped to her knees, supporting herself and her son by the back of a pew.

"God forgive me," she muttered, not knowing all that she might need forgiveness for.

But in fact, perhaps she was not the worst of sinners. She could not recall a single thing she had done that was not done from love. She kissed the baby at her breast, gathered her market bag, and hurried home to make dinner.

Chapter Thirty-three

Even before Lantry reached the door he inhaled the aroma wafting from the open window, roasting *poblanos*. *Chiles rellenos* for dinner—one of his favorite meals. It had been a good day at work, conducting interviews and writing a story about the plan to build the *teleférico*, a cable car that would whisk residents and visitors to the top of Cerro del Borrego, the high hill west of the river valley where in 1862 a division of Mexican rebels battled the French in the war that eventually drove them out. The fight was a sequel to the famed battle of Puebla celebrated on Cinco de Mayo, and a crucial battle in a locally-revered historic place. On a recent Sunday afternoon Lantry and María had climbed the long trail to the top and explored the remains of the old stone fort. From there the Pico de Orizaba glacier was in full view.

Lantry's stock in trade as a reporter had always been digging into dirt, looking under rocks, examining subjects that specific interests might wish to keep hidden. Stories like the contamination and sickness in the valley on the other side of the mountain. Such stories took a toll in stress and anxiety, so it was good now and then to work on something that was fun, inspiring, a story about people looking forward and upward, trying to build a better community. Lantry's spirits were high.

When he opened the door, María was at work at the stove, turning *chiles* with one arm, cradling Ángel in the other. She did not turn to greet him as she usually did. He stepped across the little kitchen and embraced the pair in his

217

arms. Only then did she lay down her spatula and turn her tear-streaked face to greet him. Lantry's hand went to María's face, wiping away the stream of tears.

"What is wrong?" he asked, pulling her face close to his.

But with her free hand she pushed him away, rushed to the bedroom and slammed the door. Lantry followed her and stood at the door, the knob in his hand. Heart-broken weeping on the other side rose to a crescendo of sobs accompanied by the baby's wail. He called her name, but she did not reply. At last he turned the knob and entered.

María was sprawled across the bed, sobbing into the pillow. Ángel lay on his back beside her, screaming at the ceiling. Lantry dropped to his knees beside the bed.

"What is it?" he begged. "Tell me what's wrong."

When at last María had reduced her sobbing to a whimper, she rolled over to face him.

"I saw Fernando in the market today, Fernando from Victoria," she wailed. "Pablo is in prison in Texas. He's coming home."

Lantry's heart stopped. His hand on María's arm turned to lead. He could not move, could not speak. When at last his heart began to beat again, he found one word.

"When?" he asked. "When is Pablo coming?"

"I don't know," María said, wiping her reddened eyes on the pillowcase. "Fernando said he's going to break out, escape from prison and come home."

To a man who knew something about illegal immigration, and indeed about Texas prisons, the idea of escape seemed unlikely to Lantry, but he didn't say so. It would take time to process what he had just heard, but his immediate thought was that this news had irrevocably changed his world. His second thought was to whisk María away, the three of them hide out somewhere together. He as quickly realized that the thought was insane, that he could not ask that of María, and that if he did she was too honorable to agree. Ever since Ángel was born and they had begun to fall in love, especially since they'd begun sleeping together, they had subtly encouraged each other to believe that Pablo would not return, that he had deserted her, or perhaps that he was not alive. Now he knew that was not the case, that Pablo was in desperate trouble, and that if he possibly could, he would be coming home.

There had been times over the past two months, in private moments for each of them and sometimes together, that feelings of guilt and fear and even remorse had risen beyond what they could suppress, but they both had worked in their own ways to set guilt aside. They had become a couple, enjoying intimacy, caring for the baby, creating a new life together as a family. Now in a moment the fiction Lantry had convinced himself was reality, the fiction they'd begun to build new lives upon, was exposed, was dead. His life with María and Ángel was surely over. If Pablo was in prison, then he had not abandoned María and his unborn son. Whether he escaped, or whether he served an unknown term of years, someday he would be coming home. Lantry felt his new life crumbling at his feet.

"When?" he asked again, as if that was the only question that mattered.

"I don't know," she said again, this time with what seemed a tinge of anger. "Fernando didn't know."

Who was this Fernando, Lantry wondered, and what did he know for sure? If this much was true, that Pablo would be returning, what else did Fernando know? Lantry would need to find out. His head was now swirling with other questions, a tangle of questions and thoughts that of course had always been there, but which he had mostly suppressed. But did any of those questions really matter? The one question that did matter had been answered. Pablo was alive and coming home. Lantry could no longer pretend that the life he and María had begun to share was not upon the ashes of another man. He worshipped their love as the thing of beauty that it was, but now it was also a betrayal, not only by him but by María as well. María should be easier to forgive; she acted first from desperation, and only later from love. But wasn't that true of himself as well, Lantry's racing, tortured mind demanded. Yes, he had acted from compassion that quickly grew to love, but first had come desire and the need to save himself.

Lantry remained on his knees, too weak to rise. He drew María and Ángel into his arms and held them until both became calm. Only then did the odor of burning *chiles* find its way into the room. María threw off Lantry's arm and struggled up from the bed. She rushed to the kitchen and dragged the skillet off the flames, uttering a sharp cry when the handle burned her hand.

Now it was only Ángel in Lantry's arms. The baby gazed into his eyes with what he imagined was love, complete innocence of all that the three adults in his life had wrought. Then it sank into Lantry's consciousness that not only María, but her tiny son was slipping from his life. Ángel would be fine, regardless of who his father was, Lantry was confident of that. But amongst the whirlwind of sad and terrifying thoughts that flooded Lantry's brain was the realization that he—his growing love, his very image—would be completely erased from the unfolding consciousness of the child. For Ángel, it would be as if Lantry had never existed.

Lantry gathered the infant and rose shakily from his knees, wiped his own eyes on his sleeve and went to the kitchen. María was scraping burned *chiles* from the skillet, preparing to begin anew. Her tears were dried now, and her strong arm worked fiercely at her task, her jaw set in a pale and stony face. He pulled a chair back from the table and sat, cradling Ángel in his arms. María did not turn to face them, but at last Lantry spoke.

"I must find Fernando," he said. "We must know all that he knows, so that we can do what is right. He mustn't know about us, and neither will Pablo know. If what Fernando told you is true, and if Pablo has an actual plan of escape, we need to know when he might come."

In the long pause that followed, María continued her work at the stove, seemingly oblivious to his words, but there was no doubt she had heard. Finally he spoke again, choking on his words.

"I love you María. I love Ángel. But your husband is Pablo, and I will have to go. Leaving you will be the hardest thing I've ever done, but I know I can't stay. I'll have to go, for you, for Pablo, and for your son."

María dragged the skillet off the flame and rushed to Lantry's arms. The embrace was long, desperate, sweet.

"Yes," she said at last. "That is what we must do. That is what is right."

Then after a pause, she asked, "Is it possible to love two men? I do love Pablo. He was my friend in the village. He was my only lover. We might not be married in the church, but I promised myself to him. He is the father of my child. When he

221

comes home, I will be his wife." Then she was sobbing again, and her tears flowed without control. "But I also love you, Lantry," she sobbed. "You are my other husband. Maybe I wish you were my first, maybe my only, maybe the father of Ángel. We cannot undo anything that is done, and I know I must pay for all of my sins, whatever they might be. But I will not forget you Lantry, or what you have done for Ángel and me."

Finally she kissed him gently and rose to put the skillet back on the stove.

"Yes," she said at last without looking back, "We must find out what else Fernando knows."

The lovers ate the meal in silence. It was delicious, no doubt, but Lantry could not have told what it was they ate. His mind was at work, sorting out new realities, struggling for a plan. Finally María prepared herself for bed, but crawled to the far side in her long gown and curled her knees to her chest. Lantry lay on his back, staring at the grim ceiling until her whimpers ceased.

Chapter Thirty-four

Lantry was at the market when the doors opened at six. He walked the aisles, looking for a man who matched the description María had given him of Fernando, a short muscular man about twenty, dark skin and hair. That would have described half the men he met, including many who were pushing dollies or pulling carts from the dock to the vendors with loads of vegetables or fruits. But when María had seen him, Fernando was wearing a jacket with the logo of the Chicago Cubs.

That made him easy to find. Lantry followed him at a distance, until he exited the building and wheeled his cart back to the loading dock. Fernando pulled out an orange to peel while he waited in line for another load. Lantry approached casually and asked about where the best avocados came from. They fell into an easy conversation, and before long Fernando was describing the valley north of Orizaba, where he said both he and the best vegetables had grown.

"And is it still a valley of *ejidos* and small farms where they grow the best foods and bring them to market?" Lantry asked.

"Things have changed," Fernando said, staring into the distance. "It is now the valley of pigs. Most of the small farms I knew now grow Monsanto corn for the hogs. Most of the men feed their families by feeding hogs."

"And you?" Lantry asked.

"For a bit," Fernando replied. "Then I went north. But that didn't work out."

A shift in his glance told Lantry that Fernando had remembered he was speaking to a *gringo*, and most of the northerners he had met had little concern for workers like him, especially not those who crossed without papers to work. He said no more.

"I hope you made it safely across," Lantry offered.

Their eyes met, Fernando searching the other's eyes for clues.

"No," he said at last. "I was in prison for a few weeks."

"*Lo siento,*" Lantry said. "I'm sorry." He asked Fernando where he was sent.

"It was Eden," Fernando replied with a sardonic laugh. "Some Eden."

"Did you know anybody there?" Lantry asked.

"One guy, an old friend from Victoria," he said.

Then another cloud of suspicion crossed his face. Was he telling this stranger too much?

"Look, maybe I should have told you," Lantry said. "I work for the newspaper here. I was just up in Victoria, where I was working on a story about the pig factories and the people who own them. Not a pretty sight. I hope your friend gets out soon."

"No telling," Fernando said. "He got two years, but when I last saw him he was making a plan. He has a wife and a kid, and from what he told me, I'm betting he'll be back very soon."

Then Fernando was sure that he was talking too much. He swallowed the last section of orange and grabbed the dolly.

"I have deliveries to make," he said, and he wheeled away toward the unloading dock.

All day at work Lantry went through the motions of writing and editing, his mind never far from the dilemma he and María faced. The big question now was whether Pablo would serve his two years, or whether he would break out as he had sworn. In either case there was little doubt that Lantry's intimacy with María was over, a conclusion he faced with profound regret. Now that they knew the truth about Pablo, he was sure that María's conscience would not permit her to continue to live with him as his wife, and in fact Lantry himself would have been hobbled by guilt. But Ángel needed María, and they both needed him. She was far from ready to look for another job, and in truth there was probably no job for her that would pay the rent and support their needs. So until they were sure that Pablo was really coming, Lantry determined that everything he did would be for María and Ángel, whether or not they continued to live under the same roof.

He loved María deeply, but their relationship was irrevocably changed. He knew that love would require putting her needs and interests above his own, which led to a simple conclusion, one he found unpalatable, but inevitable. If there was anything he could do, he had to help bring Pablo home. On his walk home from the office he considered two possible plans. A friend from law school, Cecilia, was an immigration attorney in San Antonio. Perhaps she could build a case that would get Pablo deported without serving all his time. The other scenario involved a man he'd come to know when he'd covered a criminal trial a couple of years back, a former gang member who, if he remembered right, was doing time in Eden.

For a certain price, the man who called himself Hondo might try to get Pablo out by extrajudicial means.

Lantry was surprised to find himself thinking this way. Whatever the mistakes of his past, he had always believed in following the law. He determined to contact Cecilia. He mentally counted the money he had remaining, something less than a thousand dollars. His salary at the newspaper paid the bills to support the three of them in their present circumstances, so he could spend his savings and they probably wouldn't starve. He would call Cecilia first; the other option he would think about. But if it came to that, he could call Hondo's lawyer and try to make some indirect contact with him in prison.

Just how far Lantry was willing to go with these steps, he wasn't sure. One part of his mind would not let go of the idea that if he honestly tried to help Pablo get out, and if all plans failed and Pablo did not come home, a slim hope might remain that his life with María and Ángel could go on. He knew that things could never be the same as they had been before Fernando's news, yet if he had done all he could do and failed — or if for some other reason Pablo did not return — then perhaps their life together could continue with something like a clear conscience. But Lantry knew that he was really only dreaming, that he could live with himself, and she with herself, only if every possibility had been exhausted to bring Pablo home.

María met him at the door. They exchanged an awkward embrace. She seemed calm, and she was kind, but clearly she too had reconciled herself to the new reality, to a future that did not involve Lantry, or at least not Lantry as lover. They sat down at the table and he told her about Cecilia. If that didn't work, he had another plan he said, which he'd explain if that became necessary. In the morning he would make a phone call to Texas. But even as he spoke he could not completely dismiss the idea—yes, the hope—that in the end all the plans might fail, both his and Pablo's, and that Pablo would not return. He could not let go the sliver of hope that in the end he would still have María, and that Pablo's son might be his.

Chapter Thirty-five

Pablo tried to stay calm and to act as if he had ceded the next fourteen months to survival in Eden. But now that he and his plan were ready, waiting for the explosion was excruciating. Was all the talk by the toughs just talk? His carefully-honed patience was wearing thin. If there was some grand plan, he had no idea what it might be, whether it might work for him or even hinder him, whether he might somehow fuse his plan with theirs. If the riot began at night he'd be locked down, far from his reconstructed uniform. Maybe he should start over, stitch another to hide in his mattress, though if that were discovered, there would be hell to pay. Anyway, whatever the plan of the gang leaders, wouldn't it be futile for them if they too were locked in their cells? Surely they were smarter than that. The fuse would have to be lit when the prisoners were out of their cells, in the exercise room, or more likely in the mess hall. So on Pablo worked in the laundry room, never slacking his pace, gaining ever more trust from the supervisors and the guards.

On a Thursday afternoon, guards arrived at the laundry room and announced that Pablo had a visitor. He was cuffed and shackled and escorted to the visiting room, where under the glaring eye of the officer who delivered him, a young Latina woman introduced herself as Cecilia Romero. She was a lawyer she said. She had been sent by a friend of María.

Pablo's initial reaction was alarm. Was this a trick of some sort? Was he being set up? And how might this visit interfere with his plan? If there was anybody not welcome by Eden's management, it was lawyers, that Pablo knew. To the warden and the guards, lawyers meant only one thing, trouble, some busybody trying to get between them and the men they were paid to keep locked up, and for good reasons. Surely for certain authorities, this visit would repaint the bulls-eye on his back. Furthermore, Pablo hadn't heard of anybody being sprung from the joint by a lawyer, and he didn't see how a lawyer could help him. He had learned not to trust lawyers after his family lost their land, and then there was the San Antonio lawyer who all but cooperated in sending him here. It surely couldn't help that this lawyer had showed up just as he was waiting for the moment to run. No doubt this visit would somehow complicate things.

All these thoughts cascaded through Pablo's head, not so much as fleshed out ideas, but more like a rash of lightning strikes. But one thing, one word, stood above the crescendo in his stunned and swirling mind: the woman said she was sent by a friend of María! Pablo was mute, only half hearing what the lawyer said. He struggled to control his racing mind and think things through. The lawyer began asking questions, many of which he didn't know how to answer, especially with the guard within earshot. But she turned her back to the guard and kept her voice low, and she seemed genuinely interested in his welfare. She asked questions about his life, about why he'd crossed the border and how, about the marijuana he was alleged to have carried. Pablo liked that word "alleged," since it seemed to raise questions about whether he had actually done what they had charged him with, about whether he was really guilty. She had notes from his record that showed it was a kilo, and she would demand to see the pot and have it weighed.

"Was it green?" she asked. "If so, its weight would have shrunk with the passage of time."

"I couldn't really say," Pablo mumbled.

Not only had he not really examined what was in the bag, but it seemed that if he answered that question, and if this was a set-up, he would be admitting to the crime that the word "alleged" called into question.

"And if they haven't saved it as evidence, that could change everything," Romero continued. "Even undocumented immigrants have rights in this country," she said.

Romero talked of appeals, of getting him out soon with credit for time served. All the while she took lots of notes, and after a time Pablo began to think she might really be able to help. He calmed himself and began to answer her questions as best he could, but speaking in a voice that he hoped only she could hear. When she was out of questions, she asked what questions Pablo had.

"Just one," he said. "Where is María and is she well?"

"I'm afraid I don't know the details," the lawyer replied, gathering her papers. "All I know is that María's friend who contacted me is a Texan living in Orizaba. He's an acquaintance from law school who works at the newspaper, and he is in touch with María. He asked me to see if I could help."

She didn't know whether María was in Orizaba too, or still in Victoria, she said. She had told him all she knew. At least Pablo knew now that Fernando must have found María. He felt great encouragement in the knowledge that she knew about his fate, and that apparently she still cared. But neither could he dismiss the possibility that this new development might somehow complicate his own plan to escape.

When Cecilia rose to go she handed Pablo a card with her name and phone number in San Antonio. She smiled and extended her hand for a firm shake. She assured Pablo that she would look into his case and would be back in touch. Speaking in a voice he made sure the guard could overhear, Pablo thanked the lawyer, but assured her that he needed no help, that he would be just fine. Then in a whisper he asked her for a piece of paper, and as best he could with cuffed hands he wrote:

"Tell María that I will come soon, very soon."

A clerk escorted Cecilia to the door by the front office. Pablo stood staring after her departing form until the guard jerked him back to reality.

"All right, back to work Real," he growled. "Party's over. And don't think she's going to get you out of here. Not gonna happen." He gripped Pablo's arm and guided him back down the corridor to the laundry room. "She did have nice legs, didn't she?" the guard added at the laundry door. "Maybe you can dream about her tonight," he said, "but believe me, dreaming is all you're gonna do."

Pablo went back to his work, nursing new glimmers of hope. He was happy to have any word about María, to know that she must still care for him. Who her friend might be and what that might mean he had no idea, but who knew, if plan A didn't work, now there might be a plan B. Yet realistically, the lawyer thing was a long shot. He'd heard of nobody getting sprung from Eden by a lawyer, so he would keep that idea on the shelf. No doubt the guards would be watching him more intently now; he must stay on the straight and narrow path and hope that the visit would not derail the plan he'd laid.

Chapter Thirty-six

Two weeks had passed since the lawyer's visit, and Pablo had heard nothing. He had just sat down to eat his breakfast when one of the thugs he had always avoided stopped at his table, stooped and spoke in a low voice.

"My name is Hondo," he said. "Today is your chance to get out of this joint. Be ready when the time comes."

Pablo's eyes followed the retreating figure, wondering exactly what that might mean. He scanned the room. He was pretty sure nobody else had overheard. Who exactly was this Hondo, and what was about to come down?

He finished his oatmeal and toast and was escorted to the laundry room. All morning as he worked, his eyes and ears were open, waiting for some signal that the time had come. Twelve o'clock came, and everything seemed normal in the cafeteria. Back to work, an interminable afternoon in the sweaty hot steam. The horn blared, signaling the end of the workday and the evening mess, and now Pablo didn't know what to do. He was about to leave his escape disguise behind. But in the moments he paused, the answer came. A loud boom rang out, and within moments Pablo's eyes were watering. He rushed to the storage room and splashed water in his eyes. The other two inmates and the supervisor followed. While they were occupied dousing their eyes, Pablo grabbed his bundle from the back of the shelf and ran to a toilet stall. He spread soap on his face, dipped the razor into the toilet water and quickly sheared off his short beard. In two minutes he had stripped off his orange jumpsuit, pulled on the flowery shirt and jeans and over them his reconstructed guard uniform. He mounted the dark glasses over his watering eyes.

Then came a sharp pop, and the stall grew dark. The lights were out and the fans had shut down. The power had been cut. He opened the toilet door a crack and peaked out. Everybody else had fled. He crept through the darkened laundry room to the outer door and peered into the hall.

Chaos reigned, flashes of orange and brown, prisoners and guards, the corridor dark but for dim outside light, a cloud of gas hovering in the air. He dragged a sleeve across his face and plunged into the din, pushing past scuffling inmates and guards, all coughing and weeping and gasping for air. When he reached the main corridor a phalanx of uniforms stood profiled against the afternoon light, blocking any route of escape. He pushed his way through the jumble until he was near the front. An officer in a gas mask stepped forward and grasped his arm, propelling him forward, out of the mass into the line of guards. Somebody handed him a gas mask and he put it on. Pablo was now one of the guards, his disguise complete.

In the gassy haze of the darkened hallway, Pablo's crude uniform looked pretty much like the rest. Gradually he inched toward the back of the confrontation line, ever closer to the door. Then a guard sprayed more tear gas, the press of inmates fell back and masked officers surged forward, leaving Pablo alone at what had been the rear of the line. He stooped low and edged toward the exit.

Now he was out the door, striding into the still-blazing sun. He crouched beside a car and stripped the gas mask off, ducked low and worked his way down the line of cars in the parking lot. He paused to peek through teary eyes into each car until he found the one he needed—keys in the ignition switch. He squatted beside the car and surveyed the parking lot. Two city cops were rushing across the lot, headed inside. He was sure he had not been seen.

When they were gone he opened the door and turned the key. The steering wheel said the car was a Chevrolet. He put the shifter in reverse and backed out. He had never driven a vehicle before, but he was surprised by how easy it was to control the car. He tested the brakes and found that they worked. As he pulled onto the road he saw three cars headed his way from town, lights flashing, sirens wailing. Reinforcements were on the way. He drove calmly toward the heart of Eden, meeting one racing squad car after another. At the center of town he turned south on US 83 and headed for Mexico.

When he reached the first dirt road he pulled off the highway, stripped off his uniform, crossed a rusty barbed wire fence and stuffed the bundle and the mask under a mesquite tree. He pulled back onto the highway, rolled down the windows, his eyes still watering, and drove into the glaring sun-drenched plain, which through his borrowed glasses looked dark, green and cool. He turned up the radio and drove, careful to stay below the speed limit. The gas gauge showed well over half, surely more than enough to reach Laredo, which he figured must be something like four or five hours away. Pablo had exactly no money in his pockets, but there was half a bottle of hot Pepsi in the door pocket. If he sipped slowly, that should get him to the river.

When he pulled off on a second dirt road to pee, he decided to look in the trunk. Besides empty pop bottles, beer cans, scattered tools and a pair of boots, he found a satchel. Inside the satchel was a laptop computer that looked like new.

The sun was slipping low when he came to Crystal City, the biggest town he'd passed. He found the light switch and pulled it on. A big yellow sign with black letters that read PAWN caught his eye. Even though it was beginning to get dark, he left the sunglasses on and entered the store. "What do you got there?" the clerk barked from behind the counter.

Without a word, Pablo set the computer on the counter. The clerk looked it over, turned it on, then looked Pablo up and down. Finally he pushed the thing back toward Pablo.

"It's almost new, but it's hot, isn't it? I'd have to pay fifty bucks to get it scrubbed, and I couldn't sell it for more than two-fifty."

"Give me one-fifty," Pablo said. The guy thought for a moment.

"I'll give you one-twenty," he said. He opened the cash register and handed Pablo six twenties. Pablo was out the door and back on the road. On the south side of town he saw a sign for a Burger King.

"Give me the biggest burger you have," he said, "with *papas fritas* and a glass of water." He wolfed down the burger and fries in the darkening parking lot, then rolled back onto Highway 83. That was when he remembered that he would soon approach the border patrol checkpoint where he'd been arrested. He couldn't believe that he'd been so focused on just getting beyond the fence that he hadn't thought through what would come next? He had no identification, US or Mexican, not even a driver's license. What if after finally escaping from Eden, he would simply be recaptured and sent back, no doubt with more time added to his sentence? Plus, by now the cops were surely looking for this car.

Now the lights of a smaller town came into view. He slowed and read the name, Carrizo Springs. He crept into town as the last light died in the western sky. Beside the highway at a tiny bar called The Outpost, three men sat on the hoods of cars drinking cans of beer. He idled up to the group and saw that they were Latinos, likely younger than him. He turned off the engine and got out.

"*Qué pasa?*" he asked.

"*No mucho*," one answered. "Want a beer?"

He extended a Budweiser can. Pablo realized he hadn't had a beer in many months. He almost said yes, but then remembered he had important business to do.

"No *gracias*," he said. "I've got to get to Laredo tonight. Anybody want to go along?"

"Are you bullshitting us," another asked in English. "What's in Laredo?"

Pablo decided to take a chance.

"Look," he said. "I have to get to the border and back home to Mexico. My wife and my baby son need me. I'll be straight with you, *amigos*, I don't have papers, not even a driver's license, and this is a borrowed car. The cops are probably looking for it right now, so I need to park it on a country road where they won't find it for a while. So that means I need a ride to the border. If one of you can give me a ride, I'll pay for the gas and I can spare a few bucks besides. Anybody got a driver's license?"

"Sure we got licenses," one said. He looked at the others. "Yeah, what the hell, I'll do it," he said. "Anybody want to go along?"

They all slid off the hoods and tumbled into a beat-up Mercury.

"You guys know the territory," Pablo said. "Turn off on the first lonely road and I'll follow you."

Pablo got back in the Chevrolet and followed the boys out of town, then their cloud of dust down a side road until they pulled off at a cattle guard and he drove into a thicket of mesquite.

"I'll need to ride in the trunk until we pass the checkpoint," Pablo said.

The driver opened the lid and he climbed in. They slammed the trunk and bumped back to the highway. Pablo shifted every which way, but there was no way to be comfortable. Half an hour passed, and the car began to slow, then came to a stop.

"Where you boys heading?" a voice asked.

"Just down to Laredo for a little fun," the driver replied.

"Could I see your license?" the officer asked.

Pablo held his breath. After a few seconds the voice came again.

"OK, you boys have a good time. And don't pick up any Mexicans on your way back."

"No, sir," the driver replied, and they were back on the road.

A couple of minutes later the car slowed again and crunched to a stop on the gravel shoulder. The door opened, and then the trunk lid.

"Ready to get out of there?" the driver asked.

"Past ready," Pablo said. "You did great. Thank you."

Pablo joined the kid in the back seat.

In another half hour Laredo's glow filled the sky. The driver followed the highway toward the border, then turned onto a side street a block from the bridge. Pablo climbed out of the back seat.

"Remember," he said, leaning into the driver's window, "the car I had was borrowed, stolen some might say. It's owned by a guard who kept me in jail for nearly a year, a guy dumb enough to leave the keys in the ignition. If he never got it back it wouldn't hurt my feelings, but you're good young guys and I don't want you in any trouble, so remember this. You'll need to keep a secret for the rest of your lives. Whatever you do, don't ever tell anybody about tonight."

"Sure," the driver said. "Good luck."

"You guys saved my ass," Pablo added. "Tell me your names. When I get home I'm going to make three more sons with my wife, and I'll name them for you."

"I'm Jorge," the driver said. "That's Héctor and that's Rafael."

"Jorge, Héctor and Rafael," Pablo repeated. "When my sons are grown I'll tell them about you."

Pablo pulled two twenties from his small wad and handed them to the driver.

"Have a nice dinner before you head home," he said.

He shook hands all around, turned his back and strolled toward the bridge.

Crossing proved easy, going south. Pablo told the Mexican agent he was born and raised in Nuevo Laredo and had just come across for the evening. The officer waved him on. Pablo remembered vaguely where the bus terminal was; he had passed it on his way north, what seemed a lifetime ago. He walked south, but stopped at a restaurant for a steaming bowl of *chile verde* and a Dos Equis beer. He paid the bill and counted his money. Seventy-five and change.

At the terminal he scanned the departure board. A second-class bus was sixty-three dollars American, and it left in twenty minutes. It was fifteen hours to Mexico City and the clock on the wall read 11:30, so he'd arrive mid-afternoon. If he didn't eat again he'd have twelve bucks left to get him to Victoria. If the ticket to Victoria was less than twelve, he could buy food with what was left.

He found his seat on the bus and settled in for the ride. It had been a long day. He closed his eyes to sleep, but images of the day replayed in vivid detail, the guard handing him the mask, Eden in the rear-view mirror, the boys whose names he'd give his unborn sons. Suddenly he laughed out loud. He had pulled it off! Yet he found it slightly disturbing that he had no regrets about what he had done. What had he become? He'd killed a man, yes, but maybe that was right, he didn't know. Now without a second thought he had borrowed—no the word was stolen—another man's car, and had sold his computer. He was not only a killer, but also a thief. Perhaps he had simply done what he had to do, but nothing in his life had prepared him to confront these facts. He resolved to set them aside for the moment and get some much-needed rest. When the bus began to move he drifted into a deep sleep, hopeful that before night fell again he would be in María's arms.

Chapter Thirty-seven

When Lantry arrived at work early Friday, Octavio called him into his office.

"I'm afraid we have a problem," he said. "It seems that our stories about the hog CAFOs and the swine flu have upset some powerful people. I got two phone calls late last night, first from *Migración*, asking about your immigration status. It sounds like they already know the answer, that you're here illegally and working without a permit."

"I was afraid that might happen," Lantry replied, "ever since the Americans threatened me in Victoria. So what should we do?"

"Then there was the second call," Octavio continued, ignoring Lantry's question regarding the first. "The guy didn't identify himself, just said he'd be coming for you, and that if *La Migra* didn't get you, he would. He said you'd be lucky if the government found you first."

Lantry stopped breathing, waiting for the news to sink in.

"OK," he said at last. "I guess it's time for me to go."

"I hate like hell to lose you," Octavio said. "You've done your work well, and if we can get your status resolved, I'll gladly take you back. I expect you'll have to go back to the US and apply for a work visa, which could take some time. But in the meantime, the second caller is the one I really worry about. I don't want anything to happen to you."

"I understand," Lantry said. "It was good of you to take a chance on me, and I've really grown to care about this city, about the paper, about everything that has happened in my life. Especially María. And now I have something to tell you. The father of María's son, Pablo, has been in prison in Texas. I contacted a lawyer and another person I know in Texas to see if they could help. I also got a call last night, from the lawyer. She'd been trying to reach me to deliver a message from Pablo to María, saying that he would be here soon. I don't know what that means, except that that part of my life, the best part, is also crumbling around me. I can't bear to leave María and Ángel, but neither can I stay. I'll have to go soon, very soon. But first I must figure a way to take care of María until Pablo comes."

"Yes, I know about Pablo, too" Octavio said. "It seems you stirred up the big boys behind Granjas Carroll like a hornets' nest, and they've checked out everything about you. They also know about María and Ángel. They wanted me to know that they even know where you live."

The last part shocked Lantry to the core. He had no idea what to say. If they were coming for him, what might they do to María and Ángel? Should he take them and flee, to the city, to the US, to some remote corner of Mexico? No, that was out of the question now that Pablo would be coming home. Maybe they could hide out temporarily in a small nearby town? But how would they live without his salary?

Then Octavio spoke again, as if answering Lantry's chaotic thoughts.

"I have a place you can go, today," he said. "There's a spare room in the back of my sister's house. I've already spoken to her, and she says you and María can stay for a few days, until we sort things out."

"I am so grateful, Octavio," Lantry said. "I'm grateful for everything you've done. You are a good man. Orizaba is a good place. If only everything else would go away and we could go on as we are. But that cannot be."

"One other thing, the immigration agent threatened to shut the newspaper down, and the thug threatened to burn us out. I'll have no choice but to say I thought you had papers."

"I understand," Lantry said. "That's the right thing to do. And I can't thank you enough for thinking this whole thing through and finding a path for us."

Octavio wrote a name and an address on a scrap of paper and handed it to Lantry.

"I'll call Beatrice and she'll be expecting you," he said.

Then he reached into his wallet and counted out a wad of pesos.

"Here's this week's pay, plus another week," he said. "You've earned it, and you'll need it." Then he stood and extended his hand. *"Buena suerte, amigo,"* he said. "Good luck friend." They embraced, and Lantry was out the door.

He walked swiftly to the little house, where he found María in the kitchen, bathed in morning sun, Ángel at her breast. "You're home!" she said, clearly surprised.

"Yes," he said.

He pulled up a kitchen chair next to her and began to relate as calmly as he could all that he had learned, at least the details she needed to know.

"So we'll need to pack our things," he said, "not that that will take very long," he added, scanning the scant contents of the three little rooms.

When Ángel had finished nursing, María laid him on the bed and they began to gather their meager possessions. Lantry's now ragged pack bulged with the clothing he had brought, and he folded the jacket and the dress shirts he'd bought for work in a cardboard box. María and Ángel's things went into a larger box, and a third box received the paltry contents of the refrigerator and the cabinets. They set the boxes near the door and Lantry swept the place clean. Then he went out to find a taxi to transport them to Beatrice's house.

"*Mi casa es tu casa*," Beatrice said as she welcomed them through her front door. My house is your house.

She showed them to a little back room, which contained a bed and two shelves on one wall. "You can put your things here," she said, motioning to the shelves. "The food can go to the kitchen."

María unpacked her and Ángel's clothing and arranged them on the shelves. Lantry left everything he owned in the pack and the box. He would decide later how much and what he could take when he went.

"I'll just leave my things in the corner for now," he told María in answer to her questioning eyes.

"*¡La comida está lista!*" Beatrice called from the kitchen.

For some time they had inhaled the aroma of hominy, *chiles* and pork, and they knew that *posole* was about to be served, along with hot tortillas. Beatrice spoke no English, so all conversation was in Spanish, Lantry contributing as best he could. He wasn't sure how much Octavio had told his sister, so when he felt the time had come, he began to provide necessary details of the delicate situation. He did not suggest that he and María had been lovers, only that he had tried to help her and Ángel as best he could, but soon he would no

244

longer be needed. María's husband, Pablo, would be coming home, and the family would be reunited. In the meantime, Lantry would soon be moving on.

The rainy season had ended at last, and the afternoon sun was warm. Lantry proposed that he, María and Ángel take a stroll up the Orizaba River walk, something they hadn't done for a while. María strapped her baby to her breast and they set out. It was a lovely afternoon, the flowers along the river in full bloom, the sky blue. Long they walked in silence, hand in hand, until Ángel woke and whimpered for nourishment. They sat on a park bench and watched the pure cold waters of Pico de Orizaba rumble by. Lulled by the soothing sun and the rhythmic sucking at María's breast, Lantry tried to imagine their life together flowing on forever like the babbling stream, their dilemma swept away by the gushing water. He would have given anything, everything, if that could be true. But Ángel finished feeding, and the spell was broken. They stood and crossed the river and strolled back south on the other side. Then Lantry spoke. "I know that you know as well as I do, María, that I must go soon. If Pablo is right, that he will come soon, it will be best if I have gone. I've been thinking, now that my mind is clear, possibly I could get my old job back in Texas. Or maybe go back and pass the bar in law. In either case, maybe I could help people like Pablo, people like you."

"Oh, Lantry, you have done everything for me already," María said, stopping and throwing her arms around him, Ángel sandwiched between. "I will always love you, I'll never forget you. And most of all I love you because you see that you have to let me go."

Lantry held her close for as long as he dared, then gently released her and wiped the tears from both their cheeks.

"You are the best thing that ever happened to me, María, and leaving you will be the hardest thing I've ever done. But I will take you with me in my heart, and I'll always be a better man because of you. Whatever my future holds, it will be inspired by you."

They walked in silence again, hand in hand, back to Beatrice's door.

"I will go tomorrow," Lantry said before they knocked on the door. "Tonight I'll make a plan. I'll leave all the money with you and Ángel except enough for a bus ticket. When I get back to Texas I'll see what else I can do to get Pablo free."

Chapter Thirty-eight

When Beatrice opened the door, Fernando was waiting for them. He had been to the newspaper office looking for Lantry, and Octavio had directed him to Beatrice's house. He stepped forward and embraced María and told her how beautiful her baby was. He shook hands with Lantry, then got to the point of his visit.

"I have a message from Pablo," he began. "Pablo arrived in Victoria last night."

"Pablo is in Victoria?" María squeaked, her shocked voice barely audible. "He's in Victoria now? When? When did he arrive? When is he coming here?"

She clutched Ángel close to her bosom, gripping Lantry's arm with her free hand to steady herself.

"My brother had told one of Pablo's sisters that both you and I are in Orizaba," he told María. "So Pablo went to the *farmacia*...."

"But when? When is he coming?" María begged.

"As I was saying," Fernando continued, determined to deliver his message intact. "Pablo went to the *farmacia*. Somebody there found the number of the Mercado manager here and let Pablo use the phone. They sent a boy to find me."

"But when is Pablo coming!" María shrieked in a voice that could no longer be ignored.

"Tonight," Fernando said. Pablo asked me to tell you that he will be in Orizaba tonight.

Now María was mute. She turned a pale face to Lantry, her eyes conveying the confusion of joy and excitement mixed with apprehension and fear. Her eyes sought from Lantry an answer to the question, what must we do now?

Lantry had tried to prepare himself for this moment, though he hadn't seen it coming so soon. His own confused eyes failed to convey the answers María sought. Yes, he had reconciled himself to the impending loss of what he held most dear. And yes he had determined to go, but that was to be tomorrow, not tonight. What he had not shared with María was the threats that Octavio had conveyed. Might Pablo arrive at any moment? And those who intended him harm, when would they come? He needed time to think, a place to think beyond the walls of the little room. It occurred to him that perhaps Fernando had answers he couldn't find.

"Fernando," he said, looking the young man in the eye, "could you step outside with me for a moment? I think we might need your help."

"Of course," Fernando replied, but with a tone of anxiety in his voice.

Lantry stepped to the door through which they had just passed and opened it on the darkening sky. He and Fernando stepped through and began to walk. Lantry did not speak immediately. He didn't yet know what to say, how much to reveal. He realized that in fact he hoped answers might come from this young market lad, this messenger of love and fate.

When they had walked half a block, Lantry began.

"Fernando," he said, "I hardly know you, but what I do know is that you are a man willing to do whatever he can to help his friends. And that is what I'm going to ask you to do.

"Of course," Fernando replied, not knowing what might be asked of him.

"I take you to be not only a faithful friend, but an honest man. But if the happiness of your friends depended upon not being completely honest with them, could you do that?"

"I guess I could," Fernando replied uncomfortably, not knowing where this conversation was going.

The two men had walked to a place where an arching tree blocked lights. Lantry stopped walking and faced Fernando, whose eyes he could barely see in his darkened face.

"You may or may not know that María and Ángel and I have lived together as a family. I love María more than anything I've ever known, and I think that she also has loved me. It didn't start out this way. In the beginning I mostly just wanted to help. But as the months went by and there was no word from Pablo, I think we both came to believe that he would not return. We needed each other, and we fell in love."

"*Sí*," Fernando replied. "I understand."

"Pablo must not know," Lantry said. "He must not. If someday María finds a way to tell him, that might be good. But for now, he must not know. What I'm asking you to do is to tell Pablo that María and I were nothing but friends, that I simply saw her need and the need of his son, and I saw a way that I could help. Nothing more. Since I don't know Pablo as you do, I can't know how he would feel if he knew there was anything more. But that's a chance we can't take. More than anything else in the world I want María to be happy, and to be secure. I want Ángel to grow up with a father who loves him."

"Yes, I understand," Fernando said again. "It might not be right, but I will do this for my friends."

"I will ask Beatrice to do the same," Lantry added. "The only other person who knows is Octavio at the newspaper, and he also understands."

Fernando extended his hand in the darkness, and Lantry took it. Then the two men embraced.

"In prison I swore to Pablo that I would find María and tell her where he was," Fernando said. "It took much longer than I expected, but I have done what I promised. I did it for the happiness of my friends, and I will also do the things you asked. And you, Lantry, I see that you will do something very difficult for the happiness of the woman you love."

"Thank you, Fernando," Lantry said, turning his feet toward Beatrice's door.

"And now I must go to the newspaper office," Fernando said. "I'll wait for Pablo there, and bring him when he comes."

Chapter Thirty-nine

Fernando sat on the office steps, watching people and the occasional car go by. It was growing late; surely the last bus from Serdán had come. Could Pablo not find this place? It had been a long day of work at the market, and tomorrow would be more of the same, beginning at six. Fernando's eyes grew heavy.

"*Hola amigo,*" a voice called. "Long time no see."

It was Pablo, standing before him in ragged jeans and a shirt covered with bright flowers. Fernando leapt to his feet and embraced his friend.

"You finally made it!" he bellowed, pounding Pablo on the back.

"And María, have you seen her?" Pablo asked. "Is she OK?"

"Yes, she's waiting for you my friend, she and your beautiful son Ángel."

"What are we waiting for?" Pablo demanded. "Let's go."

Fernando pointed down the street the way he had come, and the pair set out, Fernando updating Pablo on the news from Victoria and now Orizaba, Pablo asking question after question about María and Ángel.

"You'll see soon enough," Fernando answered. It's just a couple of kilometers to Beatrice's house where they're staying.

By now it was past ten o'clock, and the streets were mostly deserted. So the pair couldn't help noticing that a car had turned on its lights and pulled out just as they left the newspaper office. Now it had circled the block and was cruising slowly by again. Also it was not the usual car, not a battered Japanese import, but a large black SUV with darkened windows.

"That's strange," Fernando said, but they continued to walk.

Another block, and the SUV rolled by again. It appeared they were being followed.

"I think it must be some kind of cops," Pablo said, alarmed. "But would they follow me all the way from Texas? Surely I'm not that important."

But it wasn't only that he had escaped from prison, he was thinking, but he had done it in a stolen car, a car stolen from a prison guard at that. Also there was the stolen computer he had sold. Maybe they really had followed him all this way.

When the vehicle turned at the next corner Pablo and Fernando ducked into the shadows and hid behind a fence. Moments later the vehicle approached again, slower this time, then sped ahead and again circled the block. Whoever was following them was aware that they had lost the trail.

"If it's you they're after, I have an idea," Fernando said. "I'll be you and you can be me. If they pick me up they'll soon find out I'm not you."

He pulled off his Lakers t-shirt and handed it to Pablo. Pablo handed over the flowered shirt he'd worn since his escape.

"Whew, this thing doesn't smell so good," Fernando said with a laugh, buttoning it up.

252

"That's Texas you smell," Pablo said. "Sorry it doesn't fit so well. I got it off a fat prison guard."

Fernando removed his baseball cap and clapped it on Pablo's head.

The SUV rushed past again, now followed by a white sedan. The sedan's door bore the name "*Migración*."

Apparently the border police had joined the chase. When the vehicles disappeared, the pair rushed from the shadows and raced down the street to the next intersection. Fernando instructed Pablo to go two blocks south, then turn west and go to the third house on the south side of the street.

"*Hasta luego*," Fernando said, embracing his friend.

Then, clad in Pablo's flowery shirt, he strolled casually down the main drag, while Pablo fled south.

Pablo turned the corner west, panting, and set his eyes on the third house on the south. Now that he was near he slowed his walk, unsure of what he soon would find. After the long separation, what would his reception be? He paused before the door to straighten his clothing and his hair. He swallowed deeply. Now that he was about to see María at last he felt suddenly shy, nervous, unsure. What would he say? Would she be happy to see him after all this time, or only shocked? Then he remembered that he was also now a father. Would his baby son be awake or asleep? Long he stood gazing at the door. He had waited so long for this moment, and now his feet seemed frozen to the ground.

Chapter Forty

Four people huddled in the tiny living room of Beatrice's home, the atmosphere thick with anticipation and dread. Lantry had managed to speak with Beatrice in the kitchen while María changed Ángel's diaper in the back room. Beatrice needed no convincing or explanations. She had already determined that what she knew about Lantry and María was nobody's business but their own, certainly not hers, and certainly business that would do no good for María and Pablo. In fact she was almost cross with Lantry for broaching the subject, as if she didn't have enough sense to reach those conclusions on her own. Still, she felt great compassion for Lantry, and admiration that he was putting María's future ahead of his own. Now the three sat in the dim lamplight and waited, for what—for Pablo to come, for Lantry to go.

Lantry's battered pack stood ready by the back door. He would never be prepared, but it was past time to go. María cradled the sleeping baby with one hand and gripped Lantry's hand with the other. Her eyes filled with anxious tears. Beatrice excused herself and went to the kitchen so the pair could say goodbye.

"I have loved you, Lantry," María said, turning her tear-stained face to his. "But I have never known what to do."

"It's very simple," Lantry lied. "The husband you love is coming home. Together you and Pablo will have a good life, and you will raise little Ángel to be a good man. And now I must go."

254

María clung fiercely to Ángel, but threw her free arm around Lantry's neck.

"Everything will be good," he told her, stroking her glossy black hair, then gently removing her clutching arm.

"You have given me my life back, María," he said, "and I could ask for nothing more. Now you must take back your life with Pablo and Ángel. We won't see each other again, and I won't even be able to contact you. I doubt you will be able to do it, but it would be best if you could put me out of your mind. I think it's OK if you love me for the rest of your life, if you promise to love Pablo more. And now I must go."

Somewhere a dog barked, and then dogs were barking all over the neighborhood. Ángel woke and began to cry. Lantry went to the front window and pulled the curtain aside a narrow crack. Two vehicles were parked out front, a big black SUV and a sedan with the word *Migración* on the door. A uniformed agent was getting out of the sedan, then two men emerged from the back seat of the SUV. In spite of the flashlight beamed toward the house, Lantry saw that one man brandished a gun. Then he saw a fourth man between them and the door, a man in a t-shirt and a baseball cap. It must be Pablo. He couldn't see the face well in the dim light, but now one of the thugs grabbed him by the arm.

"There are men outside," he told María. "But don't worry. They haven't come for Pablo. They have come for me, but they won't find me." Lantry kissed the weeping mother, then the crying baby in her arms. "And there is another man," he added. "I think Pablo has come."

There was a loud rapping on the door.

"¡*Abrir*!" a voice shouted. "Open the door. We know he's here."

"I will never forget you, María," Lantry said, "nor you Ángel. And now you must answer the door, María. I left yesterday, you will tell them, and you have no idea where I've gone."

Lantry shouldered his pack and crept toward the back door. He slipped quietly through and faded into the darkness of night.

Chapter Forty-one

While Pablo had hesitated at the door, two pairs of headlights had rounded the corner. The SUV screeched to a stop and the window purred down. A man leaned out the window and cast a powerful flashlight beam at Pablo's eyes.

"Fernando?" the voice barked.

"*Sí*," Pablo replied.

"So where is your friend Pablo?" the menacing voice demanded. "And your friend Lantry?"

The flashlight beam dropped from Pablo's eyes, and now he saw that the man wore an official uniform of some kind.

"I don't know where Pablo is," Pablo stammered, "and I've never heard of anybody named Lantry."

"Don't bullshit me buddy," the voice growled.

The back door of the black SUV opened and two men stepped out, one with a pistol trained on Pablo's heart.

"How about you get in the car and take a ride with us," the gunman said. "Maybe we can find your friends. Or is this by chance the house where they're staying? You were standing by the door."

A hand inside the house pulled a curtain aside and a narrow sliver of light fell across the strip of grass that lay between Pablo and the gunman.

"OK" the man with the pistol said. "Maybe we'll just check this out ourselves."

He strode across the lawn toward Pablo, grabbed him by the arm and dragged him toward the door. He knocked loudly on the door, but it did not open. He knocked again.

"Open the door!" he demanded. Still no response. Now the third man was at their side. He delivered a mighty kick and the door crashed open. The intruders rushed in, Pablo still in the gunman's grip.

"Pablo!" María cried.

She rushed to Pablo, Ángel screaming hysterically in her arms. The free arm she threw around Pablo's neck and she began to sob.

Now Beatrice was in the gunman's face.

"Get your hands off my brother," she screamed. Surprisingly, the thug let go of Pablo's arm.

"OK, so where is Lantry Barton? the man demanded. "He's the one we came for."

"*Lantry quién?*" Beatrice demanded coolly. "*No lo conozco. No Lantry aquí.*"

"Out of my way woman," the gunman snarled.

He shoved her aside and plunged toward the back room, throwing open doors and hurling things aside. He found nobody, only an open door through which whispered the sweet evening breeze from the Peak of Orizaba.